THE ABERRATION OF EDEN PRUITT

THE ABERRATION OF EDEN PRUITT

BOOK 2

K.E. GANSHERT

Copyright © 2022 by K.E.Ganshert

Cover Design by Courtney Walsh

All rights reserved.

This novel is a work of fiction. Any resemblance to peoples either living or deceased is purely coincidental. Names, places, and characters are figments of the author's imagination.

No part of this book may be reproduced in any form or by any electronic or mechanical means, including information storage and retrieval systems, without written permission from the author, except for the use of brief quotations in a book review.

ALSO BY K.E. GANSHERT

THE CONTEST

THE GIFTING TRILOGY

The Gifting, book 1

The Awakening, book 2

The Gathering, book 3

Luka, a book 1 companion novel

For Courtney

If you weren't such an amazing human, I'd probably be sickened by your level of talent. Thanks for giving these books such pretty, pretty faces!

ABERRATION

*THE ACT OF DEPARTING FROM
THE RIGHT COURSE;
AN ERROR*

1

Eighteen-year-old Eden Pruitt walked toward a set of stairs that weren't hers, away from a father that wasn't hers either. At least not in the way she'd always thought.

Seven days ago, her not-father almost died.

Seven days ago, she'd handed herself over to the enemy.

Seven days ago, that enemy got away, and she was reunited with the two people she'd always called mom and dad. In the process, that dad was shot twice. The first bullet hit his left thigh and grazed his femur, barely missing his femoral artery. The second entered his chest and exited his back, barely missing his heart. If not for the circumstances that led to the life-threatening altercation, one might call him lucky. For against all odds—thanks to a retired military doctor, the world's most brilliant neurosurgeon, and the fast-acting instincts of a once-lethal fighter—he survived.

Eden pushed thoughts of that fighter aside. Feelings, too.

Behind her, Mom and Benjamin Norton, the retired military doctor, encouraged Dad to rest. Instead, he asked for his spirometer. Over the past hour, he'd been alternating between leg and breathing exercises, his frustration mounting every time he inhaled or flexed his quad muscle. Dad rarely swore, but the last sixty minutes had turned him into a sailor.

The real enemy had escaped, so he made fatigue his scapegoat. He seemed to be operating under the delusion that seven days was enough time to recover from a collapsed lung, extraordinary blood loss, cardiac arrest, and emergency surgery. A ridiculous assumption, even if he hadn't been unconscious and on a ventilator for three of those seven days.

Her father was a regular man with normal human limitations. Unlike Eden, his composition didn't include microscopic robots that made things like getting shot no big deal. And yet, he pushed himself like his body should be better, stronger. Eden suspected he wanted to be up and walking by the time their enemy stepped out of the shadows.

Mordecai.

He was out there somewhere, plotting and planning

his next move. Eden knew this as certainly as she knew Erik spelled his name with a K. As certainly as she knew the Eiffel tower had one-thousand-six-hundred-sixty-five steps. He would not hide forever. Not when he'd gone to such great lengths to get her. Whatever plans he had, he wouldn't let them go so easily—an unspoken understanding that had the tension in the home thickening by the hour. Not her home. But Dr. Beverly Randall-Ransom's, the brilliant neurosurgeon.

"When can I get out of this bed?" Dad growled.

"As soon as you're okay with using that," Dr. Norton replied.

Her father scoffed.

That was the wheelchair.

"You have broken ribs, Alaric."

The name came like a jarring hiccup.

Alaric.

Her father's given name. One she didn't know until recently. To her, he was Alexander Pruitt—a fit, fifty-three-year-old accountant. But to Dr. Norton, who had known her father before he changed his identity, he was Alaric Taylor, a fellow soldier turned CIA agent.

Eden shook her head. How was this her life—gunshot wounds and parents with different names and an enemy lurking in the shadows? She was supposed to be in school. First period in the first quarter of her senior year. In Iowa. She thought the worst part of her senior year would be missing Erik. Never in her wildest dreams would she have imagined getting drawn into an illicit world of gamblers and fighters and hackers and terrorists. Not just any terrorist, but the most notorious of all terrorists. Karik Volkova. A man responsible for an incomprehensible number of deaths. Somehow, he was her beginning and because of that, she wasn't in first period in the first quarter of her senior year. She was here. In the brilliant neurosurgeon's home, trying not to think too hard about this new reality lest she lose her mind completely.

"You can't support your weight with crutches or a walker," Dr. Norton said. "Nor are you supposed to bear any weight on your leg. Not unless you want to impede your recovery. Which means it's the bed or the chair."

Dad swore.

Mom sighed.

Eden climbed the stairs, shifting her focus to the sounds above her. Concordia in the Morning played on the television, a show her father watched every day for as far back as Eden could remember.

"Time will bring it back," a familiar voice said. It belonged to Brenna Lemming, one of the show's most beloved hosts. "In my opinion, it's not a matter of if, but when."

"You think we'd let ourselves go back to that place?"

"I think it's already happening. Look at the rising

crime rate. Look at what happened at the SafePad compound right here in Chicago." Brenna was referencing the place Mordecai had been imprisoning her parents. She was referencing the break-in and the dead guards. Eden hadn't killed them. She'd rendered them unconscious. After Cassian left, the guards were killed. "Listen when you're out and about. Just the other day, I overhead two people talking about approval ratings for our Board of Directors. Does that sound familiar to anyone? The whole point of having a Board of Directors was to avoid such nonsense."

A debate ensued. All four of the morning show hosts broke out into a robust, short-lived argument, which proved Brenna Lemming's original point.

Her voice rose above the others. "Look, I'm simply stating that human memory is short. History loves to repeat itself. And if we're not careful, we could find ourselves in familiar territory. I think it's safe to say that we can all agree—none of us want that."

Her voice was familiar. Comforting. Mingled with one that absolutely wasn't.

Eden stopped.

Intellectually, she understood that this voice didn't belong to an enemy. But her body wouldn't listen to intellect. Her body responded in the same visceral way it used to respond to Jack Forrester. Her body needed time to adjust to what her mind already knew.

Jack Forrester was on her side.

So was his wife, Annette.

The two people who arrived at Eagle Bend's police station pretending to be her parents.

Earlier this morning, Jack had returned from Dr. Norton's secluded cabin in the woods, several miles northwest of Milwaukee. He arrived beneath a cloud of frustration, reeking of cigarettes and sweating nicotine. While her father dove into rehab like a bull seeing red, Jack had been spending his time trying to crack into the networks of Subjects 003 and 004—a pair of eighteen-year-olds just like Eden. Freaks of nature. Experiments that shouldn't exist.

Subject 004 was Barrett Barr, a boy whose face had been splashed across national news ever since his disappearance in July. Subject 003 had no name at all. She was an unidentified girl they were calling Jane Doe. Unlike Barrett, Jane wasn't listed anywhere as a missing person. All they had was her face and the information in her file.

Her parents' names were listed, but like Alaric Taylor, those names appeared to have been abandoned long ago—after receiving what must have been the most bizarre phone call of their lives. They had a child. A biological child. A frozen embryo stolen from an IVF clinic, then grown in a test lab. What kind of parents took that child in—put their safety in jeopardy—only to let that child go missing sixteen-and-a-half years later without filing a report?

Perhaps they had hired a private investigator to find her like the once-lethal fighter had been hired to find Eden.

Cassian Gray.

A boy she hadn't spoken with in seven days.

A fact that filled her with equal parts confusion and betrayal. Eden set her teeth against the unruly emotions and focused instead on Annette Forrester's voice.

"When will that be?" she asked.

"When it's safe," Jack replied. "We're working as hard and as fast as we can."

"Ellery is struggling."

Eden closed her eyes, her hearing so good she could practically see with her ears. Jack was on a video call, sitting on a chair in Beverly Randall-Ransom's state-of-the-art kitchen. Eden could hear the unique hum his computer made whenever he connected via live video feed. She could hear the subtle creaking of wood as he shifted in the chair. The slice of skin against scalp as he shoved fingers into his thinning hair.

"It's her senior year, Jack," Annette said. "She wants to be with her friends. She doesn't understand why we're here. She doesn't understand why you're not with us. She keeps asking questions. I don't know how much longer I can go before I give her real answers."

"You can't give her real answers, Annette. It's too much."

"Well, you're going to have to talk to her then. I can't lie anymore."

"Put her on," Jack said.

With a start, Eden crept up the remaining stairs. If Ellery Forrester was coming on the video feed, superhuman hearing would no longer do. Eden had to see her. When she reached the landing, she pressed her back against the wall and peeked into the kitchen, waiting with bated breath as Ellery took her mother's spot on the screen. Eden had only seen her in a photograph. An age-progression photo. Now here she was in real time, with long, auburn hair and the same flawless skin and faultless symmetry as Eden. They possessed the kind of perfection other girls envied. And yet, Eden would trade hers in a heartbeat if it meant getting rid of the reason for it.

"Hey, Peanut," Jack said, leaning toward the screen like a father who wanted to fall through to the other side, where he could hold his distraught daughter.

"I don't understand what's going on." Ellery's light brown eyes filled with frustrated tears. Eden's were a combination of blues and grays with specs of green.

"I know, sweetheart. But you have to trust us. As soon as it's safe for you to return, I'll make sure you and your mother are on the first flight home."

"What does that even mean, Dad? Safe from what?"

"Elle." He spoke her name on a weary sigh.

"It's my senior year! I was supposed to be going to the homecoming dance tonight."

Jack's knee bounced beneath the table. The second this call ended, he'd probably let himself outside to smoke another cigarette. "You're in Rome, Elle. Rome! Enjoy yourself. Go sightseeing with your mother. You don't want to look back on this time and regret the missed opportunity."

Rome.

Jealousy flashed like a bolt of lightning.

Eden tried to fathom it.

Being overseas with her mother—oblivious to the truth of who and what she was.

Her life swapped with Ellery's.

If, instead of Eden, Ellery made a dumb choice on the cusp of her senior year. Ellery ended up with a rap sheet and a mug shot. And because of that, Cassian Gray found the redhead instead of the blond. Would Eden be somewhere across the Atlantic with her mom while her father helped the Forresters hunt down a high-stakes gambler who went by the name Mordecai? Would Eden care about missing her senior year if she was in Paris? Would she push for answers with the same ferocity that Ellery was pushing now, or would she take advantage of the unexpected opportunity and go sightseeing?

A stair creaked behind her.

"Good morning, Eden." Dr. Norton stepped past her into the kitchen.

Eden cringed.

"Who's that?" Ellery asked.

"Sorry, Elle. I've got to go. Talk soon." Without giving Ellery any time to object, Jack snapped his laptop shut, as if the mere glimpse of Eden would be the death of his daughter.

Eden joined them in the kitchen.

If Jack was upset by her eavesdropping, he didn't let on. Maybe he'd wanted to get off the call and her arrival had given him a reason. He leaned back in his chair. "How's the patient?"

"Ornery." Dr. Norton poured himself more coffee and tipped his chin at the laptop. "Have you made any insightful discoveries?"

He was referring to the networks. The ones that belonged to Subjects 003 and 004.

Before Jack could reply, Milly—the Randall-Ransom's housekeeper—bustled into the kitchen, bringing their conversation to an awkward halt. While Milly loaded dishes into the dishwasher and wiped down the stovetop, Concordia in the Morning continued playing in the next room.

Another pipe bomb was sent in the mail. This one resulted in a casualty. According to Dr. Beverly Randall-

Ransom's daughter—Cleo the Conspiracy Theorist—these bombs were a scare tactic enacted by their own government in an attempt to lull the stirring public back to sleep. Eden, who hadn't yet reached that level of cynicism, had a hard time getting on board with the theory. She wondered what Brenna Lemming might say.

Milly pulled the carafe from the coffeemaker and held it up in the air, the black liquid swishing inside. "You want rest?" she asked in her thick Bulgarian accent.

Dr. Norton raised his mug. "I'm good, thank you."

She shut off the machine and rinsed the carafe in the sink. Eden watched her work, wondering what Milly thought about her employer. Wondering what she thought about the swearing patient in her employer's basement. He wasn't the first patient to be treated here. Milly picked up a piece of mail from the counter and stuck it to the front of the stainless-steel refrigerator. She muttered something about Dr. Beverly needing to RSVP, then exited the room as abruptly as she'd come.

Eden glanced at the invitation.

Dr. Beverly Randall-Ransom was invited to attend the Prosperity Ball on October the Fourth, the twenty-first anniversary of The Attack. The date was quickly approaching. Only a few weeks away.

"Is it me," Jack said, running his hand down the length of his haggard face, "or is it starting to feel crowded here?"

Dr. Norton smoothed his mustache. "It's not you."

If Eden were to look up the word mansion in the dictionary, there might be a photograph of Dr. Beverly Randall-Ransom's home. A grand estate on the Gold Coast of Chicago. Five stories high, with meticulously manicured grounds. It didn't seem possible for such a residence to feel crowded, but somehow, Jack was right. And sooner or later, the neurosurgeon's hospitality would have to end.

"My place is better suited for rehab," Dr. Norton said. "Fewer stairs, with the right equipment, too."

"And privacy," Jack added, eying the entryway where Milly had disappeared.

Dr. Norton took a sip of his coffee. "I imagine it will be easier to do your work with all three in the same place."

Jack nodded.

The two men turned to Eden, as if she had the final say. The thought of leaving Chicago tied her stomach into knots. Not because it felt safer here, but because this was where Cassian Gray had left her. If she returned to Milwaukee, would she ever see him again?

She didn't know where he was or what he was doing or why he hadn't called. According to Jack, he was looking for Mordecai. But Jack hadn't heard from him in a few days. A fact that tied Eden's stomach into knots.

Cassian had been hired by the high-stakes gambler to

find her and instead helped her find the high-stakes gambler. He betrayed a man who put a single, cold bullet through a bookie's head like remorse was as foreign as Jupiter's rings. For all they knew, Cassian had met the same fate.

"Eden?"

She blinked away the cloying concern and the unsettling imagery that came with it.

"What do you think?" Dr. Norton asked.

She knew why he was asking.

How did she feel about being in such close quarters with Subjects 003 and 004? Ever since learning the truth about what she was, she'd felt like a grenade without the pin, clutched tight in someone else's hand. If she returned to Dr. Norton's, there would be three grenades under one roof. It was a recipe for disaster. But Eden couldn't deny the morbid curiosity bubbling inside of her any longer. Barrett Barr and Jane Doe were exactly like her, only they were stuck in some unnerving state of unconsciousness. Maybe seeing them would help her see herself. Whoever and whatever that was.

"If you think it's a good idea," Eden said. "Then we'll go to Milwaukee."

Dr. Norton set his mug on the counter. "I'll get the patient ready. We can head out in an hour."

2

Cassian Gray stepped off his bike and strode toward his destination with a decisiveness that contradicted the weather. It had gone from sunny to cloudy, hot to cool, then back again, like a fickle child unable to decide.

After a week of searching, he'd finally found him.

Mordecai's real name.

First and last.

He reached Cleo's residence hall as two girls exited. They looked from him to each other, exchanging approving looks as he snagged the door, bypassing the retinal scan needed to unlock it. He walked through the lobby and into the elevator, behind a skinny kid with a stocking cap and scruffy facial hair.

They reached for the same button, their fingers

knocking into one another. With a pitchy laugh, the kid yanked his hand away. Cass jabbed the button with his thumb and lifted his gaze to the numbers above the door. He felt surly. On edge. The last week had been a brand of torture to which he wasn't accustomed. He didn't miss people. He made sure that kind of attachment wasn't a part of his life. And yet, he missed Eden Pruitt in a way that made him want to bury his head in a pillow and growl.

"You know," the kid said in a voice as pitchy as his laugh, "if this was a rom com, that would be our meet cute."

Cass had no idea what he was talking about. Nor did he care to inquire. He kept his gaze on the escalating numbers while the kid shifted nervously and stared from the corner of his eye.

"I have a girlfriend," the guy blurted as the elevator came to a slow stop. "I'm not gay, I mean. Not that there's anything wrong with being gay. I just ... didn't want you ... to think ... that I was ... hitting ... on you." He spoke the words in awkward intervals, like he wasn't sure if he should keep going but kept going anyway, then grimaced when he was finally done.

The elevator doors slid open.

Angry punk rock thumped from down the hall, filling Cass with relief. Cleo wasn't at a lecture or a study group like most college students tended to be on a Friday. She was in her room, listening to music at the ear-splitting decibel she seemed to prefer.

He strode to her door, then pounded on the wood like he had when he arrived with Eden a few weeks earlier, when he still wasn't sure whether he should help her or finish the job he'd been hired to do. How could so much have changed in only a few weeks? He pounded again, then shoved his hands into the pockets of his motorcycle jacket.

The scruffy-faced kid stopped beside him.

He gave Cass an apologetic look. "You know Cleo, too?"

Cass blinked at the guy, then raised his fist to pound a third time when the door flew open. Cleo stood on the other side with her hair in its usual style—Bantu knots, she called them—and a stick of licorice tucked into the corner of her mouth.

He let himself into her room and shut off the music.

"Please, come in," she said with a heavy dose of sarcasm. "Make yourself at home."

"Did I get the wrong time?" Cleo's visitor asked with lips that barely moved, as if talking like a ventriloquist might conceal his question.

"Nope," Cleo said. "But could you give us a second?"

The guy took a giant step backward. "I'll just be right out—"

Cleo shut the door before he could finish. She pulled

on the licorice stick, taking a bite with her. "You met Finn."

Finn.

Her partner in crime. The two were working together on an illegal newspaper called The People's Press, a deviant act that could get them both expelled. Maybe arrested.

"He's a total freak. But you should see his writing. Wicked funny in the most honest and brutal way." Her attention dropped to the papers Cass was pulling from his back pocket.

"I've got his name." He handed the articles he'd printed to Cleo. For the past week, he'd been searching. Determined to find Mordecai's real identity so he could then find Mordecai. "It's Nicholas Marks. He's thirty-four."

"That's young," she said.

Too young to be in league with Karik Volkova, the infamous leader of Interitus, the terrorist regime responsible for The Attack. The terrorist regime that had created Eden. At thirty-four, Nicholas Marks would have been thirteen when America was brought to its knees. Sixteen when Eden was born. Seventeen when Volkova was publicly executed. And yet somehow, he knew about Eden. "He works for SafePad."

"Think Oswin Brahm knows that one of his employees is a psychopath?" Cleo asked.

Oswin Brahm was, among many things, the founder of SafePad Elite—a company that built luxury bomb shelters, which skyrocketed in demand after The Attack. There were compounds all over the country. One was located outside of Chicago. This was where Mordecai had kept Eden's parents. This was where Mordecai had taken Eden.

"His credentials are impressive. He graduated from Harvard with a degree in finance. Worked his way up the corporate ladder until he became SafePad's chief investment specialist."

"With access to their facilities."

"His home address isn't listed in public records. But he works in SafePad's office headquarters. Downtown Chicago. Every time I call, his voicemail answers."

"Think he's out of the office?"

"He could be in meetings."

Cleo scanned the second article and pulled another bite from the licorice, tapping her snakebite piercing with the tip of her pinkie as she did.

"The building requires retinal scans upon entrance." Cass couldn't have his retinas scanned. Cass didn't have an identity. The second the infrared light touched his pupils, the police would be notified. Living off the grid was as illegal as Cleo's newspaper.

"Which means you need someone to do your dirty work," Cleo said.

"You interested?"

Her face split into a grin. "Let me reschedule with Finn and we can hit the road."

———

Cass watched from the passenger seat of Cleo's Tesla as she exited the front doors of SafePad headquarters and crossed the busy street. Overhead, the sky darkened. Cleo climbed into the car, a gust of cool wind swinging the door open wide. She sat behind the wheel and wrestled the door shut as raindrops splattered the windshield.

"He's not in. And they wouldn't tell me whether he would be. Which means …" She reached into the back seat, yanked up her backpack, and began pulling out items from inside. A bag of warheads. A bag of Takis. A pair of binoculars. "We've got ourselves an official stakeout."

Cass raised an eyebrow. "Why do you own a pair of binoculars?"

"So I can watch people in the residence hall across the street when I'm bored."

"Do you ever study?"

"I inherited my mother's brains. Do you think I need to?" Peering through her binocs, Cleo popped a Taki in her mouth. "Maybe he's out for lunch."

The rain turned into a sudden and violent downpour. Not even the windshield wipers could keep up. For two minutes and thirty-one seconds, they could see nothing outside other than the deluge. Then it came to a stop as suddenly as it started, a ray of sunshine peeking through the passing clouds.

"We could have missed him," Cleo said.

Cass tapped his foot impatiently, his attention zeroed in on the front doors as people peeked out from beneath their umbrellas and Cleo unwrapped a warhead.

"So, fill me in."

"On what?" Cass said.

"What's been going on? I know the basics. Six's parents are safe …" Six. As in, Subject 006. Cass didn't like the nickname. He didn't think Eden liked it either. "Her dad's a little beat up. Mordecai got away but left behind some important contraband."

By contraband, Cass assumed she meant Subject 003 and 004.

"One of which is Barrett freaking Barr."

The kid who had been on Concordia National news since his disappearance this past summer.

Cass wondered who had provided Cleo with the basics—her mom, who was currently playing hostess to Eden and her parents? Or Eden? He pushed his finger across his bottom lip, resisting the pathetic urge to ask Cleo if Eden had said anything about him. Whoever had coined the phrase "out of sight, out of mind" was an idiot. It had been seven brutal days since he'd seen her and the longer she remained out of sight, the more space she filled up in his mind.

He cracked his knuckles and relayed what he could to Cleo. He told her about the unconscious guards. About interrogating the man with the tattoos. He told her about the cyanide pill and the odd thing the guy said before swallowing it.

For the Monarch.

Cleo made a face like she was trying to place something. Or maybe it was a reaction to the warhead. "That sounds vaguely familiar."

"The Monarch?"

"Yeah." She brought the binoculars into her lap. "Do you think it's another name for Mordecai?"

"How many names does a guy need?" Cass shook his head, his agitation growing. "What's his end game? What does he want with them?"

"The guy's a gambler. Maybe he wants to invest in some fighters who can't lose."

Cass frowned. It seemed like a lot of trouble for someone who was doing more than okay without the sure thing.

Cleo peered at a man heading toward the front doors of SafePad. "It's not him," she said.

Cass scratched his ear. "So ... how's her dad doing?"

Cleo stared at him. He could feel the heat of her gaze boring into the side of his face. "Wait. Have you not talked to her?"

He pled the fifth.

"Cass?"

"What?"

"When's the last time you spoke?"

The night they kissed. The night she left. The night he watched helplessly from inside Beverly's home, unsure if he'd have to do what Eden had invited him back into her life to do—carry out a command that would end her existence. The memory haunted his sleep. "Last week."

"Last week? Why haven't you called her?"

Cass clenched his jaw.

"Seriously, what are you waiting for?"

"Mordecai's head on a stick."

"How very Macbethian of you." Cleo resumed her people-watching. "And here I thought you were more informed than me. Turns out, I know more than you. They left this morning, you know."

"Who?"

"Eden. Her parents. The whole crew."

"Where'd they go?"

"Back to the doc's place."

"Why?"

"Why don't you call her and ask? I'm sure Six would appreciate it."

"Can you stop calling her that?"

"Fine. Eden. Eden would appreciate it."

Cass pulled at his collar. He wasn't sure what Eden would appreciate. Not long ago, she told him she never wanted to see him again. She only invited him back into her life to do the work nobody else was willing to do. The kind of work perfect for a guy like him. "I will. Once Mordecai's dead."

"Unfortunately, I don't think that's going to be today." She glanced at the clock.

Lunch hour was long gone.

Still, they remained.

Long enough for the stake-out to lose its shine.

Cleo took a bathroom break.

Went on a beverage run.

Took a call with Finn.

Now she was scrolling through her phone with one foot on the dash. "Maybe we should write him a letter."

"Who?"

"Oswin Brahm."

Cass kept a steady eye on the front doors of SafePad's office building while Cleo launched into an idea.

"Someone should fill him in. Let him know one of his employees is a big-time gambler in the world of Underground Fighting and was carrying out his schemes on company property. For all we know, this Mordecai has ties to the very terrorist who made things like SafePad necessary."

Cass wondered if Cleo's idea didn't have merit.

Oswin Brahm helped rebuild the nation after Karik Volkova attacked it. He even started a foundation that served those suffering from chronic health problems because of that horrible day. Maybe the quickest way to take down Mordecai was to call SafePad's founder and leave an anonymous tip.

A lady and a gentleman exited side-by-side. Cass peered at them, wishing he had a better angle on the man.

Cleo took her foot off the dash and sat up straight. "Holy freak."

"What?" Cass said.

"Look who it is." She turned her phone screen to him. She'd pulled up a guest list for the Prosperity Ball. Talk of Oswin Brahm had undoubtedly given her the thought.

Good thing, too.

Because right there, in the very middle, was Nicholas Marks.

3

Eden stood on the threshold with her breath in her throat. One more step and she would see them. Subjects 003 and 004 lying like cadavers on gurneys in Dr. Norton's medical room. Only they were warm. Their vitals steady.

Dr. Norton entered the room from behind her. "The patient is resting. Your mother is with him."

The patient was Eden's father. The fact that he was resting, a testament to how difficult the brief trip from Chicago to Milwaukee had been for him in his fragile state. By the time they reached the secluded cabin, Dad had been pale and clammy.

Jack swept past, giving Eden's shoulder a small squeeze of support as he went. Perhaps he remembered the last time Eden had stepped into this room, when she thought Jack was the enemy and Dr. Norton was Mordecai. Or the time before that, when she was a four-year-old operating under the assumption that she was getting tubes in her ears. Eden could remember how scared her parents looked, and how hard she worked to hide her own fear to be brave for them. She had no idea that in actuality, the retired military doctor was about to insert a microscopic scrambling device in her ear. No idea that her parents were afraid, not because the procedure came with any danger, but because of the newly circulating rumors of weaponized humans.

Who had started them? It was just one of the many questions to which they didn't have answers.

Now here she was for the third time, about to see a boy and a girl who had never received scrambling implants. And because of that, they were in the states they were in now.

With a steadying breath, Eden stepped inside, her attention moving to Barrett first.

Subject 004.

She'd seen him plenty of times on the news—round-faced and smiling the kind of smile that made his eyes disappear. A strategic photograph that depicted a happy, well-adjusted kid, circulated by distraught parents who didn't believe their son ran away and didn't want the public to think so either.

Ever since she discovered the missing eighteen-year-old was Subject 004, Eden had done a significant amount of research on him. Unlike herself and Ellery, Barrett Barr had siblings. Two older brothers—fraternal twins who attended Boise State University, one on scholarship for football. According to his mother, Barrett had a creative mind and was a budding entrepreneur who'd already started two businesses and designed his own website. His family made their home in Idaho and had been vacationing in coastal Maine when Barrett disappeared. He was last seen on the beach. There was no evidence of foul play, which was why most of America believed he ran away. Despite the happy picture.

But Barrett Barr hadn't run away.

Barrett Barr had been taken.

And now here he was, in Dr. Norton's basement. Not smiling a smile that made his eyes disappear, but unconscious. His face relaxed—almost serene. His hair longer than in the pictures in the news, curling slightly with the length. The strangeness of his coma made Eden so unsettled, her bones felt cold. He'd been forced to sleep against his will. For how long, none of them knew.

With a shaky exhale, she turned her attention to the question mark. The girl. The Jane Doe. Subject 003. With raven hair cut into a shag—choppy layers and fringe bangs with wide-set eyes and a fan of straight, dark eyelashes. She looked like she might be of Asian descent. At least, partially. Not Filipino like Erik, but somewhere further east. Other than the name of her parents—who were no longer on the grid—they had no idea who she was or what her life had been like these past sixteen-and-a-half years.

Dr. Norton shined a light into her eyes, one at a time, as Jack set up his laptop on the desk. Norton checked her vitals, then set to work inserting a scrambling device into her ear. The same kind he'd reinserted into Eden's last week.

"You can take that off," Dr. Norton said, nodding toward the device clipped to the girl's finger. It reminded Eden of a pulse oximeter, but was, in reality, a makeshift scrambler useful in a pinch. In case Mordecai was monitoring their location. Now that Dr. Norton was here, he was giving them something more permanent.

"Can you help me move her to the flat bed?" Dr. Norton said.

Subject 003 was going to have a body scan in hopes that the result would provide something useful for Jack. Some insight into how and why Barrett and Jane remained in their unresponsive states. As Eden slipped her hand beneath the girl to lift her, a brush of cool metal rubbed against her thumb. Upon contact, a powerful shock jolted against her skin.

Eden yanked her hand back.

"What is it?" Dr. Norton asked.

She rubbed the spot on her thumb, then lifted Jane's head, swept her hair aside, and found a small disc adhered to the back of the girl's neck. It was a disc Eden had seen before.

Are you sure you should take that off?

The gruff voice played in her memory. The man with the rough hands and the tattoos. The man who was now dead because of a cyanide pill. When he asked the question, Eden had registered a missing blip of time, like the world had momentarily lost reception, noticeable because of the drone. One second, circling overhead. The next, floating right beside her.

"Eden," Dr. Norton said, bringing her back to the present.

"This disc." She lifted Jane's head so Dr. Norton could see it. "Mordecai had one with him at the abandoned power plant in North Allegheny. I think he used it on me."

Dr. Norton came around the gurney and bent close to inspect the new discovery. Then he moved to Barrett Barr and found that he had one, too.

"What did it do?" Jack asked.

"I don't remember," Eden said. "I think it made me black out."

Jack sat up straighter. "Do you think it's the reason I can't find a signal?"

"We could take them off and see," Dr. Norton suggested.

"No," Eden quickly replied.

Jack and Dr. Norton looked at her.

"That could be exactly what Mordecai is waiting for. Maybe he wants us to take them off." Maybe this was the reason he left Subjects 003 and 004 behind. Mordecai was waiting for them to take off these discs, and when they did, he would force the pair to attack. Who would win between Eden and another one of Volkova's weapons? The problem was, there were two of them and only one of her. The fight wouldn't be fair. And her dad was upstairs—weak and sleeping. Mom by his side. "I think we should do the scan first."

So they did.

Unfortunately, the scan didn't work. Not a single image loaded on the screen.

Dr. Norton checked the machine to make sure nothing had malfunctioned.

When all appeared to be in working order, they tried Barrett. The same thing happened. Whatever was blocking Jack from breaching their networks must have blocked the scanner, too.

They were stumped. It seemed too dangerous to remove the discs without getting more information, but they couldn't get more information without removing the discs.

"What about tranquilizer?" Jack finally said.

Eden looked at him.

"We know sedation works for a short time."

He was right.

Sedation had worked on Eden.

Jack himself had administered it. Inside the Eagle Bend police department. And again and again and again in their home in Milwaukee.

Dr. Norton nodded slowly, looking very much like a man who couldn't believe he hadn't thought of the idea first. "We could use a continuous stream of anesthetic gas."

"Remove the discs while they're under sedation," Eden said, "and see if anything changes."

The three of them looked at one another excitedly.

It was their best option.

Dr. Norton made the preparations. When he finished, he slipped the mask over Jane's mouth and nose. They counted from ten to one. Then he removed the disc.

Eden watched warily—her entire body on high alert—as Jack hunched over his laptop and opened the list of networks. His eyes widened.

She stepped behind him and sure enough, there it was, right beneath Eden's network. Tres. The Latin word for three. Only ... "Why is her signal so weak?"

"I don't know." Jack's fingers flew across the keyboard. Then he stopped, sank back, and stared in disbelief. "I'm in."

He'd done it.

After a week of dead ends and frustrating failure,

Subject 003 very suddenly had a visible network and Jack was in. The same method he'd used to hack into Eden's network had gotten him into this one. After the short, stunned moment, Jack's fingers flew back into motion. Eden didn't understand anything he was doing. But he worked quickly and efficiently, like a man who'd been practicing for this very situation—pulling up windows, loading lists of code, copying and pasting and hitting various keys. Then he released a disbelieving squawk. "She's disconnected."

"What does that mean?" Eden asked.

"There's no sign that she's connected to the host." Jack set his hand on top of his thinning hair. "If Mordecai is out there waiting to control her, he can't. He needs to be connected to her network to control her, and he needs her location to re-connect with her network. Her location is scrambled. We should be safe."

"Let's try the scan again before we wake her," Dr. Norton said.

This time, it worked. A treasure trove of images loaded on the computer, ready to be studied. But first, they needed to wake the patient.

With a great deal of caution, Dr. Norton turned off the gas and removed the mask.

Eden waited, oxygen stagnant in her lungs.

A moment later, the girl squeezed her eyes.

She scrunched her nose.

She blinked—several times in rapid succession—her confusion giving way to fear as she jerked upright, her attention darting left, then right.

All three of them held up their hands in a gesture of no harm.

But the girl jumped off the table and skittered into a corner.

"We're not going to hurt you," Dr. Norton said in the same soothing voice he'd used on Eden after she sliced her hand open and watched it heal before her eyes.

The girl was not soothed.

She patted herself. Looked down at her clothes. Reached deep inside her pockets. Then cowered like a wild animal in a cage, her attention jerking from Barrett on the gurney, to the medical equipment in the room, then back to them with their hands held aloft. Erratic movements that filled Eden with apprehension. If they were grenades, she was an unstable one.

"You were taken," Eden rushed to explain. "By a man named Mordecai. We got you away from him and you've just woken up."

The girl squeaked.

"You're safe," Eden said, staying in place. Not daring to step closer. Trying to imagine how disorienting it would be to have been unconscious for as long as this girl was, only to wake up in a completely foreign environment, surrounded by strangers. "We aren't going to hurt you. We're on your side."

Jane Doe didn't move.

She stayed in the corner, crouched in her defensive position, her hooded eyes partially hidden beneath the choppy layers of hair that had fallen in her face.

"What's your name?" Eden asked.

The girl's attention darted about the room once again —from Eden to Jack to Dr. Norton to the unconscious Barrett, to the medical equipment all around. With another squeak, she squeezed her eyes shut.

Eden tried again. "Can you tell us what you remember?"

Nothing.

Dr. Norton scratched his mustache.

And another sound came.

Not from the girl.

But from above.

From outside.

A sound Dr. Norton and Jack Forrester couldn't hear. But Eden could hear it. And judging by the way Subject 003 opened her eyes and tilted her head, she could hear it, too.

The distinct rev of a motorcycle.

Cass shut off the motorcycle.

Cleo parked behind him. As soon as she had made her discovery, they returned to Milwaukee. He'd jumped on his bike, which he'd left parked outside her residence hall, and Cleo followed him here, to Dr. Norton's cabin in the woods on the lake at twilight.

Crickets chirped.

Geese honked.

The sinking sun peeked through remnants of storm clouds, creating a masterpiece over the water.

For the past week, Cass had hunted. His vision, a tunnel leading to one goal and only one goal—find Mordecai. Currently, Eden was safe. Reunited with her parents. Mordecai had not possessed her. He hadn't touched the core of who she was. But the threat remained and would remain for as long as Mordecai remained. So Cass searched harder than he'd searched for anyone, determined to stay away until he eliminated the threat.

He failed.

The threat wasn't eliminated. But they had a promising lead. And he couldn't stay away any longer.

The front door swung open.

Eden stepped outside.

Cass drank her in like a man in the middle of the

Sahara without a canteen. The last time he'd seen her, she'd been covered in her father's blood. Now she stood silhouetted by the cabin, her eyes wide, her lips parted, her long hair a tumble around her face—innocent, unguarded. Much too young. Staring back at him as if the past seven days had tortured her as relentlessly as they had tortured him.

He imagined striding forward, pulling her to him, and repeating the kiss they'd shared outside Beverly's home. His body flooded with the acute need to do so. But Cleo's car door slammed shut—a reminder that they weren't alone.

"He's going to the ball!" Cleo exclaimed.

Forrester stepped outside with eyes like an insomniac, the screen door slapping shut as Cass and Cleo came forward to meet them.

"Who's going to what?" Forrester asked.

"Mordecai," Cass said, cutting a quick glance at Eden, who was refusing to meet his eye. "His real name is Nicholas Marks. He's the Chief Investment Specialist for SafePad."

"He's on the guest list for the Prosperity Ball," Cleo said. "My mom can get us tickets. We can surround him on all sides like an old-fashioned ambush."

"You think he's still going?" Eden asked, her attention trained on Cleo.

It was a question Cass had asked himself. Mordecai

could have RSVP'd when his plans were succeeding. Maybe now, with those plans in disarray, he no longer had anything to celebrate.

The hinges of the screen door groaned as Dr. Norton stepped outside in his tweed flat cap, coaxing someone to join them like one might coax a frightened animal.

A girl appeared—slight and skittish, shielding her eyes like it was high noon.

"Jane," Cleo said.

Cass gaped.

Subject 003 was awake.

4

Eden's emotions swung on a violent pendulum.

Surprise.

Relief.

Confusion.

Anger.

Back and forth with such velocity, she felt nauseous.

She'd spent the last week using an extraordinary amount of energy suppressing thoughts of him. Distraction was the name of the game. Help her father with his exercises. Learn as much as she could about Barrett and the girl without an identity. It worked, to an extent. Until night came. Nothing could distract her in the dark. Thoughts of him came like a deluge as she tossed and turned and dug her head beneath her pillow.

Her father almost died. The bad guy got away. Subjects 003 and 004 were comatose in Dr. Norton's basement. Eden was a freak of nature infested with microscopic robots that could—in the wrong hands—make her do things she didn't want to do. Life, as she once knew it, was irrevocably lost. Yet this was what occupied her mind. A boy. Where was he? Why did he leave? Why hadn't he been in touch? What was he doing now? And the most incessant of all—was he okay?

Now he was back as suddenly as he'd left.

With Cleo.

Not shot dead like Yukio the Bookie but perfectly intact.

They found Mordecai's real name. He was going to the ball. The girl they were calling Jane was awake but not talking. Whether she could but wouldn't or couldn't but wanted to remained unclear. For all they knew, removing that disc had damaged her in some way that weakened her network and stole her voice. Maybe they did it wrong and now Jane was stuck in this weird limbo they couldn't fix without asking the bad guy for help.

The only way to find out was by waking up Barrett Barr to see if his condition was the same. Which led them to the basement, where the pendulum swung, and Eden avoided Cassian's stare like the plague.

As Dr. Norton brought the mask toward Barrett's mouth and nose, Jane let loose another one of her strange squeaks.

Dr. Norton stopped and looked at the girl, as if

waiting for her to object. Instead, she scurried to the corner of the room, sat down on the floor, and wrapped her arms around her middle.

"Maybe she's hungry," Cleo suggested.

"Do you want something to eat?" Jack asked.

Jane doubled over her crossed legs, her hair falling to the ground like choppy curtains.

Cleo shrugged.

Dr. Norton resumed, bringing the mask to Barrett's face. He counted down from ten, then removed the disc.

"There he is," Jack said. "Quattuor."

It was the Latin word for four.

Another network.

Jack's brow furrowed as his attention hopped around his computer screen.

"How's the signal?" Eden asked.

"Strong." Jack went to work and, a few minutes later, came to the same conclusion. Barrett Barr wasn't connected to the host, either. He had been at one time, but not any longer.

Dr. Norton performed the body scan.

And a few minutes later, Barrett Barr awoke.

He didn't squeak or cower, but remained prone on the gurney, looking from one person to the next like a football player on the ground, regaining consciousness after a blindsiding blow. "Uhhh," he finally croaked. "Where am I?"

THE ABERRATION OF EDEN PRUITT

"He talks," Cleo said.

Barrett sat up slowly, rubbing his forehead. He looked past Cleo toward Jane in the corner, who was no longer bent double, but watching suspiciously.

"What's going on?" he asked.

"What do you remember?" Eden replied.

Barrett scrunched his face, then gave his head a rattle. "The beach? In Maine."

"Do you know who took you?"

"Someone took me?"

Eden stared.

Had he been unconscious this whole time? Ever since his disappearance this summer? If so, then he would have no idea what was going on. How did one jump in to such a story? She recalled standing in the kitchenette down this very hallway, a knife clattering to the floor. The shock of hearing the truth for the first time, even after watching her hand heal in a way no hand was meant to heal.

Dr. Norton placed his own over his chest. "My name is Dr. Benjamin Norton. You're in my house and we've just woken you up."

From there, Dr. Norton continued. The more he explained, the bigger Barrett's eyes grew. And the more often he inserted disbelieving quips.

It's September?

I'm in Wisconsin?

41

My face is on national news?

When Dr. Norton reached the part about nanobots and Interitus and Karik Volkova, Barrett started to laugh. It took him a while to stop. When he did, he wiped his eyes. "Which one of my brothers put you up to this? Or was it both of them?"

Nobody replied.

Barrett shifted so he could look past them, toward the hallway, as if fully expecting his brothers to walk in with laughter and smiles. "Good one, guys," he called. "You can come out now."

Nobody came.

Barrett's attention returned to his audience of six. "How much are they paying you?"

"This isn't a joke," Jack said.

Barrett quirked his eyebrow.

"Everything we've told you is the truth."

"The truth?"

Eden nodded. So did Dr. Norton and Jack and Cleo. Whether Cassian nodded, she couldn't tell. She was still determinedly avoiding his gaze.

"I'm supposed to believe that I was created by Karik Volkova and I'm basically some sort of ... superhero?"

Superhero was a strange word choice, one that implied goodness and bravery. They were weapons of terror. When nobody jumped in to correct him, his expression turned into a corkscrew—his mouth and nose scrunched and twisting to the side. Like he was thinking very, very hard.

"Arm wrestling," he mumbled.

"What's that?" Dr. Norton asked.

"I beat my brothers in arm wrestling." Barrett looked up, his expression elongating into wide-eyed amazement. "We were on vacation in Maine. We go there every summer. All five of us. Graham said he'd give me fifty dollars if I could last thirty seconds against Jameson in an arm-wrestling match, which is basically impossible, but I had nothing to lose, so we got into position and I ... I beat him. Graham got pissed. He thought Jameson threw the match on purpose so he'd be out fifty dollars. So Jameson says to Graham, 'Think I'm joking? You try it. I'll give you a hundred dollars if you can beat him.' And I won! I beat Graham. I thought they were both messing with me. I don't beat my brothers in arm wrestling. Nobody does. Then we went to the beach to look for crabs and the rest is just..." Barrett brought his fists to his temples, then made a sound like an explosion while moving his hands away and spreading his fingers wide. "Totally blank."

Silence filled the room.

Cleo was the one to break it. "One doesn't talk at all. The other is a veritable fount."

The stairs creaked.

Eden turned.

Her mother stepped into the room with a crease on the side of her face, like she'd just woken from a very hard nap and was trying to gain her bearings. She looked from Jane cowering in the corner to Barrett, sitting on the gurney, to Cleo with her skull and bones necklace and snakebite lip piercing, to Cassian in his motorcycle jacket —unreasonably gorgeous and excessively brooding, looking every inch the fighter.

Barrett lifted his hand. "Hi."

Mom blinked dumbly. "You're ... awake."

"And very chatty." Cleo stepped forward and shook Mom's hand. "You must be Ruth. Or should we call you Molly?"

Molly was her mother's former name when her father was still Alaric.

Eden laughed nervously, then cleared her throat. "Mom, this is Beverly's daughter, Cleo. And this is ... Cass." As soon as she said it, her face went Florida summer hot. She could feel everyone's stare. Even Jane's was unwavering.

She was introducing her mother to Cassian Gray in front of a captivated audience. Her stomach twisted with nerves. Here was a boy who lived off the grid. Spent a decade of his life as a ruthless underground fighter, only to go into early retirement because he killed his final opponent in the ring. To pay off his debt for the advance he'd already been paid, he became a tracker for a bookie named Yukio, which was how he found her, and their lives flipped upside down.

She'd had seven days to fill her parents in on the details. But she hadn't told them any of these particulars. And now, her mother was staring at Cassian with tears in her eyes. She stepped toward him, grasped his hand between hers, and said in the most genuine of ways, "Thank you."

Cassian looked completely disarmed by the gratitude.

"For coming when you did," her mother added.

His posture stiffened slightly as he gave Mom a curt nod.

Mom had expressed the gratitude Eden felt when her father squeezed her hand three days after surgery. She'd been flooded with relief. And appreciation. For it had been Cassian's fast thinking that brought them to Safe-Pad's compound so quickly. With Dad on the brink of death, every second counted. In a way, he had saved her father's life. But as the days passed without a word, her appreciation waned.

Now it threatened to return.

She steeled herself against it. "He found Mordecai," she said.

"I found his name," Cassian corrected, trying to catch her eye.

Eden refused to be caught.

He rubbed his jaw and addressed her mother. "He's on the guest list for the Prosperity Ball."

"I'm going to see if my mom can get us tickets," Cleo said.

Her mother looked like a deer in the headlights. Barrett and Jane, awake. Cleo and Cassian, here. Mordecai's real name. And the prospect of attending a national celebration on a day her mother never wanted to celebrate. "Your father's asleep," she finally said. "I'm hoping he'll stay that way through the night." She looked from Cleo to Cass to Barrett to Jane, still huddled in the corner. "This will be a lot to wake up to."

5

Your father's asleep.

Father.

The name rang in her ears. Amplified inside the confines of her skull. Until there was nothing but the shrieking sound of it, burrowing into the folds of her brain like sharp claws. Once fully entombed, the name expanded until she was consumed with a bloated need to escape. Stand up. Leave. Run through the wall. Fast, before Father wakes. Get out of this horrible room filled with horrible equipment.

Get out, get out, get out!

Instead, she pushed deeper into the corner. Wrapped her arms tighter around her waist. There was more than one Father. She had learned this a long time ago, from the books Mother had left her.

Mother.

Where was Mother?

She patted her pockets once more, but the picture wasn't there. The picture was gone. These weren't her clothes. And the woman with the crease on her face wasn't talking about her father. The woman didn't look at her at all when she said it. She'd been looking at the blonde.

Father was not here.

Father *was not* here.

So where was he?

A hand touched her shoulder.

Her eyes flew open.

She jerked away.

The man with the silver mustache was crouched in front of her. The man who had used some of that horrible equipment on the boy. He held up his hands, the blue of his eyes unsettling. She looked past him to the others. They were staring at her, every single one.

The tall, thin gentleman with bloodshot eyes and stubble on his chin. The woman with the red line on her face. The girl with brown skin and metal in her lip. The blonde with the sleeping father and the young man who kept looking at the blonde. Even the round-faced boy was staring—the one who'd woken up on a gurney the same as she had.

There were so many of them.

Too many of them.

Standing amongst all that disconcerting equipment.

"It's okay. Everything is going to be okay." The mustached man spoke in a voice every bit as unsettling as his eyes. His name was Dr. Benjamin Norton. He introduced himself when it was just the two of them, after the blonde hurried up the stairs and the tall, thin gentleman followed. He had coaxed her to come outside with him. Now they were back in the basement, and he introduced everyone else. "This is Eden. Cleo. Cassian. Jack. Barrett." He said the names slowly, nodding to each person in turn—the blonde, the girl with metal in her lip, the young man who kept staring at the blonde, the tall, thin gentleman with the bloodshot eyes, the boy on the gurney. "And this is—"

"Ruth." The woman with the red crease lifted her chin and shot a quick glance at the blonde. "Ruth Pruitt."

Dr. Benjamin Norton nodded, then turned back to her. "Can you tell us your name?"

No, she couldn't. The words would not come. They were trapped. Deep down inside, where they'd been trapped ever since that awful day.

"We've been calling you Jane," Cleo said.

Jane.

She knew a Jane. In one of the books that belonged to Mother. She tried it on in her mind. Wrapped it around herself like a heavy cloak that could hide her from all the bad things that came with her old name.

Jane.

Jane.

She could be Jane.

A new name. With new memories.

"I think it might be a good idea to get you two something to eat. You can shower and rest." Dr. Benjamin Norton looked from her to Barrett, then stood from his crouched position. "We'll have to come up with some new sleeping arrangements. There's the den down the hall. It has a pullout sofa." He turned to the blonde. "I can bring a cot into your parents' room. If you don't mind sleeping in there, that will free up another bed."

"I don't mind," the blonde said.

"Can I call my parents?"

Everyone turned to look at the boy. Barrett. They did so in perfect unison, like they weren't six individuals but a singular entity made of six parts.

"I need to tell them I'm okay."

"You can't," Jack said in a voice much different from the doctor's. In a voice more reminiscent of Father's. "It's not safe."

"But I've been missing since July. I can't imagine how worried they are."

"Worried is better than dead."

The blonde named Eden frowned at Jack. But she

took his side in the end, telling Barrett about the bad guy named Mordecai again. About how he took her parents. He would have killed them too if she hadn't gotten to them first. "I know it's difficult, but you have to leave them out of this."

"For how long?" Barrett asked.

"I don't know," Eden said.

The boy deflated.

Jane wondered if this was a trick. A clever skit performed to deceive her, compel her to stay until Father arrived. And this time, she would never get away. She would be trapped forever.

The doctor invited Jane and Barrett upstairs.

She followed quickly.

Whatever this was—whether a trick or the truth—she was eager to leave this room with the horrible equipment behind. He led them up a set of stairs into an open living room with big windows. Twilight was gone. Night had fallen.

The doctor stepped into the kitchen. "You can help yourself to whatever you'd like. I imagine you're both hungry."

"Is it weird that I'm not?" Barrett said with a deep furrow in his brow. "I mean, I've been asleep since July, but somehow my body has sustained itself. Do you think Mordecai was feeding us?"

"I'm not sure," the doctor said. He smiled encouragingly at Jane, who hid behind her hair, convinced this was another trick. She'd never—not once in her whole life—been given free rein in a kitchen. Food had always been meticulously monitored and then, when she ran away, nearly impossible to come by.

She took a wary step toward the refrigerator.

Dr. Norton's smile remained.

She took another step, then flung the refrigerator wide open.

The doctor did nothing. He just stood there, smiling placidly.

Without breaking eye contact, she grabbed a loaf of bread from the top shelf and tore it open. She pulled out a slice and stuffed it in her mouth. She followed this with two more. Then she tucked the loaf under her arm and took a gallon of milk, uncapped the lid, and drank. When she was finished, she wiped her chin with the back of her hand.

The boy gawked like he'd never seen anyone eat before.

The doctor didn't bat an eye.

"What would you like?" he asked Barrett.

"A hot shower, actually," Barrett said slowly, his eyes never leaving Jane.

Dr. Norton led him down the hall, and suddenly Jane was alone. After an entire year of picking through garbage cans and restaurant dumpsters, she was standing by herself in a kitchen filled with food.

She glanced over her shoulder, then dug in. She crammed more bread into her mouth. She chugged the milk until the gallon was nearly empty and her stomach was full and distended.

Voices and footsteps were coming up the stairs.

Jane scuttled away—down the hallway—like a bug seeing the light.

Directly behind her, a door opened.

With a yelp, she spun around.

Barrett stepped out into the hall with a cloud of steam and a towel draped over his shoulder—his dark hair wet and dripping, his light brown eyes as disconcerting as the doctor's. He told her the bathroom was all hers. She quickly closed herself inside.

She stared at the shower stall, unsure how to use it.

Father made her wash in a barrel.

Then she ran away and hadn't washed at all.

She sniffed her armpits.

Somehow, she was clean.

Maybe the bad guys cleaned her.

A shudder rippled up her spine.

A memory, too.

One that had started so blissfully—a rare, heavenly moment filled with warmth and wonder. She had discovered a treasure in the back of a dark alley. Babies. Darling little puppies, so tiny they could barely open their eyes. And their proud mama standing guard.

Then the memory went to rot.

Danger came like a sharp scent in her nostrils.

The dog could smell it, too, for its ears flattened and its hackles raised, and a low growl rumbled in the back of its throat. Jane had curled her hand around a broken piece of glass and turned to face the peril. She would defend this mother and her babies. She would not fail. Not this time.

A pair of men stood at the mouth of the alley, blocking her escape, one of them covered in tattoos. They looked from her to the shard of glass. Father must have sent them. This was the last thought Jane remembered having and then ...

She rubbed a circle in the foggy mirror. She batted her hair from her face and stared hard at her reflection. What happened to the mother? What had become of the babies? What did those bad men do?

Her stomach rolled.

The bread and the milk revolted.

She pitched herself at the toilet. Grabbing the basin, she heaved. Over and over until the sick was gone and her stomach was empty. She flushed the toilet and rinsed her mouth at the sink. She splashed her face and patted it dry with the folded towel. It was so soft—that towel. Closing her eyes, she pressed it against her cheek. Then she turned around and faced the shower stall.

The nozzle was round. She tried twisting it—first one way, then the other. Nothing happened. She wiggled it, seeing if it might go up or down. Then she pulled. Water came streaming from the shower head and splashed against the floor.

Jane lurched back.

Hesitantly, she reached out and stuck her hand into the stream. It was cool. She turned the nozzle. The temperature changed to cold, colder, freezing. She turned it the other way. The temperature went warm, hot, scalding. Jane took her hand from the stream as more steam eddied into the air.

It's a dangerous slope.

Father's words came like a whisper.

Pleasure was a distraction.

Seeking after it—a descent into ruin.

And it wasn't only her life at stake.

According to Father, the slope started with warm baths. Soft beds. Enjoyable food. It ended in hedonism. For Jane, there had been none of those things. She didn't know there could be. Until Mother gave her the books. Until Mother brought her to town, and she saw how other people lived. Father had been furious. Jane was not supposed to go to town.

She was special.

Town would contaminate her.

Barrett had been amazed at the doctor's story. Shocked, even. As though he'd never thought of himself as anything but ordinary. But she knew. She'd always known. It was why Father ran so many tests. It was why he caused so much pain. She had powers, and it was his job to unlock them.

Jane looked down at her upturned palms. She traced her finger up the length of her forearm. Her skin was smooth and unmarred. There were certain tests she always passed. Her body knew how to heal itself. She could do it without even trying. The other tests, however...

No matter how hard she tried, no matter how desperately she wanted her powers unlocked, she failed and she failed and she failed. And her words sank deeper and deeper and deeper until that awful day when they left altogether.

But something changed in that alley when the bad guys came. The power finally broke free. She had felt the shift. She smelled those men before she saw them, and they were standing at the opposite end of a very long alley. If only the powers had unlocked themselves sooner.

What happened to the dog?

What happened to the babies?

With the shower still running and the steam thickening, Jane opened the bathroom door ever so slightly. She closed her eyes and focused on her ears. She imagined casting them into the next room, where there was a deep, rhythmic breathing and the rustle of sheets and two beating hearts. She cast them further away, into the kitchen. Two more beating hearts and the crunch, crunch, crunch of masticating food.

"You're welcome to crash on my futon." The voice belonged to the girl with the metal in her lip. Cleo.

"I'll be fine here."

There was a heavy sigh and then, "I guess I'll see you in the morning, then."

Footsteps moved to the door, which opened. Then closed. And only one heartbeat remained. Jane walked her ears down the stairs. Into the room with the horrible equipment.

Two more heartbeats.

The clacking of computer keys.

Another conversation.

"Her network is different," said the tall, thin gentleman with the bloodshot eyes. Jack. His heart beat faster than the others. "Do you have the initial images from when they were first brought in?"

"They should be in her file," the doctor said.

Papers rustled.

Buttons clicked.

"What about Eden's and Barrett's?" Jack asked.

"They're right here."

A chair squeaked.

A long pause with more rustling papers.

"They were all the same," Jack said. "Something must have happened to change hers." Whiskers were scratched, the sound like peeling Velcro. "I'd like to run some tests."

Jane pulled the bathroom door shut with a decisive click.

But her ears were still downstairs.

"Let's give her some time first," came the doctor's reply.

She reeled her hearing in like a frantic fisherman, shaking her head all the while. Backing away until her shoulder blades met the wall behind her. With nowhere to go, the memory pounced. She felt the weight of it in her arms. The cold, lifeless weight. Her only friend since Mother left. Her best friend. Dead because she failed. Dead because of these tests.

And now these men were going to run more.

What happened to the dog?

What happened to the babies?

They wouldn't survive without their mother.

She cast her ears down the hallway again.

The refrigerator opened, closed. Boots clomped across the living room floor to the door that led to a back deck. The door slid open, and the night sounds screamed. The young man who was going to sleep on the couch slid the door shut, his heartbeat joining another.

Jane peeked into the hallway.

Behind her, the shower was still running. The bathroom was a steam cloud. She stepped out and shut the door.

On silent feet, she hurried into the empty living room and the empty kitchen. A bowl of reddish-orange chips sat on the counter. Jane opened cabinets until she found a bag. She dumped the contents of a fruit bowl inside—bananas and apples. She dumped the chips inside, too. Another loaf of bread and a block of cheese.

Someone sneezed in the bedroom down the hall.

Jane stopped, then tied up the bag and ran on tiptoe to the front door. She opened it quietly and backed away, her ears inside, so focused on the heartbeats in front of her she didn't register the one behind.

"Hey."

With a jump, she whirled around.

Barrett stood on the lawn beneath the light of a lamppost, his eyes bright as he pushed his hands through still-damp hair. "This is so wild. I can hear everything. I can see everything, too. Look at that, over there." He nodded toward an opened book leaning against the trunk of a far-off tree. The lamp light was too far away to illuminate the pages. There were only the stars. And yet,

Barrett read the words like the book was right in front of him.

Then he wrapped his fingers around the lamppost. With a slight bend of his wrist, the post bent. He straightened his wrist and the post straightened with it. "This is made from cast iron, and I can bend it like it's rubber. Even my sense of smell." He inhaled through his nostrils. "Chimney smoke. There aren't any houses nearby, but I can smell chimney smoke. And ... barbecue."

Jane hid the bag she was holding behind her back, as if this might mask the smell of the chips she'd dumped inside.

"Caramel and burnt sugar. Katsura trees in the fall. I know that smell. I love that smell." He peered into the dark woods. "There aren't any Katsura trees nearby either, but I can smell them, which means they must be somewhere. Graham and Jameson are going to freak when I tell them. Absolutely lose their minds. And my parents—" A small frown dented his enthusiasm. "I guess they already know."

He scratched his earlobe, then ran his hand through his hair, which flopped in the wake of his palm. "Apparently, I can't get hurt. At least not easily. They must know that, so they can't be too worried. I don't think—" He stopped mid-sentence, his attention dipping to the bag she had unsuccessfully hidden behind her slight frame. "Are you leaving?"

Heat poured into her cheeks. She looked down at the grass, her hair falling in her face like a curtain.

"Where are you going?" Barrett asked.

Jane's heart punched a bruise into her sternum.

Barrett must have heard it. "You don't have to worry. I won't tell anyone."

The mama dog. Her tiny puppies. She needed to get to them. She needed to save them. But they were in an alley in a giant city far away. One much closer to Father. Fear came like a flood. It zipped through her veins and sloshed in her belly, making her knees tremble. She didn't want to be near Father. She couldn't be near Father. But then, what about the babies?

"Are you all right?" Barrett asked, taking a step closer.

Jane stepped back and closed her eyes. She squeezed them tight, commanding herself to go. Don't be a coward. Save the babies. But despite Father's visions, she couldn't save anything. She only made things die. And the babies were in July. According to the doctor, it was the middle of September. Which meant it was probably too late.

Her insides howled.

"I don't know what you've been through or where you're wanting to go. But for whatever it's worth, I think we're safe here. For now. I think we can trust these people."

Safe.

Trust.

They were foreign words that belonged to a foreign language.

Jane looked up at the sky and the stars. There were so many of them. She'd spent a year in the city, where the lights were too bright for the stars and her powers were still locked away. But she could see them now. If she shut out everything else—the sounds and the smells—she could see each one with astounding clarity. She imagined gravity letting go. She imagined falling into space until she was part of those stars. Far away. Out of Father's reach.

"Besides," Barrett said, running his hand back through his hair again. "If you leave, I'll be all alone."

She blinked at him, startled by his statement.

Afraid of his statement.

Alone was better.

Alone was safer.

But then, Barrett was special, too. He was special, like her, which meant he couldn't be hurt. Father couldn't hurt him. In fact—if they wanted—they could hurt Father.

The terrifying thought skittered up her throat and released in a small squeak that she covered with her hand.

Barrett tilted his head, as though trying to interpret

the noise. "I hope you stay. I mean, we're kind of in this together, right?"

Together.

Jane should not like that word.

Did not like that word.

But maybe staying one night, beneath all these stars, in a warm bed with a full kitchen would not be the end of the world.

6

Eden stood on the large deck beneath a clear, moonless sky that stretched above her—an expanse of twinkling stars while all around nature performed its nocturnal symphony.

If she listened carefully, she could differentiate the sounds. Like a well-trained musician at the orchestra, able to discern which notes were being played by the concertmaster and which were being played by the second violinist. There were cicadas and crickets and katydids and bullfrogs and the intermittent call of a loon.

Her parents were asleep.

Dr. Norton was getting Jane and Barrett settled, although Eden couldn't imagine either were in the mood for slumber.

Cleo had left—gone back to her dorm in the city.

Eden wondered if Cass had left, too.

It wouldn't surprise her.

He had a knack for leaving.

A gentle breeze danced with a wisp of hair that had fallen loose from its tie.

Outside was peaceful.

Inside, a tumult.

Her emotions continued their violent swinging. Anger. Gratitude. Anger. Gratitude. Eliciting a dizzying turbulence that made her chest tight and snarly.

Behind her, the door slid open.

She glanced over her shoulder, and her stomach swooped.

Cassian stepped out into the night.

He hadn't left.

Not yet anyway.

She turned back to the lake, her body tensing at the sound of his approaching boot steps. Her grip on the banister tightened as the dueling desires to thank him and slap him waged war. The longer he let the silence stretch between them, the stronger the urge to slap him became. Until her fingers dug into the wood and her knuckles grew white with impatience. How could he be so unaffected while her insides scratched and twitched?

When she could bear it no longer, she spun to face him.

He looked at her in response and what she saw knocked her off balance. He didn't look unaffected. He looked mad. The same unwarranted animosity he'd displayed all those weeks ago—when he was a stranger in a coffee shop with no reason to hate her. It simmered in his golden irises now like it had then. A fury that heightened her own.

"You stayed," she said, heatedly. Accusatorially.

He said nothing while a muscle ticked in his jaw.

"I'm surprised."

"Why?"

"You didn't stay last time. You left without a word."

"To go look for him," he said, his voice a low rumble.

"My dad might have died, and you didn't even call."

"I called."

"You called Jack. Not me."

"What did you want to talk about, Eden? What did you want me to say?" His words were biting.

She gaped in the wake of them. He had no right to his anger. He was the one who brought this trouble on her doorstep. And he was the one who left like none of it mattered. With her father on his deathbed and her sanity unraveling like a spool of thread. She gawked at him—disbelieving. Incensed. "I needed you."

"To push three buttons!" His voice erupted, so loud that for a moment, the nocturnal chorus stopped.

Eden and Cassian glared at one another in the silence.

He broke it first, his voice low, anger rolling off him in waves. "You have no idea what it was like. Watching from Beverly's home. Not knowing if you were under his control. Not knowing if I'd have to …" He pressed his lips together and shook his head. "You kissed me like you cared—"

"I did care!"

"It was your insurance policy. To make sure I'd do your bidding."

Eden huffed—a heated exhale from her nose. "I was leaving. I had no idea if I'd ever see you again, and you were just going to walk inside Beverly's house without a word. Without a goodbye. Like I didn't—" She bit her lip to keep the vehement statement inside.

His eyes bore into hers with breathtaking intensity. Searching. Waiting. His attention dipping to her lips, then shifting back up again. "Like you didn't what?"

"Like I didn't matter. Like I meant nothing—"

She didn't get the chance to finish.

Cassian took her face between his hands and covered her mouth with his—their anger colliding in an explosion of need.

Her fingers curled into his hair. His hands moved to her waist and spread up her ribcage, turning her insides into liquid warmth. He tasted like mint and desire—one so deep and fathomless it completely undid her. He kissed her as expertly now as he did then, when she wasn't sure if they would ever see each other again. He kissed her so thoroughly, her anger melted into an intoxicating heat that zipped through her veins. And when it was done—when she was *undone*—he tipped her chin, his eyes filled with ferocity. "Don't ever ask me to do that again."

He wasn't talking about the kiss.

He was talking about the command.

The reason she'd invited him back into her life.

Or maybe it was an excuse.

"I won't," she said.

He pulled her against him, his arms wrapping around her. His heartbeat strong in her ear. His chin resting on the crown of her head. She nuzzled against the curve of his neck and for the first time in a long time, the panic stopped clawing. For the first time in a long time, she felt … still.

"I'm sorry for not calling," he said, his voice a rumble against her ear.

She took a deep breath, inhaling the scent of him. Sandalwood and pine and the leather of his jacket. With a long exhale, she let herself completely relax. "Do you really think Cleo can get tickets?"

"She has a better chance than most."

"My parents won't want me to go."

Eden had spent her life playing it safe. Avoiding risk. Toeing the line. Following the rules. Ignoring her attraction to danger. She did it all for them—her parents. But they were the ones taking a risk. From the beginning, they'd known what she was, but they'd taken her in anyway, fully aware that things could go terribly wrong. Otherwise, they never would have set up an emergency plan with Dr. Norton that involved an alarm system.

"What do you want?" Cassian asked.

She wanted her parents to be happy. She wanted to be good despite everything that had transpired to make her otherwise. She wanted this boy in front of her. She wanted him to kiss her again and again and again. She wanted to live without the cloying fear of being controlled. Of having no control. She wanted to belong to herself. But she didn't. She couldn't. Not until Mordecai was gone.

"I want this to end," she said.

"Then we'll make sure it does."

On the fourth of October. The twenty-first anniversary of America's darkest day. The world's darkest day.

Maybe after this year, it would hold a different meaning.

Maybe after this year, Eden would finally be free.

7

Another front rolled in overnight. This one lingered with a steady rain that ran down the windows in lazy rivulets. Cass watched them meander as he leaned against the counter, sipping the last of the coffee from his mug.

The girl who had yet to talk rummaged for food in the pantry. The boy who hardly shut up sat at the table amidst a pile of books—an eclectic mix of biographies and medical journals, true crime, and military fiction. At the moment, he was finishing a particularly thick volume, flipping pages like an enthusiastic reader in the throes of a manic episode.

Out in the living room, Forrester examined the discs that had been removed from the chatterbox and the mute while Concordia News played without sound on the television.

Eden had yet to join them. She was still down the hall, in a room with her parents.

Her parents.

Cass dragged his hand down his face. What was he doing?

Barrett snapped the tome shut and came to his feet. "Somebody quiz me."

The girl grabbed a jar of peanut butter and a can of Pringles and set them on the counter. Then she opened the refrigerator and pulled out a bottle of spicy mustard and a half-empty jar of pickles.

Barrett looked from her to Cass and held out the book. "Ask me anything about his life. I bet you I know the answer."

The life in question was Dietrich Bonhoeffer.

The book, a biography by Eric Metaxas.

Cass arranged his features in a way that clearly communicated how disinclined he was to *quiz him*.

Barrett caught the message. He took a small step back, then watched curiously as the girl began concocting the strangest sandwich Cass had ever seen. Peanut butter and spicy mustard and chips and pickle juice, which she poured over the bread like one might pour malt vinegar on fish and chips.

When she caught them staring, she smashed the sandwich beneath her palm—making the chips crunch—then lifted it into the air and took a big bite, her hair curtaining her face so only the center portion was visible.

Barrett brought the biography to Forrester, who was no more inclined to quiz him than Cass. He was too focused on the discs, which he called EMPs. He said they generated electromagnetic disturbances that disabled whatever they were attached to. He'd modeled the phenomenon on his phone earlier this morning when Cass hadn't yet poured his first cup of coffee. The screen had gone black the moment the disc clamped to the phone's back. Now Forrester was using a pan-balance to take the discs' measurements, trying to figure out their composition.

"Reminds me of physics class," Barrett said with a shudder. "Although I bet now I could ace it without even trying. I should look up a picture of the periodic table."

Forrester rubbed his chin. "It's too dense to be iron."

"Is that liquid inside?" Barrett asked.

"Looks like it. But I have no idea what. And I'm not willing to break it open and see."

Cassian thought this wise. If the discs were another one of Volkova's inventions, the substance inside was probably deadly. Maybe nuclear.

Barrett grabbed the remote and turned up the volume. Concordia was running another snippet on him. He watched in amazement as his face filled the screen.

In the kitchen, the girl squeaked.

Cass looked at her.

She sat cross-legged on top of the counter, her sandwich held aloft as she eyed the hallway with fear so palpable, his own muscles coiled in response.

The light in the hallway turned on.

"If I'm going to use this thing," a man grumbled, "at least let me wheel myself."

"You have broken ribs, Alexander." Mrs. Pruitt came into view, pushing her irritable husband into the room. He wore a cannula and a massive leg brace, all while sitting in a wheelchair. Even so, he looked markedly better than the last time Cass had seen him.

Eden appeared behind them, her attention quickly moving from Forrester and Barrett to Cassian in the kitchen. She smiled, her anger from yesterday long gone.

Cass felt himself smile, too.

Mr. Pruitt cleared his throat.

He wasn't smiling.

During the two weeks Cass had tailed them, he'd never seen the man looking anything less than amiable. But then, that was before he and his wife were kidnapped. That was before he was shot and almost killed. Eden's father glanced at Forrester, gave Barrett and the girl a perfunctory nod, then pinned his attention on Cassian.

He pulled off his cannula. "You must be Cass."

Cassian stepped forward to shake the man's hand.

Despite his weakened state, his grip was firm. "My daughter tells me you found Mordecai's name."

Cass nodded.

"And he's going to the Prosperity Ball."

"He's on the guest list," Cass said. "We don't know if he'll actually be there."

"He will if he knows I'll be there," Eden said.

Her father frowned.

"You know," Barrett mused. "If you really want to make sure he shows up, you could get all three of our names on the list. Of course, we'd have to know her name for that to work." He looked pointedly at Subject 003, who had resumed eating her sandwich.

Throughout the morning, Barrett had been trying to get her to write her name on a sticky note. But she was as reticent to write as she was to talk.

Barrett shrugged. "I'm game."

"You're a missing person," Forrester said.

"Exactly. If my name shows up on a guest list, the media will be all over it. It's bound to grab this dude's attention."

"We're trying to stay off the radar," Forrester said. "Not jump into the center of it. And besides, I wouldn't have enough time to create another doppelgänger network. Not when the first one is still so glitchy."

"Eden's not going," Mr. Pruitt said.

"Yes, I am," Eden replied, her jaw set with a stubbornness Cass recognized. "He used you and Mom as bait to get to me. This time, I'm going to be the bait so we can get to him."

"Eden …"

"We can't keep hiding. It doesn't work."

Cass agreed. It didn't. Those who hid were eventually found. His mother was proof. But he kept the sentiment to himself. He didn't think it would do him any favors with the dad.

The front door opened and Norton stepped inside, holding the screen door as he shook rain from his flat cap. "Look who I found."

Cleo stepped in behind him.

She looked as surly as Mr. Pruitt.

Eden's face fell. "Your mom couldn't get tickets."

"Oh, she got them."

"That's great!"

"Two. She got two. And she's forbidding me from using either of them."

Beverly Randall-Ransom was a mother who had always allowed her daughter a certain amount of freedom. Like publishing an illegal newspaper, of which Beverly was fully aware. But when it came to Cleo's physical safety, she could be more protective than Alexander and Ruth Pruitt.

Cleo shrugged off her slightly damp zip-up hoodie. She wore a graphic tee underneath with the words Rebel

Yell. She plopped onto the sofa beside Forrester and nodded glumly at Eden's father, whom—as far as Cass knew—she had yet to officially meet. "Rough week?"

"You could stay that," he said, a ghost of a smile tugging at his mouth.

Cleo leaned her head against the couch's back. "I guess this means it'll be Eden and her plus one. Whoever that is."

"If my daughter insists on going, then I will join her."

Everyone stared at the man in the wheelchair.

"Don't be absurd," Norton finally said, hanging his jacket on the coat rack. "You are supposed to be non-weight bearing for five more weeks. The Prosperity Ball is in three."

Eden's father didn't back down. He looked at the doctor with an expression every bit as unrelenting as his daughter's stubbornness. "It's a good thing I'm a fast healer."

8

Dad tackled rehab like his asinine plan might be an actual possibility. He did breathing and leg exercises like the fate of the world depended on it. He iced. He took pain meds. He pedaled on the stationary bike, so eager to be upright and out of the wheelchair that Mom and Dr. Norton were in a perpetual state of exasperation.

In an ironic twist of fate, the most bothersome injury came not at the hands of the enemy, but the doctors who saved him. Aggressive but necessary chest compressions that resulted in several broken ribs. Now a burr in her father's side, for how could he support his weight on crutches or a walker when doing so put pressure on bones in need of healing?

There was such a thing as pushing too hard, Dr. Norton cautioned. Of prolonging the healing process.

Her father ignored the warnings. And when Jack created a fake identity for Cassian, Dad objected vehemently. There was no need, he insisted. He would escort Eden to the ball.

Jack created the identity anyway.

For backup, he said.

Just in case.

Other than the sporadic and odd squeak, Subject 003 remained silent. She was wary of Jack. Terrified of Dad. And watchful of everyone else. Meanwhile, Barrett Barr hardly stopped talking. Of all his newfound powers, the photographic memory delighted him the most. He kept consuming and regurgitating large quantities of facts and data nobody else cared about, stopping only long enough to ask the same question he always came back to: When could he contact his family?

"I keep waiting for you to punch him," Eden said with a hint of amusement.

She was outside in the woods with Cassian in the same clearing they'd used the first time he showed her how to fight. The weather was cooler now as October approached, the leaves starting to change. And they were practicing moves much more advanced.

"He's like a golden retriever puppy," Cass said.

They moved through a series of takedowns, wherein he approached from behind as stealthily as possible. Eden executed them easily, if not a little distractedly.

They'd been coming out here every day and much to her dismay, there'd been no more kissing. Not since the night of his return.

She could hear him behind her.

Only this time, he didn't attack.

He set his hand on her waist—the unexpected contact a shock to her torso, making every muscle in her core go tight. His broad palm pressed against her hip. His breath tickled her ear. Eden's own caught in her throat, the tiny hairs on the back of her neck tingling.

"The power comes from your abdomen," he said. "So, if I were to do this—"

He shifted.

Almost imperceptibly.

But Eden could feel it before the shift even began. She grabbed his left forearm and with a quick and decisive pivot, threw him over her body and brought her knee to his neck.

He looked up at her, his full lips curved into a slight but satisfied smile, a gleam in his golden eyes.

It never got old.

Impressing Cassian.

Eden did so as often as she could.

She helped him up and they began again.

This time, they ran through an entire series—a back-and-forth dance of blocks and attacks until Eden grabbed his opposite elbow and spun around. They stood face-to-face, so close she could see each of his individual eyelashes.

His attention dipped to her lips, which had—according to Barrett—over a million different nerve endings. The human fingertip contained over three-thousand touch receptors.

Now, with their chests rising and falling in unison, Eden could feel every single one of them.

He leaned slightly forward.

She held her breath.

Waiting.

Yearning.

And then, "As-salamu alaykum."

Cassian pulled away, his retreat a bucket of icy water against her back.

She grit her teeth and glared at Barrett, who approached with an oblivious grin.

"That's Arabic for hello," he said, sliding his hands into the pockets of his jeans. The last time Dr. Norton went into the city, he'd returned with a small but sufficient wardrobe for each of them. Jane had stared at the gift in the strangest way before stuffing each item into a pillowcase, which she now carried with her wherever she went. "Mr. Pruitt asked if I'd come get you."

Fetch, like an actual golden retriever.

"I'll be there in a minute," Eden said.

"Not you. Him."

Cassian raised his eyebrows. He and Dad didn't do a lot of conferring. Cassian tolerated her parents with a guarded politeness. Mom tried hard to get past the barrier. Dad didn't bother. He was too busy with rehab.

Barrett raised his eyebrows back.

Cass met Eden's eye, like she might know what this was about.

She shrugged.

He pocketed his phone, tucked his gun into his waist belt, and headed toward the cabin, leaving Eden and Barrett alone. Despite her annoyance over Barrett's timing, her heart was soft for the guy. The novelty of seeing his face on national news had worn off. He tried his best to stay positive, his disposition upbeat, but Eden could tell he missed his family. She knew what that felt like.

She picked up her hoodie and gave it a shake, then pulled it over her head. "You doing okay?"

"Oh, you know." Barrett shrugged. "Niko sawa."

"I don't know what that means."

"It's Swahili for I'm fine." Two squirrels scampered after one another in a nearby tree, scrabbling from one limb to the next. He looked up at them, then dug his hands deeper into his pockets and released a heavy sigh. "Jane squeaked twice yesterday. I think she might be on the brink of talking."

"Her first words might be shut up."

Barrett smiled good-naturedly. "I'm surprised she's still here."

"Surprised?" Eden pulled her long hair free from the hood of her sweatshirt.

"I keep waiting for her to run away. She was going to the first night, you know. I think I convinced her to stay, but I'm not sure she wants to be here."

Eden raised her eyebrows, wondering where she would go. If Jane left, Jack would lose his mind. He was borderline militant about keeping phones away from Barrett. Adamant that his wife and daughter stayed in Rome. He wanted no cracks in whatever ship they were building. Jane leaving would be a gaping hole.

Barrett scratched the back of his head. "Do you know how many frozen embryos have been created in the twenty-first century?"

"I have no idea," she said.

"Over twelve million. Want to guess how many of those were implanted?"

"Not really."

"Less than five million, and only twenty-three percent of those resulted in successful pregnancies. That leaves seven-and-a-half million. Which means that if you crunch the numbers, we had a ninety-one percent chance of never existing. We either would have failed to implant, been donated in the name of scientific research, discarded, or stuck in a weird state of pre-existence in some lab with a bunch of other frozen embryos."

Eden frowned. "What's your point, Barrett?"

"My point is that in a strange way, statistically speaking, we sort of owe Karik Volkova our lives."

Cass found Eden's father in the basement rehab room, a trip he made often thanks to an elevator that went from the master bedroom to the utility room below. He sat at a machine doing a quad press with his left leg, a walker in the place his wheelchair used to be.

The ball was in less than a week.

"I've been talking with the doc," he said, grimacing as he pushed himself onward. "Obviously I'm not as far along as I'd hoped to be."

Sweat trickled down his face as he struggled to get through one last rep. He lifted it halfway before the weight came clanking down.

Cass imagined the frustration Eden's father must be feeling—having to battle against such a small amount of weight. Cass sustained his fair number of injuries over the years. They were always infuriating. How much more infuriating would those injuries have been had Eden's life been on the line?

Mr. Pruitt sank back against the seat and grabbed the towel resting over his right knee. "He's told me some things."

Cassian shifted uncomfortably. There were a number of things Norton could have told Eden's father—all of them incriminating. Cass braced himself for an interrogation. One that could very well end with a one-way ticket to the exit. But he wouldn't take it. He would stay for as long as Eden allowed him to.

"You're a fighter," Mr. Pruitt said.

"Was a fighter."

"And a tracker."

Cass looked away, heat rising up his neck. They were close to it now. Uncomfortably close. The reason they were in this predicament to begin with. Cass had been hired to find a girl and now here they were.

"Ben also said he trusts you."

Cass's attention jerked upward.

"And you will be an asset by my daughter's side."

The two of them stared at one another, Cassian's heart thudding uncertainly.

"I won't be." Mr. Pruitt cast a dirty look at his walker. "We managed to get a room at The Sapphire. Jack and I will use it to set up surveillance and communicate with you throughout the event." He mopped his brow with the towel. "I need you to understand something."

Cass stood straighter, giving the man his full and undivided attention.

"My wife and my daughter are my entire world. I'm putting half of that world in your hands." Mr. Pruitt's gaze was locked and unwavering. "I'm counting on you to protect her."

Cass didn't look away. He stared back with the same fervency as Eden's father. "With my life."

9

"Have you seen Jane?" Barrett asked outside on the back deck.

She ducked further into the closet, behind the hanging coats. She had to be as a quiet mouse. Barrett didn't use his ears as much as she did; he preferred his mind. But that didn't mean he couldn't detect the smallest of sounds.

"I haven't," the doctor said as a loud sizzle hissed through the air, and the smell of grilling meat filled the dark space.

Jane stuffed her hand into one of the coat pockets and came back with nothing. She looked down at her collection. One crumpled bill, seven coins, two buttons, a piece of gum, and a tube of Chapstick. Her conscience twinged. She didn't enjoy stealing from the nice doctor. But steal, she did. At first, she justified it; she didn't trust niceness. Not when Father had used the trait like a trap whenever he wanted to conduct a particularly nasty test. But Jane had been here for a while now and the doctor's niceness hadn't waned. Nor did he force her or even suggest she return to that ominous room in the basement. After twenty-two days, she suspected his niceness wasn't a trick, but the real thing. Still, she stuffed her hand into the last pocket and pulled out another coin.

She dropped her treasures into the sack and listened to make sure the coast was clear. She listened to Barrett's heartbeat and the doctor's heartbeat—both of them outside on the deck. She opened the closet door, tucked the sack beneath her arm, and raced to the bedroom.

She locked the door and dumped the contents from the sack onto the soft bed—*her* soft bed. There were the brand-new clothes Dr. Norton had given her. Four cans of tuna. A jar of half-eaten peanut butter. Eight ketchup packets she'd found in a kitchen drawer. A map she'd torn from one of the doctor's books. A broken pencil. A headband. Three toothbrushes. An empty container of floss and its long tangled innards she'd pulled from within. She had no idea what it was until she saw Barrett using it on his teeth. Now there were the two buttons. A Chapstick. And more of the treasure she'd been collecting.

Just in case.

Four crumpled bills and twelve coins.

She sat cross-legged in the middle of the bed, twisted the lid off the jar of peanut butter, and scooped her finger inside to grab a large dollop. She unfolded the map and studied it while she licked the peanut butter. Two of the cities were circled—Milwaukee and Chicago. This was where the others had gone. For the ball. One city was crossed off with dark, angry lines.

For an entire year, Jane had lived like a street urchin in the city of Minneapolis, creeping through back alleys like a frightened, feral cat. She knew the name of the city because she heard people talk and she could read signs. She hadn't, however, known what it meant. It turned out Minneapolis wasn't the world; it was a small dot in the world. The doctor lived near a different big city called Milwaukee. It was three-hundred-forty miles away from Father. Thanks to this map, Jane now knew that when she left, she would travel east, where the distance between her and Father would grow.

Sometimes at night, she woke up thinking about the puppies. How she failed them like she failed Kitty. But then she would shove those memories away, in the deep place where her words hid. Those memories weren't hers anymore. They belonged to Violet. She was no longer Violet. She was Jane.

She sucked the remaining peanut butter off her finger and picked up the headband. She pressed it against her nose. It smelled like honey and vanilla. It smelled like a mother. Not hers. But a mother all the same. Jane hadn't smelled her own in over a decade. Even so, she could remember the familiar scent—sesame oil and talcum powder.

Last night, Eden's mother had fallen asleep on the couch while the others worked in the basement, getting ready to carry out their plans. Jane had tiptoed close, taken the mother's hand, and pressed it against her cheek. This was a foolish thing to do, for she had woken up and Jane had skittered away.

She hid in this very room and told herself she would leave tomorrow. Just like she did every night. But then morning would come, and something would convince her to stay. The soft bed. The warm showers. The mother. A kitchen full of food. The boy named Barrett, who was every bit as nice as the doctor. She was descending into debauchery. Father would be irate.

In the evening, other things would convince her to leave. Like Jack, who watched her as closely as she watched him. He wanted to run tests. The doctor had told him to give her time. How much time, Jane didn't know. The father was named Alexander Pruitt. She didn't like him either. Even though he was different from her own father. Even though she knew he couldn't hurt her—he couldn't hurt anyone—no matter how hard he was trying to get stronger. Then there was the young man named Cassian. He could definitely hurt someone.

Jane could tell. But he didn't notice Jane. He didn't notice anyone but Eden.

Down the hall, the back door slid open. The television turned on. Voices filled the living room. Familiar ones from Concordia Entertainment. All day long, the people inside the television had been talking, remembering, honoring those who had died in an event they were calling The Attack. Jane had never known about The Attack. Over the past twenty-two days, she was discovering a lot of things she'd never known. Now, the familiar voices were talking about The Prosperity Ball, which was where the mother had gone, along with the others. They had gone to fight the bad man.

The back door slid open again.

The scent of grilled meat intensified.

Dr. Norton's heartbeat joined Barrett's as he walked through the living room and into the kitchen.

"That's a lot of famous people in one building," Barrett said.

And then suddenly, something happened.

A frightening blast of overwhelming noise, so piercing and loud and abrupt, Jane clapped her hands over her ears with a scream and doubled over her legs.

Her heart pounded against her ribcage—angry, violent beats. She kept her hands clamped over her ears, afraid to peel them away even though the blast was gone. It was as if her hearing had lost its filter and all at once, every sound within a ten-mile radius coalesced into a monstrous scream that shattered her eardrums.

Slowly, she straightened, wondering what had just happened and whether it might happen again when a knock sounded on her door.

She squeaked and ducked under a pillow.

The knock came again. "Jane? Are you okay?"

It was Barrett, who had given up on trying to get her real name and resorted to calling her Jane, like everyone else.

"We heard you scream," he said.

There was a long pause.

Jane's heart continued to crash.

"The hamburgers are ready and the Prosperity Ball coverage is on. We have to keep our eyes peeled for Mordecai. Maybe we'll see him in the crowd."

Her hands slid away from her ears.

The door handle twisted. "Jane?"

Hurriedly, she stuffed her collection of items into the pillowcase. She hugged the bulging sack to her chest and peeked out the door where Barrett was waiting. He shoved his hand through his still-longish hair and cocked his head, like he often did. At least with her.

She should feel safe in this house with the nice doctor and the nice boy, three-hundred-forty miles away from Father. But her heart continued to thud. In the aftermath of that awful noise, an equally awful feeling was growing in her stomach. The same feeling she used to get whenever Father took Kitty.

She followed Barrett into the living room.

She sat on the couch with the sack on her lap and a plate of food on the sack, watching Concordia Entertainment. Barrett knew the name of every person interviewed. Actors and singers and athletes and authors and scientists and politicians. Parading along a length of red carpet while cameras flashed and reporters jostled to get interviews.

For the first time since waking up twenty-two days ago, Jane couldn't eat.

There was no room for food.

The awful feeling expanding in her belly was too big.

10

Long before Eden moved to San Diego and became best friends with a brilliant but geeky kid named Erik Gaviola, when she still lived in Seattle, she used to play tag with her classmates at recess. The tall, swirly slide was home base. Home base was safe. She and Camila, a girl who'd moved to Seattle from Guatemala, would crawl inside the tunnel and hide. Camila wore special braces on her ankles to prevent muscle contractures, which made running hard. She preferred the safety of base and Eden preferred Camila. Sometimes, they'd become so engrossed with their silly, whispered conversations, they'd forget they were playing a game. They'd forget that outside, someone was after them.

The luxurious bathroom inside their suite on the sixtieth floor of The Sapphire Hotel felt like that swirly slide. It had turned into home base. Only her mother, who was pinning Eden's hair into a thick updo, had replaced Camila.

"Do you think Erik's watching the coverage?" Mom asked.

Last year, the two had watched the live event together in Eden's living room with a bowl of popcorn. They'd wanted to attend via the Prosperity Ball metaverse, which was entirely affordable for middle-class families such as theirs. But Eden's parents had objected. At the time, Eden thought their objection had to do with the significance of the day and their discomfort with celebrating something so tragic. Now, with the gift of hindsight, she could see the full picture. They wanted to keep their daughter off the radar. Attending the Prosperity Ball, even if only virtually, would have put her on it.

So, Erik and Eden resigned themselves to watching the festivities the old-fashioned way. In an attempt to distract Mom from her melancholy, they convinced her to join them while Erik provided a stream of hilariously biting commentary on the partygoers' attire.

"I think he knew the name of every celebrity who walked the carpet," Mom said.

"His brain is a vast ocean," Eden replied.

And now, so was hers.

She imagined how crazy this would drive him. Her

newfound ability to memorize the numbers of pi. Or every gambit ever played in the World Chess Championship, a tournament Erik followed with the same fanaticism most boys his age followed March Madness.

She missed him terribly.

Coverage of the event played on the flat screen outside the bathroom. Paparazzi descended around a red carpet outside The Sapphire, where cameras flashed, and reporters called out celebrity names as they filed inside. All the while, her dad and Jack turned their suite into a surveillance room worthy of the CIA—breaching security, checking connections, monitoring check-in to see which guests already had their retinas scanned and which guests were not yet accounted for.

Nicholas Marks belonged to the second category. So did Cassian Ransom—twenty-two-year-old nephew to two-time Nobel laureate, Dr. Beverly Randall-Ransom, the world's most esteemed neurosurgeon—and his plus one, Eden Pruitt. Thanks to Jack Forrester, Cassian was now on the grid. His past, squeaky clean. Or rather, nonexistent.

Mom secured her hair with another pin as Eden forced her fists to unclench in her lap. Her palms were clammy. She was more nervous now than she'd been when she'd gone off to rescue her parents. Then, the adrenaline coursing through her veins had been much less nervous uncertainty, much more ferocious determination. She'd been zeroed in with laser focus. Now, the goal was murkier. What if Mordecai didn't show? What if he wasn't looking for her like they assumed he must be and this ended up being the most extravagant date of Eden's life, all while her parents and Jack Forrester eavesdropped via Bluetooth?

Out in the suite, Jack and her father discussed the hotel's layout.

Eden tried to block out the unfolding conversation. She ignored the ornate double sink, the Jacuzzi bathtub, the high-end soap and shampoo on the marble-topped vanity and focused instead on the mirror, as if doing so might trick her nerves into thinking she was in San Diego, getting ready for homecoming with her date, Erik. But then, homecoming didn't involve celebrities. Homecoming didn't involve this level of surveillance, or a psychopath named Mordecai. Nor was it held on such a morbid anniversary.

She peeked at her mother in the mirror's reflection.

Oswin Brahm might want to celebrate how far the nation had come since The Attack twenty-one years ago, but the Pruitts would always mourn. This day and two days after, when Eden's parents watched with utter helplessness as an asthma attack stole their firstborn.

Their only born.

Christopher.

His death had a profound impact on Eden's life.

She'd always known this. She just hadn't realized how big. His absence left a void. It took Mom's breath away. Without that absence, they never would have taken Eden at all. There would have been no void to fill. No breath to give back. But Christopher had died, and the void was there, and Mom's breath wasn't, and so they took her. And in an ironic twist of fate, Eden had nearly taken her mother's breath away permanently when she wrapped her hands around her mother's neck.

"Mom?"

With a bobby pin clamped between her teeth, her mother murmured a muffled, "Yes?"

"I'm sorry."

Mom paused from the hair styling.

Eden could feel muscle and sinew beneath her fingers as she squeezed. Squeezed. Squeezed. "I—I almost killed you."

Mom took the bobby pin from her mouth.

But Eden rushed onward, before her mother could interrupt. "I've always tried so hard to make you and Dad happy. I know you get sad. I know you worry." Because of Christopher and his death. Because of Eden and what she was. "You say that I saved you. That after Christopher died, I—I filled a hole. But I almost killed you."

"Eden." Mom took her shoulders and turned her around so they were no longer looking at one another in the mirror, but face-to-face. Eye-to-eye. "I need you to listen to me, and listen well, daughter of mine."

But Eden didn't want to listen.

She knew what her mother was going to say.

The same thing Dr. Norton said after she saw the footage on Cassian's phone. After she saw the horrible thing she had done to them.

That wasn't you.

But it was her.

Her hands had done the squeezing.

Only, that wasn't what her mother said.

"It was never your job to make your father and I happy." She spoke in a gentle voice that shook with strength and conviction. "I am so sorry I ever made you feel it was."

"But—"

Mom shook her head, like that was enough—no buts allowed. Then she cupped Eden's chin. "And if it is forgiveness you need, I will forgive you a hundred times over."

Eden's chin trembled.

"I love you. To the moon and back. Nothing you could ever do will change that. Do you hear me?"

A tear pooled.

Mom brushed it away with her thumb. "Now we need to stop this, or your mascara is going to run."

A laugh tumbled up Eden's throat.

Mom's, too.

She gave Eden's shoulder a squeeze, then resumed her work, sliding one last pin into place and picking up the can of hairspray.

Eden held her breath.

Mom pressed the nozzle. The spray hissed from the can, falling like mist over Eden's hair. When she finished, she waved the air clean. "What do you think?"

Eden turned her head from one side to the other. "I'm impressed."

"So am I." Mom winked, then picked up the cosmetic bag. "Now for some eye shadow."

Eden closed her eyes, enjoying the soft sweep of brush against her eyelids. And yet, she couldn't ignore the slight tremble—the subtle unsteadiness—in her mother's touch that made it impossible to forget why they were here. With her eyes closed, it was also harder to block out the conversation between Jack and her father in the next room.

A knock sounded on the suite door.

Eden's nerves quadrupled.

"I've got it," Jack said, probably stopping her father from trying to stand.

A few seconds later, the door opened.

Eden pictured Cass on the other side in his tuxedo and swallowed the jumble of nerves in her throat.

"Any sign of him?" Cass asked, his footsteps padding across the carpet.

"Not yet," Jack said. "But it's early."

"Think he'll show?"

"We've made her pretty easy to find. And he must be searching."

"He's going to know we're up to something," Dad said.

"Hopefully, he will assume he can outsmart us." Clacking computer keys followed Jack's words. "This should be ready for you."

There was a pause.

And then, "Testing, testing. 1, 2, 3 ..."

"It works."

Someone took a deep breath.

"I'm putting a lot of faith in you," Dad said.

"I know," Cassian replied.

Mom finished Eden's left eye and moved on to her right.

Brush, brush, brush ...

"You care about her," Dad continued.

"Yes," Cassian said.

"Then make sure this ends. If he shows his face, take him out."

"Without hesitation."

"There!" Mom, oblivious to the conversation Eden couldn't help but overhear, stepped back to survey her handiwork. She nodded approvingly, then pulled Eden's dress off the hook, where it hung on the back of the bathroom door. Eden slipped off the white terrycloth robe and stepped inside. The dress slid up her body like a glove—black, floor length, strapless.

Then her mother opened a black velvet box. Inside, a breathtaking choker sparkled. A piece of jewelry that rivaled Marie Antoinette's infamous diamond necklace and that—many argued—had been so valuable, it led to the unfortunate loss of the queen's head.

"Beverly said you needed to look the part." Mom fastened the choker in place.

Eden touched it lightly with her fingertips. She'd never in her life looked so expensive—her flawlessness accentuated by the make-up, the dress, the accoutrements.

Her mother put on a brave face. "All ready?"

Eden nodded, and together, they walked out of the bathroom.

Dad and Jack were bent together over the surveillance equipment. Beyond them, next to the floor-to-ceiling windows that boasted a brilliant view of downtown Chicago at night, Cass stood, dressed in a sleek, perfectly tailored tuxedo that highlighted his broad shoulders and lean torso. He turned, as if sensing her presence, and the way he stared made her skin hot and tingly.

Dad cleared his throat.

He was sitting in a chair next to the empty one Jack had been using, wearing the giant brace he cursed several times a day, looking unsettled and tense. Eden couldn't blame him. He was sending his daughter off with a twenty-two-year-old boy to hunt down a man with mysterious ties to Karik Volkova. Dad hadn't made it a secret that he didn't want Eden to go. But Eden was eighteen. She could make her own decisions, and even if he wanted to lock her up, no lock could hold her. She was going to that ball, and while perhaps in his prime—at the height of his days in the CIA—her father would be an asset at her side, he'd finally come to terms with the fact that he wasn't now.

Cass, on the other hand, was strong, resourceful, highly trained, unafraid, and familiar with a gun. He was also four years older, experienced in the ways of the world, with an obvious appeal that spelled danger for fathers everywhere. While he may have been the perfect escort given these particular circumstances, Eden's dad was far from comfortable with the arrangement.

"You look handsome," Mom said.

Cassian responded with the same guarded politeness he'd been using whenever her mother tried interacting with him.

Dad picked up the gun strap resting by Jack's laptop.

Once they passed through security, it would hold a

9mm Hellcat. A black pistol easily concealed. Cassian stashed two of them inside one of the bathrooms early this morning.

Yesterday, Dad taught her how to shoot. She feigned ignorance, like she didn't already know. Like Cassian hadn't already taught her. She pretended she didn't have a better shot than he did. Her father needed to feel like he was contributing to her safety. She played along.

Mom looked away with an anxious bob in her throat while Dad handed the strap to Eden. She sat down on the bed, secured it around her calf and slipped on her shoes while Dad reviewed the plan. All the while, Eden tried regulating her temperature, but Cassian's stare was generating way too much heat. When her father finished, Mom gave Eden a hug, embracing her for a moment longer than comfortable. Then Dad moved like he was going to do the same.

Eden objected.

He stood anyway.

Foregoing the walker, he wrapped Eden up tight, completely enveloping her like he did at the police station in San Diego. Eden had been awaiting his arrival, convinced her father would be furious. Instead, he hugged her with a fierceness she knew she didn't deserve. He hugged her with that same fierceness now, his healing ribs be damned.

When it was over, Jack checked the doppelgänger signal one last time.

And Cassian opened the door.

"You okay?" he asked as she stepped past him out into the hallway.

It wasn't a compliment.

But a simple, perfect question.

One that grounded her as her hand moved to Beverly's diamond choker.

"I will be," she said.

Oswin Brahm was determined to turn the country's mourning into celebration. According to him, the bad guys only won if America let them. This was his motto, and tonight, it would become Eden's, too.

She would not let Mordecai win.

This was going to end.

She couldn't consider any other alternative.

Cassian held out his arm and led her away from the safety of home base.

11

Cass fought his first fight when he was thirteen. Vick put him in the ring way too early—only six months into training—against a kid three years older, and three years stronger. Within a year, he was beaten to a pulp twice. First by his father. Then by a sixteen-year-old fighter nicknamed The Bull. A lot of people thought Vick foolish. It was a big risk to take with a kid so full of potential. But Vick was no fool. If he was going to invest as much time and energy as he planned on investing into Cassian Gray, he wanted to see his young prospect in action. He wanted to make sure Cass was a sure bet.

Vick got his wish in spades.

Never had a crowd seen anyone lose so relentlessly. The boy would not stay down. He got up again, and again, and again—filled with grit and tenacity—fueled by a dogged, unyielding anger that raged like a fire in his belly. It was a quality Vick could not teach. Some fighters had it. Some didn't. Cass had it. He was pulverized that first fight, beaten to the point of death. And instead of slinking away in humiliation or fear, the loss became more fuel for the fire. He only trained harder.

It was the first and last fight Cass would ever lose.

Fans of the sport called him fearless. And he was. Because what did he have to fear? The worst had already happened. His father had found them. His mother was dead. Cass had been powerless to save her. Pain was a relief. Death would be welcome. He had nothing to lose.

Until now.

Until her.

This girl he was hired to find. He said yes, hoping to pay off his debt and start a new life. Somewhere new. Somewhere without memories, without ghosts. Instead, his target caught him off guard—because she wasn't a typical target. Then she captivated his attention—because she wasn't a typical high school girl. Every time he thought he had her figured out, she would do something that would force him to reconsider. And that was only watching from afar.

Now he was up close, and the past several weeks had been a brand of torture to which he wasn't accustomed. Every day with Eden awakened feelings better left dormant. And now here he was, not walking into a ring, but zeroed in with the same laser-like focus he had before every fight. His body wound tight—his muscles coiled and ready to spring. But without that fearless edge. For the first time in a long time, there was a cautiousness that tempered the hungry lion. A concern that dug like a burr under his skin. Cassian couldn't protect his mother from his father when he was a kid. What if he couldn't protect Eden now?

As they reached the elevators, an entourage approached from the opposite end of the hallway. A man and a woman walked toward them, flanked by three bodyguards. Cass couldn't tell who the star of the show was—the tanned, comically muscled Fabio with short hair or the woman gliding beside him in a black dress like Eden's, only much more revealing. With a neckline that plunged in a deep V all the way to her navel and slits so high on each side they might as well have reached her navel, too. When they stopped, she pinned her attention on Cass—her eyes roaming up his body, then back down—making Fabio shift uncomfortably beside her.

The woman stared—boldly, openly. "How do we know each other?"

"We don't," Cass replied.

"I'm positive we've met."

Upon closer inspection, there was something vaguely

familiar about her face, but he had neither the patience nor the inclination to place her. Perhaps she was a fan of Underground Fighting. If that was the case, she'd have a difficult time placing him. "If we have, I don't remember."

Her eyes flashed, like a person who wasn't used to being forgotten.

The woman's attention flitted to Eden.

So did Fabio's.

Cass shifted closer, wanting to shield Eden from their perusal. Instead, the scent of her perfume distracted him from the entourage. Eden smelled like heaven—so good he could drown in the scent and die a happy man.

The elevator doors slid open and a sprightly, white-haired gentleman dressed like a bellhop greeted them with a funny little bow. The woman sauntered into the elevator with her chin raised. Fabio followed, and the three bodyguards as well.

Cass placed his hand on the small of Eden's back, and they stepped inside, too.

"Don't stop until we reach the ballroom floor," the woman said.

"Y-yes, ma'am," the operator stammered.

They reached the bottom quickly—the elevator so fast and smooth it was hard to tell it was moving at all. With one last affronted look, the woman and her posse swept past them into the crowded lobby. Cameras flashed. Reporters descended.

Eden thanked the operator.

He blushed all the way up to his tuft of white hair, like people didn't thank him often. It reminded Cass of the old woman at The Roast and her fallen change. Eden had been quick to help when nobody else had bothered. When nobody else had even noticed. But she had. Because that's who Eden was. She saw people others didn't. Befriended people others wouldn't.

When they stepped off the elevator, she turned to Cass with a quirked eyebrow. "Do you know who that was?"

"The elevator operator?"

"The woman."

"Should I?"

"She has over two million followers on Perk."

"Why?"

"Because she sings. Songs people really like."

Ah. So that explained the vague familiarity. He'd probably seen her in passing on magazine covers sold by street vendors, on the side of buses, on flashing billboards.

"Most guys your age are obsessed with her."

Looking at Eden, Cass couldn't help but think most guys his age were obsessed with the wrong woman.

"Her name's Star."

"That's it?" He lifted his eyebrow dryly. "The whole thing?"

Eden bit back a smile, amusement sparkling in her eyes. And Cass—the hopeless fool—felt a swell of victory more powerful than anything he'd ever felt after a win in the ring.

12

Star was only the first celebrity they encountered.

The red carpet teemed with them inside the expansive lobby. A conglomeration of the Oscars and the Grammys and the ESPYS with a healthy dose of influential politicians and prize-winning professionals peppered throughout. Every variety of the rich and the famous posed for the cameras and interviewed with Concordia's most well-known entertainment reporters while starry-eyed, over-stimulated lottery ticket winners ogled the A-listers behind the velvet stanchions, unable to believe their good fortune.

According to Dad, who was speaking in Eden's ear, Mordecai had yet to pass through check-in. If he was here, he was in the crowded lobby. She searched the throng as they bypassed the reporters to a pair of beefy-looking bouncers scanning the incoming guests. One took care of the A-listers, who were swept inside without a wait. The other scanned the rest. Eden and Cass stood at the back of the line. The closer they got to the front, the tighter her stomach clenched.

Last night's dream was still fresh in her mind—a nightmare in which security scanned Cassian's retinas and a SWAT team descended, dragging him away. He wasn't Dr. Beverly Randall-Ransom's nephew. He was an infamous underground fighter wanted for murder. In the dream, Eden had remained in line, her entire body covered in a film of cold sweat. When they scanned her retinas, she was in the system as Ellery Forrester, a disturbed teenage runaway. They brought her to a holding cell where she waited for her parents. Only instead of Annette and Jack arriving, it was the dead man with the tattoos.

As if sensing her distress, Cassian placed his hand on the small of her back. The gesture didn't calm her nerves, but it did distract her from the nightmare.

When they reached the front, Eden held her breath as the guard scanned her eyes. Then her body. He checked the screen and nodded in a bored sort of way, motioning for her to step forward.

She held her breath as the guard scanned Cassian.

With another bored nod, he let Cass through.

Eden exhaled.

"We're in," she whispered into her earpiece as Cassian came beside her, and together, they entered the ballroom.

Eden's mouth went slack as she took in a scene straight from Cinderella. Not on a screen. Not virtually. But in actual, real life. All glitter and hanging stars and fancy food and sparkly drinks and handsome tuxedos and expensive jewelry and gowns so extravagant some bordered on obscene. It was a party fit for royalty. And there, in its center, like a king on his throne, sat the host —Oswin Brahm.

Cassian took her hand and led her through the ballroom to a set of double doors on the opposite side, where a pair of bodyguards stood sentry, their beefy hands folded in front of them, square faces devoid of expression. Eden looked down as they walked past them, out into a quieter hallway.

Cassian's stride was confident, his grip on her hand firm. He stopped in front of the men's room and slipped inside. Eden waited, her heart pounding. The hallway wasn't crowded, but it wasn't empty either. There were guests loitering about and more bodyguards, too. She looked for a dark corner, a safe place where he could hand her the gun he had stashed and she could tuck it in the strap around her calf.

The bathroom door opened.

Cassian stepped outside with a troubled brow.

"What is it?" she asked.

His lips turned up into a perfunctory smile as he nodded at a gentleman walking past. "They aren't there."

Eden's heart rate doubled.

Not there?

How could they not be there? Her attention lifted to the surveillance cameras. They were everywhere. Undoubtedly in the bathrooms, too. Had Cass been caught stashing the weapons? Were bodyguards on the lookout for him now?

Cassian nodded at another passerby, then escorted Eden back to the ballroom. "It's going to be fine," he whispered in her ear.

She took a deep, rattling breath and silently repeated his words. They would be fine. They would be fine. They would be fine. If he'd been caught on surveillance, surely they would have stopped him at the security check. And if ever a pair were equipped to succeed without the help of guns, they were it. She was indestructible and his fists might as well be registered.

They stood at the periphery of the ballroom, Cass alert beside her, listening carefully to a combination of directives and information. Still no sign of the man who held Eden's freedom in his hands. The two of them attempted to blend in while they waited for his arrival. They tasted the food, sipped some drinks, mingled with acquaintances of Dr. Beverly Randall-Ransom.

"So," a man who introduced himself as Dr. Fields said. "Beverly is your ... aunt?"

It was the second time Cass had fielded the inquiry.

Beverly was Black.

Cassian, white.

And she'd never mentioned a nephew.

"Beverly's late husband was my mother's eldest brother," Cass said in a straight, unaffected voice that wasn't friendly, but wasn't rude either. If mentioning his mother—even in a fictitious sense—bothered him, Eden couldn't tell. His expression remained as unaffected as his voice.

"Ah, I see." Dr. Fields took a sip of his Champagne. "It was a terrible tragedy, what happened to your uncle. But I suppose it's what drove Beverly to the level of success she's reached now."

Not too far away, the point guard for the Chicago Bulls side-eyed Cassian like he recognized him, and Eden's stomach clenched into a hard, tight fist. What if he made a habit of betting on the Underground like Mordecai made a habit of betting on the Underground? What if he alerted a reporter outside or whispered to a bodyguard standing by the doors?

"That guy over there," she imagined him saying. "He's an illegal fighter. How'd he get in here?"

Her nerves wound tighter, and the small talk with Dr. Fields was tedious. Which was probably why Cassian politely excused himself and asked Eden to dance, where they could avoid the idle chatter and covertly survey the massive room. Mordecai still hadn't checked in, but that didn't mean he wasn't there. In fact, there was a good chance that as soon as he saw her name on the guest list, he'd begun concocting a plan that didn't involve him checking in at all.

Eden's heart skipped as Cassian's hand slid to her back. He drew her close until her body was flush against his, her lips a mere centimeter from his neck, where his pulse thrummed and warmth radiated from his skin. The air in her chest crackled with heat. She inhaled the enticing scent of his cologne, completely forgetting the point guard for the Chicago Bulls and the missing guns. It would be so easy to close her eyes. Get lost. Imagine for one heady moment that she was not invincible and there was no Mordecai.

Cass's thumb slid to the spot where her waist met her ribcage and a shiver rippled deep down in her abdomen.

Now was not the time for her eyes to roll into the back of her head. If she didn't say something—distract herself in some way—they might. She regarded the cameras over Cassian's shoulder, imagining Erik spotting her in the background. Rewinding the footage. Pausing. Staring. Blinking. Wondering if his eyes were playing tricks. Eden swallowed. "Cleo thinks all of this is smoke and mirrors."

Cassian exhaled—a short, amused huff, his breath tickling her ear. "That sounds like Cleo."

"She thinks The Attack put us to sleep. And the further we get from it, the more we start to stir awake." Her thoughts flitted to Cleo's map. The uptick in riots. Not a single one of them shared with the public because the government controlled all forms of media. She still couldn't process it—the blatant duplicity involved in such cover-ups. How easily Eden herself had been deceived. "She thinks the pipe bombs in the mail are a ploy to keep us in hibernation. And this ball is a ploy to keep us happily distracted."

Cass turned her in a circle, his posture alert as he perused the crowd.

Eden's hands slid to his shoulders. She leaned back and peered up at him—this boy who surely had opinions. "What do you think?"

"I think there are times when Cleo's theories hit uncomfortably close to the truth."

"You believe the government was responsible for The Attack?"

"I think the government wields unity like a weapon."

He sounded very much like Cleo, who had once referred to unity as code for silencing the oppressed and preserving the power dynamics. Inside Cleo's dorm room the first time they met. "So you think unity is a bad thing."

"When it's valued over truth and justice."

Eden's brow furrowed.

"The people who hold tightest to unity are usually the ones with the most to lose."

"Should truth and justice prevail."

Cassian nodded.

Cleo's words rang within his. The people with the most to lose were the ones in power. Which included the government. And almost everyone in this ballroom.

"Was Erik one of the guys?" Cassian asked.

She blinked dumbly at the conversational pivot—no doubt intentional. The topic she'd chosen for distraction wasn't a safe one in such a public venue. Not to mention, her parents were listening. "One of the guys?"

He nodded to Star, the singer who was currently laughing with Oswin Brahm and his pretty wife.

"Oh. No. Star isn't his … type." She smiled. "Erik was actually obsessed with Cleo's mom."

Cassian quirked his eyebrow.

"If he knew I was here on behalf of Dr. Beverly Randall-Ransom …" She used the doctor's full name, a call back to the time Cassian poked fun at her. When they rode in the back of the neurosurgeon's fancy car on their way to Angelica's. "He'd probably lose his mind."

The crowd shifted around them.

Cameras followed as Oswin led his wife onto the dance floor.

Eden glanced toward the doors. "What if he doesn't show?" Her life spanned in front of her—years and years of waiting, of watching, of knowing he was out there somewhere, biding his time until he could make another move. Until he could force her to do what she didn't want to do. The prospect left Eden feeling like she might crawl out of her skin. "What if we never find him?"

"We will," Cass said, his golden eyes filled with conviction.

Eden looked at the doors again.

Mordecai had to be looking for her. For Barrett. For Jane. Eden's name was on the guest list, available to the public. Surely he wouldn't have missed it. Surely he wouldn't pass up such an opportunity. Her mind circled around the same frustrating questions it had been circling for weeks now. He had treated her like a prized possession. Like a creepy obsession. He kidnapped Barrett and Jane only to put them to sleep and store them away on two cots in an underground compound. What did he want with them? What was he up to?

She slid her fingers beneath the lapels of Cassian's tuxedo.

His breath hitched, making her wonder if she was every bit as distracting to him as he was to her. It was a distraction that didn't wane with time—but grew.

So did her worry.

The night was slipping away, and they had yet to find their target.

Her thoughts turned despairing. Her body on sensory overload. Everything became too much—the music, the crowd, the intrusive cameras, the intermittent communication from Jack and her father—no sign of him, no sign of him, no sign of him. The conversations and the laughter and the tinkling of silverware and the clatter of plates. All of it spun around her, making her dizzy, making her sick. Until a faint, far-away whisper arose from the jumbled din.

Come.

She cocked her head. Where had it come from—her parents? Jack? It didn't sound like anything she'd heard all night. But there it was again—a soothing voice that made her stop.

Cassian stopped with her, glancing over his shoulder at the vague spot captivating her interest. But before he could ask what it was, her father's voice came through the Bluetooth. "He's here."

Cassian pressed his fingers against his ear. "Where?"

"Watch the doors. His retinas were just scanned."

Eden's heart raced as Cassian pulled her off the dance floor. "Do you see him?"

"Not yet," her father said.

Up above, on the sixtieth floor, her parents and Jack

were monitoring the security cameras and Concordia's news coverage. Down below, in the ballroom, Cassian's attention swiveled from the main entrance to several side doors.

Eden accidentally bumped into two excited girls clutching pens and an autograph book. She mumbled an apology, feeling strangely off balance. Like she had stood too fast and now she was dizzy, only she hadn't been sitting.

Come.

There.

Again.

For a third time.

This one louder, more insistent.

"Eden?" Cassian said.

"Did you hear that?" she asked.

He cocked his head. "Hear what?"

"I think ..." She shook her own, attempting to clear it. But the dizziness only grew. The fog in her brain, too. She cupped her forehead, her body overly warm. "I think I need to use the restroom."

"Now?"

"Yes."

The furrow in his brow deepened.

Eden began walking toward one of the side exits.

Cassian followed, communicating with her father and Jack as they went.

"That's him," Jack said as they passed through the doors, out into an expansive hallway. "Right there."

"He's in the north lobby, opposite side," Eden's father said. "Where are you two going?"

Before Cassian could answer, Eden pushed inside the nearest ladies' room, feeling unreasonably irritated—a staticky heat that scratched in her lungs. She didn't need an escort to the bathroom. She was perfectly capable of going by herself.

She stopped in front of the sink, ignoring the chatter in her ear as she turned on the water.

Come.

Her hands jerked away like the water was scalding.

The lady beside her—heavyset, red-cheeked, dressed in an emerald green sequined gown—gave her an unfocused smile, the kind people gave when they'd had too much to drink. "That is a gorgeous necklace."

Eden touched the diamonds around her throat.

"This is some party, isn't it?" The lady hiccupped, then covered a childish giggle with her pudgy fist. "The Champagne tastes like fizzy gold. Probably costs as much, too. And the food!" She leaned closer and shot Eden an exaggerated wink, then turned to her reflection and ran her hands down her smooth but ample waistline. "It's a good thing I'm wearing this body shaper under here. Cost a small fortune, but worth every penny."

The hair on Eden's arm stood on end.

Something was about to happen.

She could feel it. Sense it.

As if calling the premonition forth, the lights overhead flickered. The crystals on the bathroom chandelier tinkled.

The lady looked up.

Another flicker.

Once, twice …

The bathroom went dark.

The woman beside her gasped.

The live music and the buzzing conversation outside ground to a halt. Goosebumps crawled across her skin as an alarmed voice spoke in her ear. "Eden? Eden, do you copy?"

She didn't have time to answer.

Before she could process the power outage, a deafening blast rattled the walls. The lady shrieked and fell to the floor as the chandelier came crashing down.

13

The voices in Eden's ear went to static.

A firm hand wrapped around her wrist. "We need to move."

It was Cassian.

In the ladies' room.

Pulling her from the bathroom, past the lady on the floor, where party guests shoved out into the smoky hallway and shock had morphed into pandemonium. Chaos and hysteria all around as people coughed and screamed and pushed maniacally toward exits.

Something terrible had happened.

There was a grotesque smoldering hole where one of the ballroom walls had been.

And yet, Eden processed it in a fog. In a cloud. A thick bubble. She was there, but none of it penetrated as Cassian's grip tightened on her wrist and he cleared a path through the scattering crowd. The sprinkler system kicked on, adding water to the panic. And blood. There was blood. Eden could see it running down people's faces. She could see it pooling around fallen bodies. She watched as Cassian bent over a dead bodyguard, his face gruesomely disfigured, and divested him of his gun.

All of it unfolded like she was at the bottom of a deep dark well, watching live coverage on a television screen high above her.

Come.

There.

Again.

The only clear thing as she was shoved from behind and Cass wrapped his arm around her waist and nearly carried her through the stampeding mob, in the opposite direction like two salmon swimming upstream. They ran through the ballroom—an inferno of fire and smoke—through another exit. Into an evacuated kitchen.

He rounded a corner, the gun poised and ready. But there was no one. The kitchen was empty. He kicked open a door that read Employees Only and stepped into a lobby with lights that flickered and hummed.

Electricity.

Cass strode to the windows, his hand pressed against the side of his head as he tried to decipher the squawks emitting from their earpieces—familiar voices chopped into indecipherable sound bites. Eden didn't try to decipher it. She was too transfixed by the elevator doors and the errant thought taking shape in her mind. A silly inclination. A tempting inclination. A strong inclination.

Come.

Cassian spoke back to the choppy voices as Eden stepped closer to the elevator. She was a fly and the button a web and she was caught.

She pressed it.

The doors slid open, as if waiting there just for her.

She stepped inside.

"We need to move," Cass said, pushing into the stairwell.

Then, as though realizing Eden was no longer behind him, he turned—his eyes widening, his pupils dilating—as the elevator doors slid shut and up Eden went.

All the way to the top.

She walked through the deserted rooftop bar, out into the crisp, windy night—her dress flapping around her ankles. Far below, people screamed, and sirens wailed while she stood on the rooftop of The Sapphire Hotel.

"You came."

She turned.

Mordecai stood in front of a helicopter, dressed in a tuxedo, his smile twisted as a holographic image projected from the device in his hand. And while a part of Eden's brain knew that this was it, the chance she'd been waiting for—she only needed to get her hands on him—she didn't move. The heavy fog in her head had become a barrier, separating her mind from her body. The two were no longer communicating. As much as she wanted to wrap her hands around his neck and end him right here, right now, she couldn't.

He walked closer, pebbles crunching underfoot. "Where are they?"

Eden stood—unmoving, unspeaking.

"Where are the other two?"

She ground her teeth, but Mordecai pressed something on the device. A portion of the holographic image lit with bright red and the word escaped without censor. "Milwaukee."

"Where in Milwaukee?"

Eden gave him the address, unsure why she was giving him the address.

"Good girl." Mordecai stroked a cold knuckle along her cheek, his eyes filled with the same unsettling awe as before, when she came to the abandoned power plant. "You, my dear, have proven to be very difficult. Which means you're strong. I admire strength. When properly controlled."

The door behind them burst open.

Mordecai grabbed her, spun her around, and used her like a shield.

"She's on the roof!" Cass yelled into his Bluetooth as he came to a stop with his gun drawn, his eyes blazing.

First with fury. Then confusion. Eden could beat Cassian in hand-to-hand combat and he was a highly trained and dangerous fighter. Which meant she could crush Mordecai like a bug. All she had to do was carry out the move Cassian had helped her perfect. But Eden didn't spin around. She just stood there like a fool as Cassian breathed heavily, his attention moving from the helicopter to the holographic image to the remote in Mordecai's hand. And then his confusion swirled into an acute point of painful clarity. "He's controlling you."

It was true.

Somehow.

Not like the first time when she attacked her parents. But it was true just the same. Eden was fully conscious. Completely aware of all that was happening, and yet powerless to make her own decisions as Mordecai hid behind her like a coward, his arm clamped tight around her waist.

"Surely you came armed." He started at her left ankle. He groped to her thigh. Cassian's chest heaved. His nostrils flared. Her skin crawled as Mordecai moved to her right leg. His hand stopped on her calf, finding the gun strap. "Empty," he said, like one might comment on a curious weather pattern. "No matter. I have what we need beneath my suit coat. Just to your left. Why don't you get it out, my dear?"

Why don't you go to hell? Her thoughts spat in reply.

And yet, she obeyed.

With her lungs caving in, she removed the gun from its holster and pointed it straight at Cassian.

He stared back at her; his expression tortured.

And in that moment, Eden knew—it was not his life he cared about.

But hers.

"What do you want with them?" Cass yelled above the wind. Above the sirens. Above the panicked sounds of a night gone horribly wrong.

"It's not what I want with them. It's what I want for them."

"Which is what, exactly?"

Eden squeezed her shaking hands tight around the metal.

Somebody help.

She didn't want this gun in her hands.

She didn't want to point it at Cassian.

But she couldn't put it down.

The plea squeezed up her throat and spluttered past her lips. "Help."

Mordecai didn't hear. He was too preoccupied with Cassian. "They have a destiny to fulfill."

Cass fired his gun.

A bullet whizzed past Eden's ear.

Mordecai ducked behind her and screamed, "You dare!"

Then he pushed something on the device. The holographic image radiated with waves of bright orange, and with a surge of intense pain, Eden pulled the trigger.

She shot the gun.

Cassian dove behind a half-wall, bullets colliding with brick, spraying crumbles of hardened clay into the air.

No!

She didn't want to do this.

"Did you really think you could outsmart me?" Mordecai yelled.

Inside, her mind yelled louder. Drop it! Drop the gun. But her hands kept the weapon trained on the half-wall behind which Cassian hid as the door burst open again.

Two people ran out onto the roof.

To Eden's horror, she turned the gun on them.

Jack Forrester.

And her mother.

I love you. Do you understand? To the moon and back.

Jack held up his hands, a gun clutched in his right.

Mordecai pulled Eden closer to the helicopter. "Drop it!"

Jack did as Mordecai said.

"Slide it this way."

Jack gave the gun a kick.

It slid over pebble and concrete and stopped two feet in front of Eden's strappy shoes.

Mordecai swept a lock of fallen hair from the side of her face, wet from the sprinklers, and poured cold words into her ear. "I would like you to shoot them."

No.

Please, no.

She squeezed her eyes—demanding herself to wake up. Right now. This wasn't real. This was a nightmare. But Eden didn't wake up. And a horrible, splitting pain burst inside her head.

"What are you doing to her?" Mom shouted.

"Nothing she can't stop," Mordecai said. "All she has to do is obey."

Cold, searing pain made her finger curl around the trigger.

"Please." Mom's pupils shrank into pinpricks as she faced the barrel. "Eden."

"Stop calling her that!" Mordecai screamed, pulling Eden further back. "She is Subject 006. She has no name until she is given a name. Now I said shoot them."

The radiating orange overtook the projected image.

Pain surged again—unbearable, blinding pain.

She was going to do it.

She was going to shoot her mother.

She could feel it in her finger, twitching over the trigger.

"Help," she cried, choking over the word.

Somebody help.

Black spots danced in the periphery of her vision.

And sound crackled in her ear.

A voice.

Not the one who told her to come.

Not the one who told her to shoot.

This voice was small and still and familiar.

Eden, can you hear me?

Her exhale was loud—half-cry, half-breath as a tear tumbled down her cheek.

"Do you see their foreheads?" Mordecai said. "I'd like you to put a bullet in the center of each."

The pain swelled—so excruciating, she would have dropped to her knees had his grip not remained tight around her waist.

"In five … "

Agony accumulated as her heart thundered and her finger trembled. But somehow, rising from the midst of it —her father's voice. Fierce and insistent. "Eden, can you hear me?"

"Four …"

"You are not Subject 006."

"Three …"

"Your name is Eden Pruitt. I gave you that name. Because I am your father. Do you hear me, Eden? Listen to my voice."

She did.

But the pain. The pain was relentless, agonizing,

impossible. She could resist now, but she couldn't resist forever. She was going to pull it. And then she was going to die.

"Your name is Eden Pruitt. You are my daughter. Listen to my voice."

"Two …"

"I love you, Eden. You are my daughter. Listen to me. Listen to my voice!"

She grabbed onto his words, her body shaking. She repeated them in her mind like she'd repeated them at the Eagle Bend police department. Her name and her identity, over and over again. Her name was Eden Pruitt. She was his and she was loved. Her name was Eden Pruitt. She was his and she was loved. Her name was Eden Pruitt. She was his and she was loved. It was a truth Mordecai hadn't counted on. A truth that overpowered the pain. A truth that gave her a voice and that voice said no.

"One."

Her head split in two. The pain tore through her as it reached its pinnacle. She resisted for as long as she could, and then she let loose a guttural scream. Cassian sprang from the shadows. She pulled the trigger as he pulled his, tackling her mother to the ground.

His bullet met its mark as the device in Mordecai's hand fell.

The holographic image disappeared.

The pain cracking through Eden's skull disappeared with it as the man behind her howled and writhed, clutching his hand. His bloodied, blown apart stump of a hand.

Cassian rolled up onto his knees and pointed his gun.

Eden dropped hers.

Mom was on the ground behind him.

Stunned.

Pale.

Alive.

They had Mordecai cornered.

But the cornered man was not giving up without a fight.

With another howl, he pitched forward.

"Freeze!" Cassian yelled.

Mordecai did not freeze.

He grabbed the gun Eden had dropped.

And Cassian fired.

The shot spun Mordecai halfway around. His eyes went wide as he clutched his good hand to his chest, where red blossomed through the white of his pressed shirt like a rose in bloom. He looked down at it peculiarly—oddly—like he didn't understand why the rose was blooming. Then he fell to his knees and toppled.

Cass raced forward and dropped beside him.

"Who are you working with?" he demanded. "What do you want with them?

Mordecai coughed, blood gurgling in his throat. Trickling from his mouth. "They were … a gift …"

Cassian grabbed him by his suit coat, lifting his upper half off the ground. "A gift for who?"

"The Monarch." With a wheeze, Mordecai raised his stump of a hand in salute. Then it dropped to his side as his eyes went glossy and blank.

14

Eden ran to her mother as Cass stared into the unseeing eyes of the man he'd been hunting.

Mordecai was dead.

Gone.

Cass had done what Eden's father told him to do. He'd taken Mordecai out. But he'd done it before getting answers. He picked up the fallen device. The one Mordecai had used to control her.

A gift.

For the Monarch.

It was the same moniker the man with the tattoos had used after taking the cyanide pill. Cass had thought—or maybe just hoped—that Mordecai was The Monarch. That the threat to Eden would end once Mordecai ended.

But he was wrong.

Mordecai wasn't the Monarch.

The threat to Eden continued.

Cass muttered a curse.

The rooftop door burst open.

Eden's father appeared.

"Dad!"

Eden pulled her mother to her feet, bearing her weight as they joined Alexander Pruitt in a family hug. He looked over his daughter's shoulder, from Cassian to the dead man on the ground to the helicopter behind them—his hair a mess, his face a bloodless white.

He was without his walker, which meant he'd gotten up here without it. An impossible feat, if not for the adrenaline. Cass knew all too well how far that particular hormone could stretch the bounds of possibility. He also knew the exhausting crash that followed. With his wife and daughter alive in his arms, Pruitt looked on the verge of collapse.

Before he could, another explosion rent the night—a colossal blast as the rooftop shuddered—so violently Cass was pitched forward. Then another as the whole of downtown Chicago went black. The screaming below intensified.

Cass ran to the rooftop banister and peered down, trying to make sense of the pandemonium. A raging inferno burned across the street from The Sapphire, where paramedics and firefighters and reporters had gathered. Another bomb had exploded.

"What's happening?" Eden asked as sharp popping joined the cacophony.

With a shriek, Eden's mom ducked like the spray of bullets might reach them on the roof.

"We need to get out of here before the building collapses," Forrester shouted.

Cass agreed. But how?

Eden's mother stood with her left foot hovering above the ground like a dog on point. Her father leaned heavily against the rooftop door, his face white as bone. They were sixty-eight stories above the ground, and the entire power grid of downtown Chicago was out. Mr. Pruitt looked longingly at the helicopter, as though wishing he knew how to fly it. Apparently, his days in the CIA had not equipped him with that skill.

He heaved open the door with the weight of his body and said with a grimace, "He's right."

"Dad—" Eden objected.

"I'll be fine," he said, cutting through her protest. "Help your mother. I'll be right behind you."

She hesitated.

"Move," her father commanded.

Cass pocketed the fallen device as Eden helped her mother inside. They cut through the rooftop bar and into a smoky stairwell. Five flights down, Eden lifted her mother into her arms while her father fell further behind.

Cass lagged, ready to help as soon as the man allowed it. So far, he hadn't allowed it.

Then another explosion rattled the walls.

Pruitt sank onto the step.

"Dad!" Eden yelled, turning around like she would carry them both.

"I've got him," Cass called, doubling back.

With a pain-soaked groan from Pruitt, Cass heaved the man over his shoulders in a fireman's carry. The weight of him multiplied with every flight they descended. Cass grit his teeth against the discomfort and kept going.

Forty stories.

Thirty stories.

Twenty.

Fifteen.

His shoulder ached.

The smoke thickened.

His lungs screamed for oxygen.

Halfway between the eleventh and the tenth, Eden ground to a halt. Cass coughed into his left bicep.

"Someone's screaming," she said.

He strained to hear, but there was nothing but the sharp hacking from Eden's mom and the roaring of fire.

Eden carried her mother to the tenth floor and pulled open the door to a hallway filled with flames.

"What are you doing?" Forrester shouted, his sweatshirt over his mouth as he slammed the door shut.

"There are people stuck in the elevator!"

"We have to get out of here," Forrester said.

"We can't leave them."

"Look at your father, Eden."

Forrester's words did the trick.

Alexander Pruitt had passed out long ago. Whether from the pain or from some other more dire reason, Cass didn't know. He coughed as Eden schooled her horrified expression and they resumed their descent.

Two floors later, they passed three firefighters going up as they made their way down. Eden told them about the people stuck in the elevator.

"Between the tenth and eleventh floors," she said.

The firefighters hurried along.

So did they.

Until they reached the third floor.

Forrester shoved the door open. They raced across the decimated ballroom lobby, smoke and fire all around, to a different set of stairs. Cass followed without question. Forrester knew where he was going. He'd spent the past few days studying the hotel's layout.

They descended five more stories and burst into a parking garage.

No smoke.

No sound.

Just rows of quiet, abandoned cars.

Forrester fell into a violent coughing fit as Cass kicked in a car window, his lungs sucking in the clean air.

The alarm blared.

Eden's dad didn't even stir as Cass unlocked the door and placed him in the back seat. Eden helped her mom inside as the ceiling above them quaked, bits of cement raining to the ground.

Cass used his bare hands to pry apart the panels on the top and bottom of the steering column, exposing the ignition cylinder. He grabbed a shard of glass by his boot and cut the power wires. He stripped, twisted, then cut the starter wires too.

A few seconds later, the car roared to life.

Forrester jumped into the passenger side as Eden squeezed into the back. Cass threw the car into reverse, and peeled away.

15

Mom gritted her teeth and Dad stirred in and out of consciousness as Cassian maneuvered through traffic, trying to get away as firetrucks and police cars and military vehicles rushed in the opposite direction. Jack tried making calls on his cell phone. None of them went through. He tried finding Concordia News on the radio, but all he got was static.

It took forever for the traffic to thin, but when it did, Cassian punched the gas.

Eden watched the speedometer climb above 100 mph.

Nobody objected but the automated voice from the car speakers kindly and calmly asking him to slow down.

Cass ignored it.

Jack gave up on the radio, but not the phone. He alternated between Dr. Norton and Annette with no luck while everyone but Eden coughed, including her father, who grimaced with every single convulsion. The further away from Chicago they drove, the emptier the world became. Until it was just them on the highway, like they were the last people left on earth.

When Cass pulled up Dr. Norton's gravel drive, he didn't even come to a stop before the front door opened and two figures stepped out into the night.

Dr. Norton and Barrett Barr.

Cassian parked.

Eden opened the door.

"It collapsed!" Barrett said, his voice tinged with excitement, like this was some game instead of a living hell. "The Sapphire Hotel. The whole thing's a giant ash heap."

Dr. Norton took one look at Dad and fetched the wheelchair as Barrett continued talking. "Four more bombs have gone off since the first blast. All downtown. All within a block of The Sapphire. And get this. There were snipers outside waiting for people to evacuate."

Eden's mind spun.

Why?

Who?

Surely not Mordecai. He didn't need to go to so much trouble to get her on the roof. Not when he had her under his control before the first explosion.

"Do they know who's responsible?" Eden asked Barrett.

"No, but reporters are speculating."

Mom hobbled out of the car as Dr. Norton returned with the wheelchair. Dad insisted Dr. Norton help Mom first, to which Mom objected. "I'm not the one struggling to breathe." It was an unconvincing statement, given the wheezing that followed.

"Let's get you both taken care of," Dr. Norton said.

Eden lifted her father into the wheelchair, his lack of complaint a testament to how much pain he must be in. Cassian took one look at Eden's mother, then swept her easily into his arms and carried her inside.

"Mordecai is dead," he told Dr. Norton, an afterthought of a statement issued over his shoulder while the doctor pushed Eden's father behind them, insisting that Jack follow so he could check him, too.

Eden stood outside with Barrett.

Her lungs were fine.

Her body perfectly intact.

She had carried her mother down sixty-five flights of stairs, inhaling smoke the whole way, and she wasn't sore. She wasn't even tired. Her hands, however? They shook like the rooftop floor of The Sapphire.

Barrett stared at her, his eyes wide in the dark. "Reporters are saying it might be Interitus."

To that, she had no reply.

Eden stood in the shower, her hands shaking as she tried to wash away the stench of smoke in her hair. Grime and ash rinsed down the drain, but no matter how hard she scoured, the smoky smell remained. Every time she inhaled, memories flashed through her mind like scenes from a horror film. The fallen bodyguard's disfigured face. Pulling out the gun from Mordecai's holster. Pointing it at Cassian. Pointing it at her mother. Pulling the trigger.

She scrubbed harder and harder, more and more frantically, until a burst of pain sliced through her temple. With a sharp hiss, she clapped her hand over the spot. Eden stood beneath the spray, unsure what had happened. What was that? An aftershock from the torment she'd experienced on the roof? Or something else? Something new? She waited to see if it would come again. She didn't move a muscle until the hard spray of hot water went cold.

When she got out, she wrapped herself in a towel and balled up the ruined dress from the floor. She shoved it deep into the trash bin with hands that still shook, pulled out the bag, and tied it tight to keep the smell of smoke inside. The diamond choker glinted in the sink's basin where it had fallen. Its velvet box lost somewhere in the rubble that was Oswin Brahm's luxury hotel. Maybe Oswin Brahm was lost there, too. After all he'd done for America, after all he'd done to rebuild this country he loved after its near destruction—had Interitus claimed him in the end?

Eden dressed in a pair of sweats, set the smoky trash outside on the front porch, and stepped into the living room, where Barrett, Jane, Dr. Norton, and a very agitated Jack sat watching the news. Her parents were asleep. Cassian unaccounted for.

If he was smart, he jumped on his bike and rode away.

Far, far away.

The shaking in her hands moved into her arms. She hugged herself in an attempt to make it stop while reporters covered the war zone that had become downtown Chicago. Barrett was right. They were already speculating, throwing out the infamous and dreaded name —Interitus.

This was a well-orchestrated attack, they said. Interitus had tried to target Chicago twenty-one years ago and failed. Now, it seemed, they'd succeeded. Hospitals were overflowing. Airports and train stations were packed with frightened travelers. The entire country was in a panic despite America's Executive Director urging citizens to stay calm.

Eden hugged herself tighter and looked away, her gaze connecting with an ominous device next to the vase of flowers on the table.

Bile rose up her throat as she stepped away, her stomach churning with nausea. Mordecai had used it to take control of her body without her consent. For several horrifying minutes, it hadn't been her own.

The bile gathered into a lump that lodged itself in her esophagus.

She felt dirty.

Ashamed.

And absolutely, horrendously violated.

She tried to take a breath, but her lungs refused to cooperate. Feeling like she might retch, Eden pivoted on her heel and escaped out onto the deck.

―――――

Cass stood in the shadowed hallway, watching Eden go.

Nobody else noticed her leave. They were too riveted by the television as media moguls speculated over who was responsible and what exactly was happening.

He grabbed a bottle of sparkling water from the fridge, popped the cap, and joined her outside, where the night was quiet and eerily peaceful in light of the chaos unfolding ninety miles south. Eden sat in one of the Adirondack chairs with her knees pulled up to her chest and her arms wrapped around her shins—like she had their first night here, when she saw herself attacking her parents, when Norton explained to her why she'd done it. As he slid the door shut, she peeked over her shoulder, then quickly looked away like she couldn't meet his eye.

He sat beside her, the night replaying itself like flashes in a lightning storm. Eden, in his arms on the dance floor. Her odd request to use the restroom. The explosion. The elevator doors sliding shut with her inside. Watching the lift climb to the top. His mad dash to the roof. Finding her with him. The terror in her eyes as she aimed her gun.

There were moments in Cass's life—horrible moments—seared into his mind like a hot branding iron, each memory saturated with the same terror that had engulfed Eden. Watching his mother die through the slats of a closet door. The roar of the crowd and the blood on his hands as he stared down at a lifeless man who wasn't his father. Standing in Beverly Randall-Ransom's conference room, watching Eden hand herself over to the enemy, unsure if he would have to carry out a command that would not only destroy her but him, too.

And now, tonight. And the helpless, panic-stricken look on Eden's face.

He took a long drink from the bottle. Coughed a few times.

Eden stared out at the lake, moonlight reflecting off her profile—her posture rigid and unyielding. He could see it in the bob of her throat. The clenched muscles of her jaw. She was a tightly twisted wire about to snap.

"Eden—"

"I understand if you want out," she said quickly—a tumble of words—as she yanked on the sleeves of her sweatshirt. As though doing so might hide the tremble in her hands.

Cass cocked his head. "Why would I want out?"

"It's too dangerous. I'm too dangerous."

"You think danger bothers me?"

"I shot at you."

"You missed."

"I almost killed my mother." She bit her lip in the wake of those words, her chin quivering tremulously, and wrapped her arms tighter around her shins. "I would have, if you hadn't pushed her out of the way."

"That wasn't you."

Her eyes flashed as she finally met his gaze. "Yes, it was."

"You hit the dead center of a target the first time you fired a gun."

"So?"

"If you were trying to hit me, you would have hit me. If you were trying to hit her, you would have hit her. You didn't."

Eden spluttered, as though grappling for an objection.

"You resisted," he continued. "And that? That was you."

She shook her head—short, jerky shakes—her lips pressed together, her nostrils slightly flared. "It was also me who pulled the trigger."

"He was controlling you."

"Because of what's inside me! Because of what's a part of me."

"A part. But it's not you." Cassian Gray was not a man given to speeches. People, in his opinion, spoke too much. Used too many words. But right then, he would give an entire address if it would get her to see what he saw when he looked at her. Bravery and goodness and generosity and resilience and a dogged determination to protect the people she loved. "And you're not the only one."

She peered at him warily.

"You don't think we all have the same struggle—a battle inside that has us doing things we don't want to do? If you're good, you fight it. You starve it."

Moisture gathered in her eyes as she continued her short, jerky head-shaking.

"I'm telling you right now, I'm looking at one of the best."

A tear tumbled down her cheek.

Cass leaned forward, reached under her chair, and swiveled it to face his, legs scratching against wood. He brought his hand to her face to still the shaking and caught the second tear with his thumb. "The world has plenty of monsters, Eden. You aren't one of them."

She stared at him like she desperately needed his words to be true.

He stared back, determined to show her they were.

With a sniff, she pulled away. Pushed all ten fingers into her towel-dried hair and clasped her hands behind her neck. "I'm sorry for shooting at you."

"I'm sorry for finding you." One corner of his mouth quirked. "Sort of."

She laughed a hoarse, teary laugh and wiped her cheeks.

Cass leaned closer, his knees on either side of hers. Her long eyelashes damp.

"I guess we're even then," she said.

"I guess so."

He couldn't resist any longer.

With a piercing softness that grabbed him by the heart, he cupped her chin and kissed her.

She kissed him back—her lips soft but hungry, like she'd been waiting for this as impatiently as he had, fanning the desire he'd been so careful to constrain. He wanted to pull her into his lap. He wanted to keep on kissing her. Erase every inch of space between them. But she'd been through hell and his body was responding a little too eagerly, so he forced himself to pull away and take a ragged breath.

She brushed her thumb over his bottom lip, her eyes meeting his as a foreign, frightening emotion slammed through him.

Love.

He loved her.

He loved Eden Pruitt with a ferocity that alarmed him.

It was too fast.

Undoubtedly foolish.

He didn't deserve her.

He didn't fit into her world.

But it was true all the same.

He loved this girl who was self-sacrificing and brave. Intelligent and kind and steadfast with an equanimity that was rare at any age, let alone eighteen.

To keep from speaking the frightening confession, he picked up his bottle and took a long swig.

Eden tucked her hair behind her ears and sank back into her chair. "Who is the Monarch?"

Cass rubbed his jaw as Mordecai's last words swirled in his mind.

They were ... a gift ...

His knuckles whitened as he squeezed the bottle in his hand. Whoever—whatever—this Monarch was, Eden was not a thing to be gifted.

16

The world has plenty of monsters, Eden. You're not one of them.

The words held her together through the night. They held her together now, as she sat on the sofa in a crowded living room, watching the news with the rest of the world, sandwiched between her mother and the boy who had spoken them.

Cassian's arm rested by his side on the couch cushion, his pinkie finger less than an inch from her thigh. A not-quite touch that was driving her mad or keeping her from madness. Eden couldn't decide.

On her right, Mom sat with a brace around her injured ankle, and next to her—the man who had worked relentlessly on rehab for the past four weeks, looking drained of all energy. Last night, he'd spent every remaining ounce and now, he sat in his wheelchair, the spirometer Dr. Norton encouraged him to use untouched in his lap.

Dr. Norton moved about in the kitchen, brewing more coffee, and chopping vegetables for omelets while Jack paced like an addict jonesing for his next fix. He couldn't get a hold of his wife. He had tried video calls and emails and anything else he could think of, but each one of his messages bounced. Every five minutes, he would stop and phone Annette. Then he would swear loudly and resume his pacing.

On the floor, Jane sat next to her sack full of clothes with Mordecai's disassembled device in front of her. Jack had taken it apart. He found a chip inside and spent an hour studying it between failed phone calls before declaring it beyond repair. Now Jane was tinkering with the pieces like tinkering was an old hobby. Only instead of using any tools, she picked with her fingernails in the same rabbity way that she picked at her food. Eden had to fight the urge to sweep the pieces into the fire crackling in the grate. She didn't want that device fixed. She wanted it destroyed.

Barrett perched on the edge of the armchair with the television remote in hand, running unsolicited commentary while flipping from Concordia Chicago to Concordia National to Concordia World, each running slightly different coverage on the same catastrophe.

Interitus had officially taken credit for the attack.

Downtown Chicago was still burning. First responders had been cleared from the site. Military swarmed Michigan Avenue, which was marked by smoldering fires and precarious wreckage with hidden pockets ready to collapse. Hundreds remained unaccounted for, many of whom were high-profile leaders and celebrities. Candlelight vigils were cropping up across the nation to honor the fallen.

Every station would intermittently show mugshots of terrorists at-large affiliated with the evil regime, the most popular being a female named Prudence Dvorak, currently in her mid-thirties with an outdated photograph that depicted a girl much younger. A girl similar in age to Eden. They had assumed Mordecai was too young to be associated with Karik Volkova, but Mordecai wasn't much younger than Dvorak. Had Volkova been recruiting teenagers? And if Mordecai was a member of Interitus, did he orchestrate the attack to get to Eden, or was he trying to get to Eden amid an already-planned attack? The latter seemed too coincidental, the former too excessive. But then, if Mordecai was part of Interitus, terror was his aim. Maybe he saw the Prosperity Ball as an opportunity to kill two birds with one stone: get Eden, sow terror.

The unanswered questions gave her a headache.

She couldn't stop thinking about Mordecai's last words.

A gift.

For the Monarch.

Nobody had heard them but herself and Cassian. And while it seemed like important information to share with her parents, she hadn't been able to bring herself to do so. Not when they both looked so weak and vulnerable.

Jack let another curse fly and fisted his hair. "The attack happened in Chicago. Why is cell service down in Milwaukee?"

His question went without answer.

On the television, a news anchor for Concordia Chicago informed the public that Perk was on a temporary moratorium to stop the spread of false information. A photograph of a well-known and deeply beloved actress replaced the mugshot of Prudence Dvorak, followed by photographs of several others. America's finest, the news anchor said. All of them gathered in one place. So many dead. So many more missing in the rubble.

Barrett flipped to Concordia National.

The press secretary spoke with reporters, sharing the same message again and again. Stay calm. If possible, stay at home. America's Board of Directors were taking every means necessary to ensure the safety of its citizens.

"This vile regime is a cancer that must be eradicated. They have struck twice. We will not allow a strike three.

The infrastructure of our great nation cannot withstand another blow, which means we must rally together and fully cooperate with these precautions to prevent another attack."

"Maybe they shut down cell service," Mom suggested.

"Like they shut down Perk," Barrett added.

"What would that do other than cause more panic?" Jack replied.

"If they think Interitus is communicating via cell, it stops their ability to communicate," Barrett said, watching as Jane smelled—actually sniffed—two of the pieces and clicked them together.

"Madam Secretary," a reporter said. "How is it possible that Interitus was able to carry out such an orchestrated assault?"

"We have reason to believe," the woman answered, "that this regime has been amassing followers amongst illegals for years."

A squeak followed the declaration.

It belonged to Jane, who hadn't made a sound all day.

Everyone in the room looked at her, like she might follow the squeak with actual words. Instead, her attention returned to the disassembled device, her choppy hair falling in her face. She never tied it back or tucked it out of the way. Eden had to repress the urge to pull it back for her and tie it into a ponytail.

"They've been building in number and strength amongst hidden communities. Confirming what we already know."

"Which is what?" the reporter asked.

"Off-the-grid individuals are a serious threat to this country."

Off-the-grid individuals.

Eden looked at Cassian's pinkie—the broad bed of his neatly trimmed nail.

"Which means we will urge all businesses and institutions to conduct proper retinal scans."

Barrett flipped back to Concordia Chicago, which ran an interview with Oswin Brahm that had played late last night. He was safe. Alive. Clean but banged up as he hid in an undisclosed location and addressed the nation like he had twenty-one years ago when Interitus first struck. Back then, he'd been composed. A beacon of calm in a storm of chaos. This time, anger radiated off him in palpable waves. His eyes, laser beams of fury aimed directly at the camera. This time, the attack was personal. His hotel had been reduced to a pile of ash. Too many of his guests were dead. Interitus would not get away with it.

Barrett flipped to Concordia World.

Tickertape scrolled on the bottom of the screen.

All citizens abroad must report to the nearest embassy.

"What?" Jack exclaimed, his hands gripping the back

of the sofa. "Why?"

As the news anchor answered his question—America's Board wanted everyone home and accounted for—he tried calling Annette again, his fingers fumbling over the buttons.

It didn't work.

Until then, Eden had always thought the Forresters were in the better position. Ellery and her mother were in Rome. Sightseeing. Jack was here, trying his best to help Eden and her parents take down the man who threatened them. But now? He was separated from his family in a time of national crisis, unable to reach them—the government on high alert for the tiniest hint of terrorist activity. His daughter, oblivious to the fact that she was a weapon created by the very regime the press secretary swore they would eradicate. Which meant authorities were as much a threat to his daughter's safety as Interitus, even if their intentions differed.

With a muttered expletive, Jack let himself out onto the deck and slammed the sliding glass door behind him. Jane let out another squeak and clapped her hands over her ears as Jack yelled at the sky—a great war cry of frustration—then pulled out a pack of cigarettes from his back pocket.

All of them stared.

Until Dr. Norton gave his throat a clear. "Who would like toast with their omelets?"

"Two pieces. Extra butter," Barrett said.

"Alaric?" Dr. Norton pointed his attention at Eden's father.

The disorienting name made Eden want to clap her hands over her ears like Jane. His name was Alexander. Alexander Pruitt. She was Eden Pruitt. They were the Pruitts. And other than the boy sitting next to her, she didn't want this to be her life. She missed Erik and the ocean and school and the neat and tidy existence that used to be hers. She missed it all so much that she wanted to scream at the sky like Jack.

Dad shook his head listlessly. "I'm not hungry."

"It's important to get—"

"No thank you," Dad said, more firmly this time. "I'd like to go rest, if you wouldn't mind."

Dr. Norton set down the knife he'd been using to chop peppers, then came into the living room to wheel her father to the guest room.

The fact that he didn't object to being wheeled carved a pit in Eden's stomach.

"I think I'd like to rest, too," Mom said, giving Eden a brave smile. She grabbed the crutches propped against the couch. And when she hobbled past, she brushed her fingers through Eden's hair. Her crutches tapped down the hallway as gravel popped in the distance.

A car was approaching.

Cassian didn't hear it.

But Eden did.

So did Jane and Barrett

All three of them looked out the window at the same time.

Cleo's Tesla came into view.

Eden stood. Cassian looked up at her, then finally heard what the rest of them already had. He joined Eden as she let herself out the front and Cleo parked her car.

"You're alive!" she exclaimed, slamming her door shut and marching toward them like a frazzled mother hen. "Every college student on campus is freaking out like these missing celebrities are their favorite aunts and uncles. Meanwhile, I had no idea if you two were still living. How'd you get out?"

Eden told her the story. The whole sordid tale.

And when she finished, Cassian shared with Cleo what Eden had yet to share with her parents.

"He said they were a gift for the Monarch."

"The Monarch," Cleo repeated. "That name again."

"Is it familiar?" Eden asked.

Cleo wedged her front left tooth between the pad of her thumb and her black-painted thumbnail. "Yeah, but I'm not sure why."

Behind them, the door flew open.

Barrett stood on the other side with a Christmas-morning smile stretched wide across his face. "You guys need to come see this!"

17

Inside, Dr. Norton and Jack were back—standing in the living room, staring open-mouthed at a holographic image projecting from the device Jane had reassembled.

Eden recoiled.

"Start it over," Barrett said, his voice brimming with excitement.

Jane pushed something that made the projection go away.

And Eden felt a strong, visceral urge to smack the device out of Jane's hand as pieces of last night flashed through her mind. Mordecai groping her legs. The gun in his holster beneath his suit coat. Her finger on the trigger. Searing pain and the horrible realization that she was going to do it—she was going to shoot Cassian. She was going to shoot her mother.

Don't touch it. Stop messing with it.

But then Jane pushed something to make the projection reappear. It wasn't the image from last night, but a three-dimensional butterfly that spun into a map.

"Did you see that?" Barrett pointed. "Did you see what it was? A butterfly. A Monarch butterfly. That dead guy who took the cyanide pill? He said *For the Monarch*, right? Here's a Monarch. Not like a king monarch, but a butterfly monarch."

A tremble took hold of Eden's limbs. She was no longer on the roof with sirens and screams and wind but outside an abandoned power plant in North Allegheny in the back of a quiet Land Rover, where a three-dimensional butterfly spun into a map just like this one, only that one had two blinking dots bouncing erratically. This one had five.

Eden stepped forward and swiped the map left, just like Mordecai had done in the back of his Land Rover.

Just as she expected, a database took its place.

"Those look like IP addresses," Jack said.

Eden swiped again, knowing what would come next.

Code.

A list of commands, longer than before.

Were they commands given to her? Commands given against her will? If they were to translate them, would they go something like this:

Come.

Aim.

Shoot.

Kill.

With a shudder, she swiped one last time.

And the familiar image appeared. The one from last night, with a vast array of dots—too many to count—not blinking or erratic but steady and different colored.

Eden took a lurching step back.

She could smell smoke.

Was it still in her hair?

Jack stepped beside her with his head tilted, moving his pointer finger from one marker to the next like an invisible dot-to-dot. Suddenly, he stopped. Then he grabbed the projection and pain seared in Eden's left temple. She clapped her hand over the spot.

"Stop," Cass said, his voice filled with tension and authority.

He was staring at her, his golden eyes teeming with concern.

They were all staring at her. Even Jane.

She pulled her hand away from her head. The pain was gone. Had it been real, or did she imagine it? The tremble in her limbs grew. She felt disoriented. Out of sorts. Like Erik's little sister whenever her blood sugar crashed. "He used that to control me," she finally said.

"I would never do that," Jack replied in earnest. "I just want to see something."

With her heart thundering, she swallowed the acidic taste in her mouth and gave Jack a reluctant nod.

With utmost care, he captured the projection and zoomed out. Then zoomed out some more. And some more. Until the outline of a human body could be seen, like a diagram from anatomy class. And above it, a familiar number.

006.

Goosebumps marched across Eden's skin.

Jack grabbed his laptop from the kitchen table and hurriedly pulled up images. A whole folder full of images, taken at various points. Some right here, in Dr. Norton's home. Others, in Beverly Randall-Ransom's. Most were recent, but some were taken years and years ago. When Eden was a baby. Again, when she was four.

"It's a blueprint. A map of Eden's entire system." Jack turned back to the holographic diagram, his eyes wild. "There's so much more detail. So much more information than we had before."

The words planted a seed of hope deep in Eden's soul. "Enough to stop it from happening again?"

Jack looked at her.

"If you studied all of this, if you figured out exactly how it works, do you think you could stop us from being controlled?"

"I think it's a possibility," he said.

The silence that followed his words hummed with

energy. She hated this device. And now she loved this device. For it could be the key. The key to defusing the bomb that was Eden. The keys to preventing last night from ever happening again. The key to her freedom. A discovery so game-changing, she wanted to sandwich Jane's face between her hands and kiss her on the forehead. But before she could even manage a proper breath, phones began to ring.

Jack's.

Cleo's.

Dr. Norton's.

All of them at once.

Jack lunged at the coffee table to answer his. His eyes went wide with relief as soon as he heard his wife's voice on the other end. He quickly let himself out onto the back deck.

Dr. Norton answered his, too.

Cleo's wasn't an active call, but several voice messages. All from her mom, who had somehow left them despite the sidelined cell service. She dialed her mother's number. Dr. Beverly Randall-Ransom answered halfway through the first ring.

Cleo assured her she was fine. They were all fine. Then she listened as her mother relayed a string of information. She searched for a pen and jotted a phone number on the back of her hand. They expressed their I-love-you's and Cleo hung up.

"She's at the hospital, along with every other doctor in Chicago." Cleo dialed the number she'd scrawled across her skin. "Mona was supposed to bring a kid who—"

Her voice came to an abrupt halt. So did her dialing.

"What?" Eden said.

"Mona." Cleo blinked slowly, then her expression brightened—like a lightbulb turning on in slow motion. "Oh my gosh, Cass. The girl with the glass eye."

His brow furrowed.

"That's where I've heard it before. That's why it's familiar."

"That's why what's familiar?" he said.

"The Monarch. I recognized the name because of the girl with the glass eye." Cleo pointed the words at Cassian like they should mean something.

The furrow in his brow deepened. "Who's the girl with the glass eye?"

"You don't remember her?"

"Am I supposed to?"

"She was one of Mona's girls."

"Mona had a lot of girls."

"Not with glass eyes!" Cleo looked at him in exasperation. "She was a few years older than us. Hardly ever talked. Dark hair. Pixie cut. Androgynous looking. At first, I thought she was a boy. But her name was something super feminine. Like Juliette or Florence."

"How is she connected to The Monarch?" Eden cut in.

"I asked her how she got the glass eye."

Eden snorted.

Cleo would ask such a question.

"She said The Monarch gave it to her."

The goosebumps multiplied. All over Eden's body. They raced up her neck and across her scalp. "Do you know where she is now?

"I have no idea," Cleo said. "But I bet you anything Mona does."

18

Dr. Norton ended his call as Jack opened the sliding glass door. He shuffled to the couch and sank onto the center cushion—staring but not seeing. "Annette and Ellery are being detained at the embassy in Rome. They're on a waiting list to come home."

Silence ensued, thick with uncertainty and the smell of burnt toast as the neglected bread popped from the toaster.

"They'll have to go through customs," he said in a deadened, faraway voice.

Dr. Norton squeezed Jack's shoulder.

"What if the wrong people are monitoring flights? What if they have the same photograph he had?" He thrust his hand toward Cassian, who stood across from

Eden with a tightly clenched jaw. He'd been hired to find not just Eden, but Ellery, too.

"Mordecai is dead," Dr. Norton said, as if his death meant the death of all threats.

But it didn't.

Jack ran his hand down the length of his face. "So was Volkova."

"Ellery has the scrambling device."

"What does that matter if Interitus sees her face on a security camera at O'Hare?"

"I don't think they're looking for us," Eden interjected.

Jack and Dr. Norton looked at her.

Eden swallowed, glanced toward the hallway where her parents had disappeared, then forced herself to say the words she'd been keeping close to her chest. "We were supposed to be a gift."

"What do you mean?" Dr. Norton asked.

"Last night. Before Mordecai died. Cass asked him what he wanted with us, and he said we were a gift. For the Monarch."

Jack cut a sharp look at Cassian. They were together when the tattooed man took the cyanide pill. They were together when he spoke his strange, final words. "So you're saying ... Mordecai isn't the Monarch?"

Eden shook her head.

Jack's face went a shade paler.

Eden rushed onward. She meant to share this as good news. Hopeful news. She didn't share it to add more worry to the equation. "By the time Dad uncovered us, Volkova had already been executed. Every Interitus member involved in the … experiment … was found and killed.

"Somehow, Mordecai discovered we weren't destroyed. For whatever reason, he was monitoring *this* when our networks came online." Eden picked up the device she both loved and hated and projected the first image. "I think it's our networks."

"If that's true, why are there five?" Jack said.

Eden stared hard at the fifth dot, which was glitching. But not in the same way as the others. "You know for a fact my dad destroyed the other two?"

"Yes," Dr. Norton said, so matter-of-factly, there was no room for questioning it. There were no more secrets. Everything was out on the table.

"Maybe that one is an error." Jane had fixed the device partially, but not completely. The fifth dot could be the result of damage.

"It could be the Monarch," Barrett said. "Some sort of control center."

Eden nodded. Which left the other four. One for her. One for Ellery. One for Barrett and one for Jane. "When Mordecai projected this image in the back of his Land Rover, there were only two."

"Yours and Ellery's," Jack said, catching on.

"Barrett's and Jane's weren't on the map because they were disabled." Eden looked at them expectantly, waiting for the dots to connect. Waiting for them to see that this situation was not so dire. But she could tell by their slightly confused expressions they weren't getting there on their own. Eden would have to connect the dots for them. "When our networks came online, Mordecai realized we were alive. He decided to find us. Then, once his collection was complete, present us as a gift to The Monarch."

"Gifts are surprises," Barrett said.

"Exactly," Eden replied. "So whoever the Monarch is, there's a good chance he or she doesn't know about us." She looked from Jack to Dr. Norton, expecting her theory to comfort them.

They didn't look comforted.

They looked deeply troubled.

"Why would he be monitoring this?" Jack asked, gesturing to the projection. "If everything was destroyed, where did he even get it from?"

Both valid questions. Eden didn't have any good answers. As hopeful as she was trying to be, there was a high probability Mordecai wasn't a lone wolf. Last night's attack certainly wasn't a one-man show. The Monarch might not know about them, but others probably did.

"IPs can be traced." Jack's face turned white as he grabbed the device and swiped to the second image—strings of numbers separated by periods. An entire database of them.

Eden's stomach clenched.

All devices had IP addresses, and IP addresses could be traced. Maybe not to an exact location, but certainly to a general vicinity. This device was here with them, in Dr. Norton's cabin.

"Can you hide it?" Cleo asked, understanding the concern.

Jack alternated between his laptop and the device in question, working like a fast and furious storm squall, while Eden's clenched stomach went hard as a rock. Instead of seeing the dot-to-dot she had created, Jack and Dr. Norton had created a dot-to-dot of their own, forcing Eden to recalibrate hers.

The picture was disturbing and mysterious, with only two certainties: this was far from over. And this was much bigger than they previously understood.

Once Jack finished, he sat on the couch, as white as the drapes that hung in Dr. Norton's living room. "It's diverted now, but if someone was already looking for it …"

The words hung in the air—a horrible question mark.

Were they safe here? If not, then where could they possibly go?

Down the hall, Eden's parents slept. Her father—a man with broken ribs and a giant brace and scars where bullets had entered and exited his body. Her mother—a woman with a broken ankle and a fragile heart and a neck that was no longer bruised but had been not too long ago. They were bruises Eden had put there.

The muscles across her chest pulled tight.

Enough was enough.

She refused to let her parents stand in the crossfire any longer. This was supposed to end last night and yet here they were, playing defense once again.

It was time to change the game.

It was time for the hunted to become the hunters.

Thanks to Cleo, they had a lead: the girl with the glass eye.

Eden looked at Cass. He stared back at her like he knew exactly what she was thinking. They would leave tonight. And they would start with Mona.

Eden walked with Cleo and Cassian as he pushed the motorcycle down the long gravel drive. At the other end, the cabin windows glowed yellow. The horizon had swallowed the sun, but the sky resisted the dark.

It was twilight.

The in-between.

No longer day, but not yet night.

Inside, Dr. Norton fixed dinner. Barrett distracted her mother with every fact and anecdote he could find on Monarch butterflies. She was too polite to dismiss him. Jane had taken possession of the remote—flipping channels so quickly the reporters sounded like a depressing remix—and Jack smoked a cigarette on the deck while filling her father in on everything he had missed while resting.

Nobody noticed them slip out the front.

By the time her parents would register her absence, they would be unable to follow. Eden would be gone.

Jane and Barrett knew the plan. Eden and Cass were going to find The Monarch. Jane and Barrett were going to stay. They would keep their eyes and ears on high alert. They were prepared to fight should the wrong people show up. At least, Barrett was. Jane neither agreed nor disagreed, but seeing as she didn't talk, Eden wasn't concerned about her spoiling the plan.

"Don't tell them anything about the girl or Mona," Eden said to Cleo. The last thing she wanted was her parents chasing her while she chased the Monarch. The goal was to get them out of trouble, not lead them further into it.

Cleo pantomimed zipping her lips.

Cassian swung his leg over the seat of the bike. "We'll

need your help after Mona gives us whatever information she's willing to share."

"My phone will be on," Cleo said.

"Give this to my parents." Eden handed her a folded slip of paper—a note hastily written but heartily felt.

I'm going to put an end to this. Then I'll come back and we won't have to be afraid anymore. Please stay safe. Please don't worry. You raised me to be strong. All my love, Eden.

"Tell Jack to study the projections. He has to find a way to keep us from being controlled." Eden climbed onto the bike behind Cassian. "His daughter's life depends on it."

Cleo slipped the note into her back pocket and gave Eden a salute. The bike rumbled to life. Eden wrapped her arms around Cassian's lean torso as he released the clutch and they sped off into the encroaching night.

19

Rocking on the floor, Jane clutched the sack to her chest and glanced at the clock on the doctor's wall. Yesterday, she'd gotten the bad feeling. Then something bad happened. Something awful. She'd watched it on the television last night. She'd watched it on the television all day. Now the bad feeling was back, wiggling its way into the pit of her stomach.

Barrett must have felt it, too, because he kept meeting her eye with a look of unease.

Any minute now, the adults would find out. Eden's father and mother and the doctor and the man named Jack who smelled like cigarettes. They would realize what Jane and Barrett already knew. Eden and Cassian were gone.

In the kitchen, Dr. Norton was getting dinner ready. The house smelled like meatloaf and potatoes and the cigarette smoke on Jack's clothes. He sat at the table, showing Eden's father the projections from the device Jane had fixed. If she'd known it was going to lead to all of this, she would have left it alone.

"It was connected to the same host Eden was connected to the first time she was controlled. But it's not connected any longer. There's this error code, see. I think it has to be connected to the host and Eden's network in order for it to work."

"What are the different colors?" Alexander asked.

"I'm not sure yet. But Eden's system has three parts, and there are three different colors." Jack zoomed closer, and closer, and closer, pinpointing a blue marker that differed slightly from the rest. A fluorescent globule floated in its center. Then he swiped to the database of numbers.

"IP addresses," Alexander said.

"That's what they look like to me, too. But when I plug them in, they don't lead anywhere."

Concordia National returned from a short commercial break.

The television had been playing all day.

The death toll was rising as first responders returned to the scene. Jeremiah Finkledei, one of America's greatest minds—a trailblazer who brought the metaverse into middle-class homes all across the country—was confirmed among the dead. Along with America's

Attorney General, Judy McGinnis. Their photographs filled the screen while ticker tape ran across the bottom, listing the phone number of a tip line people could call if they witnessed any suspicious activity or knew of anyone living off the grid.

The footage cut to a long line outside a hospital where queues of people waited to donate blood. The anchor's voice wobbled as she commended America's generous spirit and its willingness to come together in this time of national crisis. Her voice cracked when she reminisced about an even darker day, twenty-one years before, and how horrifyingly familiar all of this was. All the while, Eden's mother sat on the couch dabbing her eyes with a crumpled tissue.

"Dinner's ready," Dr. Norton said, setting a pan of meatloaf on top of the stove.

Ruth collected herself, then glanced around the room, finally noticing the absence of her daughter. "Where's Eden?"

Jane rocked faster.

Silence descended.

A bloated, disconcerting silence.

Dr. Norton peered out the kitchen window. "Cleo's car's gone."

Jack joined him. "So is Cassian's bike."

Ruth rose from the sofa and called Eden's name. When there was no answer, she hurried down the hall and called her name again. She returned, looking frazzled. "Where is she?"

Barrett, who'd been sitting in the armchair opposite Jane, shifted in the seat. "They ... left."

Everyone turned to look at him.

"What do you mean 'they left'?" Alexander said.

"Cleo went home, to her dorm."

"Did Eden go with her?" Ruth asked.

Barrett reached inside his pocket and handed her the folded note.

Ruth took the letter with trembling hands. She unfolded it and read a few of the words. With a gasp, her hand flew to her mouth. Her eyes filled with tears.

"What is it?" Alexander asked.

Ruth passed him the note.

He skimmed the contents, shaking his head as he read. "I need a phone."

Jack handed his over, peeking over Alexander's shoulder as he dialed Cassian's number.

There was no answer.

Ruth's face had gone chalky white. Alexander's, a pinkish-red.

Jane tried to imagine Father's reaction after she ran away. The thought scared her. So, too, did the very real knowledge that he was still out there. In the crossed-off city. Probably looking for her. The urge to run east—to put more distance between them—swelled. She would run and run and run until she reached the giant body of water called the Atlantic Ocean. Then she would start to swim.

Alexander tried Cleo's number next.

She didn't answer either.

Ruth went to Barrett. She knelt in front of him, grabbing his hands and squeezing them tight. "Please tell us where they went."

"I-I don't know. They didn't tell me."

He was lying.

He was lying to Eden's mother.

Ruth turned to Jane with a look of such desperation that, for one intense moment, Jane wanted to speak. She wanted to tell Ruth the truth. About Mona and the girl with the glass eye. She wanted words to break free so she could help Ruth feel better. But the words weren't there. They left with Kitty.

"It's going to be okay," Barrett said. "Eden can't get hurt."

"But she can be taken!" Alexander slammed his fist hard on the table.

Jane startled.

The room fell into a hush.

Alexander tried calling Cassian again. Then Cleo. This time, his call went straight to her voicemail. Jane could hear Cleo's recorded voice on the other end. "Hey,

I don't listen to voicemail, so if you want to waste some breath, speak into the void."

A beep followed the outgoing message.

Alexander wheeled himself to the front door with a pain-laced grimace.

"Where are you going?" Dr. Norton said.

"To Cleo's dormitory. If she's not going to answer, then I'll talk to her in person. I will make her tell me where they went."

"Alex," Ruth said.

He shouted a curse.

Jane squeaked and ducked beneath her sack.

"Eden has a plan, Mr. Pruitt," Barrett said, his voice a little unsteady. "She's going to be okay." He stood and went to the table. "The most helpful thing we can do right now is stay here and study this." He picked up the device. "We can't be taken if we can't be controlled. Cass and—"

He stopped abruptly.

They waited for him to continue, but he seemed to be in some sort of stupor.

"Cass and what?" Alexander finally said.

Barrett cleared his throat. "Cass and ..."

He stopped again. This time, less abruptly, a deep furrow divoting his brow.

"What's the matter?" Jack asked.

"I can't remember her name."

Jane watched the doctor and Eden's parents exchange confused looks.

"Whose name?" Ruth said.

"Your daughter's."

"Eden?"

"Eden," Barrett repeated, his eyes darting back and forth in a state of confusion and unease. He rubbed his forehead, then peered at the books on Dr. Norton's shelf, all of which he'd read. He grabbed one—a collection of poems—and thrust it at Dr. Norton. "Flip somewhere random. Tell me the page and line number."

"Barrett—" Dr. Norton started.

"Just do it!"

The shout was so unlike him that Dr. Norton obliged. He opened the book to the middle. "Page fifty-seven," he said, running his finger down the margin. "Line eighteen."

Barrett looked as though he were skimming a giant, invisible book hovering in the air. He started to nod. "My captain does not answer. His lips are pale and still. It's from 'O Captain, My Captain' by Walt Whitman. Try another."

"Barrett," the doctor said. "What's going on?"

"Please. Just one more."

With a sigh, Dr. Norton flipped deeper into the book. "Page 102, line ... ten."

Barrett started skimming the invisible book again.

"Where never kings connive nor tyrants scheme. 'Let America Be America Again' by Langston Hughes."

Ruth placed her hand gently on Barrett's arm. "Sweetheart, what are you doing?"

"I forgot her name."

"What do you mean?"

"I mean, it wasn't even on the tip of my tongue."

Jane stared.

They all stared.

It was normal to forget things. But Barrett wasn't normal. Not more than thirty minutes ago, he'd been telling Ruth every fact a person could ask for about Monarch butterflies, all of it committed to memory. Because Barrett didn't forget things. Neither did Jane.

He set his hand on top of his head. "It's like it fell right out of my brain."

20

Eden had no idea silos existed inside Chicago. Yet here they were—stark and towering against a night sky that had gone gray from smoke as the Magnificent Mile smoldered across the river. A chain-link fence surrounded the expansive property, posted with signs that warned against trespassing.

Cass parked his bike.

Eden stepped off behind him. "What is this place?"

"The Damen Silos," he said, pocketing the keys. "They used to be owned by the government, but a private citizen bought them years ago at an auction."

"Why?"

"To keep them from being leveled." Cass moved a few lengths forward where the chain link had come loose from its rusted pole. He pulled it up and motioned for

Eden to crawl inside. When she was through, he ducked in after her.

"What are we doing here?" she asked.

"Visiting Mona," he said, cutting through tall grass and waist-high weeds under the light of a hazy moon.

Eden gaped. Mona lived here?

The place was long abandoned. The perfect setting for a zombie apocalypse movie, with no signs of life that she could see. She followed Cass along a strip of land strewn with crumbled brick and debris. On her left stood the skeletal frame of what might have been a warehouse once upon a time. On her right, a polluted canal for ships and barges.

Cassian's phone began buzzing inside his jacket.

He pulled it from his pocket and glanced at the screen. Eden glanced, too. There were three missed calls. All from Jack's number.

Her insides twisted. It was a cruel time for Eden to leave, even under normal circumstances. They'd reached that point in the year when her parents became a little extra tender, their protectiveness bordering on over, their affection and concern tipping toward needy. For Mom, at least. Now Chicago was burning. The country was on high alert. Their enemy was out there somewhere at large. And Eden had left.

The phone started buzzing again.

Eden steeled herself against the sound. "You should block the number."

"Are you sure?"

"If you don't, they'll just keep calling." And they couldn't be distracted. They were on a mission. Feeling guilty about leaving wouldn't help her accomplish it.

Cassian dismissed the call. He blocked the number, pocketed the phone, and stopped in front of a large sheet of corrugated metal covered in graffiti. He pulled it back and invited her to slip through. As soon as she did, the sound of crumbling rock had her looking left, where a gangly boy hopped from a rusted metal beam.

Eden startled as Cass slid inside behind her.

The boy was stretched thin. He had the look of a kid who'd grown too fast to fill, with bare feet and a dirty face and hollowed cheeks. If Eden had to guess, she'd say he was thirteen. Maybe fourteen.

"This is private property," he said in a voice caught between boy and man, his gaunt shoulders squaring. Then he scuffed his bare foot in an arc along the ground.

Cass looked down at the arc, then used his boot to do the same—a mirror to the boy's, creating a two-dimensional shape like a football in the dust.

The boy looked up, suspicion easing into curiosity.

"We're here to speak with Mona," Cass said.

The kid stared for a moment, then led them through the warehouse, out into the night. Toward a hole in one of the silo walls. They climbed in and descended crumbling stairs into a dank labyrinth of underground tunnels and rooms lit with kerosene lamps. Populated with people.

Eden gawked, unable to hide her shock and bewilderment.

Cleo had told her once that it was easier to live off the grid in cities like Chicago because there was a community. At the time, Eden imagined a network of dodgy crooks living on the streets. Cassian's mother was the exception, not the rule.

But this place told a different story.

Young children peeked out from soiled sheets that hung in the doorways. A baby's cry and the soothing sound of a mother's lullaby. Coughing and whispers as older children loitered in the tunnels, watching as Cass and Eden followed the barefooted boy deeper into the maze.

At this very moment, reporters were claiming Interitus had been building in strength and number in communities like this one. But all Eden could see were malnourished kids and haggard-looking mothers. Concordia was feeding them a lie. Concordia had always fed them a lie. And Eden was the fool who'd swallowed it whole.

Anger stirred.

This place was dark and damp and depressing.

Children and babies should not be subjected to such living conditions. But here they were, subjected all the same. Was it always this somber? Did they look at every stranger in the same suspicious way they were looking at Eden and Cassian now? Or was this the result of the ruined smoking buildings across the channel?

The boy led them around a corner, then swept aside a sheet and gestured for them to enter a dark room. He lit the kerosene lamp inside, giving light to their surroundings. Eden was surprised to see a computer and a metaverse headset on top of a desk. Beside them, a battery-operated generator. There was also a neatly made cot and wooden crates filled with a variety of supplies, and stacks of boxes marked with numbers.

"I'll fetch Mona," the boy said.

When he left, Cass leaned against the desk and crossed one boot over the other, his knuckles white as he wrapped his fingers beneath the desk's ledge.

"So, people live here," Eden said.

Cass nodded.

"How many?"

"Fifty, give or take a few. More in the winter. Less in the summer." There was a stiffness to his words. The set of his shoulders, too. Like he was every bit as upset by the conditions as she was.

"Isn't there somewhere better they could stay?"

Somewhere above ground. Somewhere that didn't smell like mold.

"Everybody here lives off the grid."

"That doesn't mean they deserve to live like this."

The tense set of Cassian's shoulders relaxed ever so subtly. So, too, did his grip on the desk's ledge. A ghost of a smile played on his lips.

"What?" Eden said.

Cassian shrugged. "You care."

Eden blinked, unsure how to respond to such a statement. Thanks to her superhuman ears, she could still hear the baby's cry and the mother's lullaby. Babies should sleep in warm cribs, surrounded by clean air.

"Most people don't," he added.

His words struck her with sadness. Perhaps because they were true. But only because most people didn't know. If this place could be documented and shown to the public, she was sure that most people would feel the same anger she was feeling now.

It was, of course, a naïve idea. If Concordia kept protests and riots hidden from the public, they'd keep this hidden, too. She thought about the map in Cleo's dorm room—marked with protests that had turned into riots over the past year. There'd been seven of them, when the year before there'd only been two. She thought about Dwight in Madison, missing. Where did he go? What did the government do with people like him? What would the government do with the people here? The whole thing made her feel untethered.

Cassian's phone began buzzing again.

He pulled it free. "It's Norton," he said, showing her the screen. "Do you want me to block his number, too?

She nodded more resolutely than she felt, then chewed her bottom lip, trying hard not to think about her parents. Not to think about that mother and her baby or what would happen to that baby if the mother was arrested. She took a deep breath. "That thing you did with your foot. The arc. Was that some sort of secret greeting?"

"It's a simple way to tell whether a visitor is friend or foe."

She nodded, then peeked into one of the crates, which housed an assortment of books. She picked up a weathered copy of *Harry Potter and the Prisoner of Azkaban*. "Where does this stuff come from?"

"Mona is very organized. And Beverly isn't the only influential person she knows."

She thumbed through the pages, dust motes collecting in the air. "Does Mona ever worry about getting caught?"

"Always."

Footsteps approached in the tunnel.

Eden returned the book to the crate as the sheet was

swept aside, and a woman entered. The barefooted boy followed.

Eden recognized the former from the photograph she'd found in Cassian's apartment. This version was a decade and a half older without the jaunty hat. Gray peppered her auburn hair, which was cut in a sharp line two inches short of her shoulders. She was squat and square with cheeks that had gone jowly. She had thin eyebrows and wore a wool overcoat that reached her ankles. She wasn't smiling in the photograph and she wasn't smiling in person.

"Cassian," she said in a manner devoid of all warmth.

"Mona," he replied in the same detached way.

The greeting was nothing like the one he'd shared with Beverly.

Mona glanced at Eden, then back at Cass. "It's been a long time."

"It has."

"To what do I owe this pleasure?"

"I'm looking for a girl."

Mona raised her sparse eyebrows. "And you need my help? I hear you're quite adept at finding girls on your own these days."

A muscle twitched in Cassian's jaw. "You've been talking to Vick."

"Unfortunately, we've had a few conversations."

"Then you know Yukio is dead."

"Men like him tend to end up that way." She stepped behind her desk and shuffled through some loose papers. "Who is this girl you're looking for?"

"She's a few years older than me. White. Dark hair. Medium height. And a glass eye."

Mona looked up from her desk, recognition sparking in her eyes.

With that final descriptor, she knew exactly who Cassian was talking about. Eden could tell. But she quickly extinguished the spark as she jotted something on a pad of paper, licked the tip of her middle finger, and tore the paper free. She handed it to the boy, who left the room. "What do you want with this girl?"

"Information."

"About The Monarch," Eden added, watching for another spark. For one fraction of a second, she could have sworn she saw one. But it vanished so quickly, Eden couldn't capture its meaning.

"And this girl," Mona said. "She has this information?"

"She might," Eden replied.

Mona eased onto her desk chair and twiddled a pen between her fingers.

"You know Cleo," Eden said.

Mona nodded.

"She remembers asking this girl about her glass eye.

How she got it. The girl told Cleo the Monarch gave it to her." When Eden finished, she cut a look at Cassian.

"Is she still here?" he asked.

Mona stared at him without blinking. He stared back —a silent face off like a pair of cardsharps at a poker table.

"I have a lot of mouths to feed," Mona finally said, setting down the pen and steepling her fingers. "After recent events, getting the rations we need will be more difficult than usual. As you well know, hardship has a way of hitting those at the bottom the hardest."

Cass removed a clip of money from his pocket. He pulled a bill free and set it on the desk.

Mona looked at it, then back up at him.

He removed another bill and set it on top of the first.

She pocketed them both, then clicked her pen and began scribbling on the pad of paper. "Technically, Beverly gave her the glass eye. But I suppose that's not what Francesca meant by the statement."

"Francesca?" Eden said.

"Burnoli. She was only here for a few months."

"How'd she get the glass eye?" Cass asked.

"Her foster parents weren't nice people."

"Her foster parents?"

Mona gave Eden a singular nod.

Francesca Burnoli. They had a name. And a story. She was a foster kid who ended up with a glass eye because of her abusive foster parents. Was one of them The Monarch? "Do you remember their names—these foster parents?"

"Bryson."

A weighted pause ensued. One Eden didn't understand. Cass must have, though, for something significant passed between the two of them. Like the name meant something.

"I don't remember their firsts," Mona said.

"Do you remember if Francesca ever referred to either of them as The Monarch?" Eden asked.

"No. Nor do I know where she is now." Mona jotted one last item on the paper. When she finished, she gave her finger another lick and tore the piece free. "This is everything I remember about Francesca. It's not much, but it might help."

She handed the slip to Cass.

Eden looked at it.

Mona had written three lines.

Francesca Burnoli

Bryson

The Orchard

"What's *The Orchard*?" Cassian asked.

"The name of the girls' home she lived in before she was placed with the Brysons. Maybe someone there can give you more information."

Behind them, the sheet swept open again.

The boy was back.

He cut between Eden and Cass and handed Mona the same piece of paper, only this time someone had added to it in neat capital letters.

Mona made a humming noise in the back of her throat as she read the words. Then she pushed to her feet. "It's late. Unless you have somewhere to be, you're welcome to stay here for the night." She unlocked the top drawer of her desk, searched through a stack of cards before pulling out two, then handed one to each of them. "We could use some extra hands with tomorrow's load."

21

Mona left.

Eden looked at the card the woman had handed her before leaving the room—blank except for two small squares. She peeked at Cassian's. His was the same. "I thought you and Mona would have a warmer relationship."

"Mona is too busy for warmth."

One could argue that Dr. Beverly Randall-Ransom was, too.

"Does she normally make people pay for information?"

"What she said was true. There are a lot of mouths to feed. With money in short supply, information is her currency." He pulled out his phone and called Cleo.

Eden was surprised he had a signal all the way down here in the dank bowels of these abandoned silos. Maybe they had some sort of cellular generator, like the battery-operated one on Mona's desk. It made sense. What didn't make sense was the virtual reality headset next to the computer. The metaverse was heavily monitored by the government. Users were required to hand over their identification in order to access it. What use would an off-the-grid person like Mona have with one?

Halfway through the third ring, Cleo answered. "What'd you find?"

"Her name was Francesca Burnoli."

"Francesca! That was it."

"She was a foster kid. The eye injury came from her foster parents. Last name is Bryson."

Eden could hear Cleo's scribbling pen.

"There's also a girls' home called The Orchard. I'm assuming it's in Chicago. She stayed there for a while."

"Anything else?" Cleo asked.

"That's it."

"Alrighty then. I'll run these through the web and see what I can find."

Cass thanked her. He hung up the phone, then held up the card Mona had given him. "Hungry?"

"I thought you said food was hard to come by."

"It is. Which is why Mona gave us these." He gave his card a flick and grabbed the kerosene lamp. They left Mona's room and headed in the opposite direction from which they'd come, deeper into the labyrinth.

"What's the story with Bryson?" Eden asked.

"What do you mean?"

"When Mona said the name, it felt like it meant something."

Cass didn't answer right away. They continued down the tunnel, Eden lengthening her stride to match his, then turned left before he finally said, "Mona had a son named Bryson."

Had.

As in, past tense.

"It's probably why the last name stuck with her all these years."

"When did he die?"

"Twenty-one years ago."

Eden nodded knowingly. When a loved one died twenty-one years ago, no more explanation was necessary. Mona lost her son the same way her parents lost theirs.

"Before The Attack," Cassian added.

Her stride hitched. "Before?"

"He died in one of the uprisings, during a riot."

Eden's mouth dropped open as Cassian continued.

"Shortly after, The Attack happened. She was listed among the dead and too depressed to correct the mistake. When she finally came back to herself, it was too late."

"What do you mean?"

"It's harder than you think to prove you're living. And anyway, there were a lot of orphaned kids. Too many for the government to handle. She started taking them in. It made her feel like a mother again."

"So that's how this all began?"

Cassian nodded.

Ahead, a small group of adolescents and young adults congregated outside a room. As Eden and Cass approached, one of the group's members broke away with an exclamation of disbelief. He wore a stained sweatshirt with the hood up, but even beneath its shadow, Eden could see the way his face lengthened in excited surprise. "Cass 'The Wolf' Gray!"

Cassian came to a sudden halt beside her.

The guy held out his hand like he wanted to slap Cassian's.

Cass didn't take the offer.

Undeterred, the kid pulled off his hood, revealing a head full of tight blonde curls. "It's me, man. Hudson!" Then he turned to the group. "You guys, this is Cass Freaking Gray. Longest winning streak in the history of Underground Fighting. And an old pal from way back."

If Cassian knew this pal from way back, he didn't give any indication. Instead, he stared—stone-faced—as the rest of the group eyed him curiously.

Two guys. Three girls.

Hudson looked over one shoulder, then the other.

Like a guilty kid in the throes of shoplifting. "Mona would kick me out if she knew, but bro, you won me some serious cash." He rubbed his thumb over his index and middle finger, grinning stupidly.

The guy was terrible at reading a room.

Nothing about Cassian's body language suggested he remembered Hudson or had any interest in reliving his glory days in the ring. With a terse, "Excuse us," Cass put his hand on the small of Eden's back and ushered her through the doorway into what could only be described as a cafeteria. An assortment of tables lit by more kerosene lamps—only one of which was occupied—and a serving counter on the far side. As Cassian walked toward it, Hudson called after them.

"Hey man, we gotta catch up! I'm dying to know when you're getting back out there."

Cass didn't stop until they reached the counter.

He gave his card to the woman behind it. She punched one square and handed it back, along with a sandwich and a red apple with puckered skin.

Eden received the same.

At one table, a woman sat alone reading a well-worn paperback with a beefy, shirtless man on the cover. Except for an apple core, her plate was empty and sat atop something resembling a newspaper.

"Can I borrow this?" Cass asked as they passed.

"Go right ahead," the woman replied, not even looking up as she turned a page.

Cassian took it, then led the way to the farthest table.

Eden sat across from him, twirling the hole-punched card between her fingers. "A ration card."

"Don't lose it," he said.

"If I do?"

"No breakfast tomorrow."

She raised her eyebrows.

"Mona runs a tight ship. These will get us two meals. Dinner and breakfast. Her subtle way of saying we're not welcome for more than a night. Long-term residents get weekly cards with twenty-one squares. Mona only keeps as many as there are rations. No cards, no room. There usually aren't any extras in the winter."

"What if someone misplaces their card on a Monday?"

"They don't." Cass unfolded the paper he'd snagged.

It wasn't Concordia, but another illegal venture. Like Cleo's *The People's Press*. Only this was thicker and more professional looking.

At the top was today's date.

Saturday, October 5th.

Underneath the date, a large title read *America Underground*.

"Is that—?"

"A newspaper that's circulated amongst communities living off the grid?" Cass turned a page. "Yes."

Highly intrigued, Eden scanned the front-page article above the fold. Like every article in the *Concordia Times*, it was about the attack in Chicago. Only this was from the perspective of a person living off the grid, discussing the ramifications for their particular communities, focusing most heavily on the retinal scan crackdown and a new hotline for whistleblowers. Below the fold was a list of safe houses and businesses. Not just in Chicago, but across the entire country.

"Does Cleo know about this?" Eden asked.

"Cleo subscribes," Cassian said.

Eden took a bite from her apple—dry and slightly bitter—her mind turning to Concordia reporters, issuing statements about the danger of these communities, where Interitus was supposedly recruiting. Amassing numbers. Building in strength. Eden saw zero evidence to back up such claims. Was the government willingly misleading the people or did they believe the picture they were painting?

The old Eden would have given the benefit of the doubt. This new Eden no longer knew what was true. Interitus had to be gathering somewhere and *America Underground* made one thing abundantly clear: there were many more communities like this one. Surely not all of them were so innocuous. There were probably plenty with higher populations of Hudsons, gambling on Underground Fighting with men like Mordecai. Men who carried on Karik Volkova's legacy.

Cass turned another page and stopped.

"What?" she asked, the word muffled by a mouthful of stale white bread and bologna.

Cass slid the paper across the table.

Eden blinked at a page full of faces. Ten, at least.

She scanned them, her attention coming to a screeching halt over the third girl in the right-hand column. "That's …"

"Jane," Cass finished.

Eden swallowed her bite.

The page Cassian had turned to was dedicated to missing people living off the grid.

And here was Subject 003.

The girl they'd been calling Jane.

Only her name wasn't Jane. Her name was Violet Winter. She was reported missing since June. Of last year. Not this past summer, when Barrett Barr's face found its way onto national news. But the summer before.

"That's why we couldn't find her," Eden said.

"She lives off the grid."

"Why has she been missing for over a year?"

Of course, Cass didn't have an answer. Cass didn't know.

"Do you think Mordecai had her that whole time?"

Cass narrowed his eyes as though considering and took a bite of his apple.

"Maybe that's why she's so …"

"Different?" Cass said, arching an eyebrow.

Eden shrugged. Maybe Jane—or Violet Winter—hadn't just woken up two months later, like Barrett. Maybe she'd been asleep inside that luxury bomb shelter for over a year. Maybe during that long stretch of time, something had short-circuited. According to Jack, her signal was weaker than Eden's and Barrett's. Maybe this explained why.

Across the room, the woman closed her book with a huff. She scooted her chair back, left the book on the table, threw her plate into the garbage, and exited the large room.

"We close in fifteen," the lady behind the counter called.

Cass got to work on his sandwich.

Eden ate as much of hers as she could stomach, flipping through the pages of *America Underground*—amazed at the quality—peeking at Cassian between articles. "So … Hudson," she finally said.

Cass scowled.

"You two were buddies once upon a time?"

"I don't remember him."

"He called you Cass 'The Wolf' Gray."

His scowl deepened.

"Is that a nickname?"

"Not one I chose."

Eden nodded and forced herself to bite her tongue. Unlike Hudson, she could read body language. Cassian clearly didn't want to talk about the nickname, despite the nickname piquing her curiosity.

She pictured the tattoo wrapped around Cassian's shoulder—a wolf woven with Celtic knots currently hidden beneath his jacket. He'd shown it to her in the middle of the night while they ate cereal in Beverly Randall-Ransom's kitchen.

According to Cassian, his mother loved wolves. She loved the sound of their haunting calls. She read him *When Pup Howled at the Moon* so many times, the binding had come loose. She thought it unfair that wolves were made into villains in fables and stories. Eden knew he didn't get the tattoo because of the nickname. He'd been given the nickname because of the tattoo. If his mother loved wolves—if she thought them misunderstood—Eden could only imagine how much he loathed that nickname. Cass 'The Wolf" Gray, a ruthless fighter who killed his last opponent in the ring, exacerbating the animal's villainous reputation.

Eden smashed a few stale bread crumbs with the tip of her finger, wondering about his former career. Where did this fighting take place? Was there just one venue or several? Before she could speculate much further, Cassian's phone lit with Cleo's name.

He snatched it off the table and answered.

There was no need for him to put the call on speaker. Eden could hear Cleo just fine, even when he got up from their table to borrow a pen from the irritated lady behind the counter, who handed him a writing utensil with an annoyed, "Ten minutes."

"There were only two Francesca Burnolis that I could find," Cleo said. "One is a thirty-six-year-old mother of three selling beauty products online. The other is a dead 89-year-old who spent the final years of her life battling dementia. Neither are our girl."

Cass sat down.

"But the Brysons, I think I found. Gage and Isabella."

His attention lifted to Eden's. "You sure it's them?"

She understood the question. Bryson was a common surname.

"They have a sixteen-year-old son named Clay," Cleo said. "Adopted out of foster care."

Eden set her forearms on the table and leaned closer.

"They live in Glencoe, a suburb on the north shore. Gage is a guidance counselor at New Tier Township, but their son, Clay, goes to Glencoe Montessori. Isabella spends her time volunteering at a pregnancy crisis center in Des Plaines. She also leads a support group."

"For?" Cass said, scribbling notes in shorthand on the margins of *America Underground*.

"Family Estrangement."

"Who's she estranged from?"

"I'm not sure," Cleo said. "I found Isabella's maiden name on an old engagement announcement. Her parents were listed as Mr. and Mrs. Jeffrey Coolridge of New York City, New York. They died in The Attack. Their obituaries said they were survived by their two daughters, Lillian Kashif and Isabella Bryson."

"So, she could be estranged from her sister."

"I doubt it."

"Why?"

"Her sister's dead. I found her obituary, too. She died four years after The Attack. On the exact same day, actually."

"That's weird."

"My thoughts exactly."

"Does it say how she died?"

"Apparently, childbirth."

Childbirth.

Eden tried to imagine it. Losing both parents only to lose your sister four years later. On a day that was supposed to be a celebration of new life—the redemption of a day that had encompassed so much death. Instead, it claimed more.

"What happened to the baby?" Cass asked.

"Passed away with the mom."

"Does Isabella have any other family?"

"A nephew named Amir Kashif, Lillian's son. He was seventeen when his mother died."

Cass tapped the pen against the table. "Do you know where the support group meets?"

"At the Wilmette Public Library. First Sunday of every month."

"That's tomorrow."

"Yep."

"Are they still meeting?"

"It says nothing about being cancelled."

When Cass hung up, Eden looked down at the notes he'd jotted in small neat script.

Gage and Isabella Bryson were a married couple with an adopted son living in Glencoe, Illinois. Gage was a guidance counselor at a high school. Isabella volunteered at a crisis pregnancy center and led a local support group.

"It doesn't exactly scream terrorism," Eden mumbled.

"No, it doesn't," Cass agreed.

"Do you think one of them could really be The Monarch?"

Cass clicked the pen against the last line of his notes.

Fam Est SG - Wilmette.

"Maybe we can find out at tomorrow's support group."

22

Eden lay on the top bunk of a bed with no concept of time.

Cassian slept below her, breathing deeply in and out.

There were no digital clocks in this underground maze. No electrical outlets in which to plug them. Just a retinue of sound unfolding in the dark as Eden passed in and out of a restless sleep plagued with nightmares. Strangling Cassian while Cleo screamed at her to stop. Pointing the 9mm Hellcat at the malnourished boy who'd taken them to Mona as the country's Board of Directors commanded her to pull the trigger.

At the sound of the deafening gunshot, her eyes had flown open. She fought sleep after that, listening as a young girl awoke with a start and whimpered about having an accident. Eden could smell the urine as the girl's mother turned on a flashlight. She stuffed the soiled blanket into a bag while her daughter shivered beside her, holding on to a book she'd pulled from beneath her pillow. Mother and daughter climbed back into bed, this time with only one blanket between them, and the woman whisper-read a familiar story while the girl yawned and turned the cardboard pages.

Goodnight stars.

Goodnight air.

Goodnight noises everywhere.

But the noises did not go goodnight. This place was far from quiet, with the low humming of generators and a sump pump interrupted by the occasional call of a train horn overhead as they rumbled through a nearby train yard. And other noises much closer. Coughs. Sniffles. Snores. A boy muttering in his sleep.

Eden thought of Cassian and the tattered book on his apartment floor. Had his mother read it to him here when he was cold and afraid? At what age had he gotten the tattoo and how much more violently did he fight when the crowd started chanting that nickname? Her thoughts turned to her own mother, reading stories about a girl in a yellow hat who went to a Parisian boarding school. Back then, it had sounded like a grand adventure. Going off to Paris. Being away from her parents, free from Christopher's death and the grief he left behind.

At some point, she must have nodded off to sleep because the sound of stirring awoke her. She blinked into the dark as Cassian crept from the room. On the other side of the makeshift door, light flickered and glowed through the thin sheet. Then faded away. Along with Cassian's footsteps.

Eden swung off the bed and silently landed on the floor. She peeked out from the sheet as the faint light of the lamp disappeared around a corner. Eden followed as Cassian made his way above ground, where fog hovered over the river and cold nipped at the air and the first vestiges of sunlight shone in the east.

Cass moved like he knew where he was going.

Along a rickety boardwalk above the canal, the silos covered in vibrant graffiti, early birds chirping in the trees, until he reached a rope dangling from a metal staircase bolted to the concrete. Cassian pulled himself up easily. Then he climbed the rusted stairs, his footsteps a gentle clanging echo above her.

Eden waited until he was out of sight.

Then she climbed up after him—a treacherous ascent to the very top, where a chilly wind blew as the days crept deeper into autumn and Chicago's skyline loomed across the river, a stunning sight with a gaping hole where The Sapphire used to be.

Cassian leaned against a half wall with his hands shoved into the pockets of his leather jacket, his breath escaping in puffs of white, his gaze set on the skyscrapers outlined by the first rays of the rising sun.

"Can't sleep?" she said, pulling the sleeves of her sweatshirt over her hands.

He glanced at her, then turned back to the sunrise—his strong profile illuminated by a pinkish gold. "No."

She sat on the wall beside him, then tentatively reached out to touch his hand. It was warm despite the chill. She skimmed her finger over a small scab on his knuckle, a nick from the rooftop when he tackled her mother, saving her from the bullet Eden had fired. If not for him, she would have become a murderer. Her mother would be dead. She turned his palm up. Traced the lines. Then slid her hand into his.

His fingers stretched, then curled protectively around hers.

"This is where you and your mom used to live," she said.

He let the statement hang in the air. And then, "We hated it here." His thumb mindlessly stroked the side of her index finger, sending a ripple of warmth up her arms, down her spine. "We stayed for two years before we could move into an apartment. It was small. Rundown. But it was ours." For a moment, his expression softened. "After my father found us, I had to come back."

His words punched her in the gut.

She imagined his father—a monster who killed his wife and left his son for dead. Her heart broke for the twelve-year-old, sleeping on a bunk bed in a dank basement without his mom. Without anyone.

"I hated it even more the second time. I spent as much time away from this place as possible, getting into scraps on the street for food. Vick saw one. Mona told me I couldn't stay if I decided to fight, like that might get me to think twice. I haven't been back since."

She didn't blame him.

Eden wouldn't have wanted to stay either.

Vick had given him a way out and Cassian took it.

"What did your mom do?" she asked.

He looked up from their hands, as though confused by the question.

"How was she able to afford an apartment?"

"Oh. Mona got her a job cleaning houses. Big ones like Beverly's."

"Did she take you with her?"

"There was an older gentleman across the hall who kept an eye on me. He was nice and he didn't ask questions, like why I wasn't in school. I didn't realize until later that he lived off the grid, too."

"And how did he make ends meet?" She was suddenly very interested in this off-the-grid world of mothers and children and nice elderly men.

"He was an investigator."

"What did he investigate?"

"Missing people, like Violet. Sometimes, he'd let me help."

Years later, he would use those skills to find her.

Cassian frowned. Perhaps he was thinking along the same lines. "She wore a lot of hats, my mom. Cleaner of houses. Teacher of me. Writer for *America Underground*."

Eden gaped.

"It didn't pay as much as the cleaning, but she loved doing it." Cassian looked at her as though amused by her shocked reaction. "She used to be a reporter."

"For Concordia?"

He shook his head. "Before The Attack. Before I came into the picture. She covered the conflict in southern France for six months. Became fluent in the language."

"Really?"

"*Voila. Tout au mieux.*" The words rolled off his tongue in a rich, alluring timbre. Had Eden not already loved the language, she would have fallen hard on the other side of hearing him speak it. "It was one of her favorite things to say."

Eden leaned closer, captivated. She wanted to hear more about her—this woman who brought Cassian into the world. Who spent six months in France. Who died in such a tragic, unjust manner.

Cass tugged on her hand like a confident leader in a dance, guiding her to her feet with a subtle pull until she was no longer beside him, but in front of him, standing between his splayed legs, her eyes level with his. "Do you remember saying that to me?"

"Saying what?"

"*Voila. Tout a mieux.*"

Eden tilted her head. She had. After accidentally hitting him with a door in the basement of Cleo's residence hall. Her eyes moved to the place where she'd applied the bandage—right above his eyebrow.

"It was the first time I heard those words since she spoke them."

She recalled the look he'd given her. Like she'd said something wrong. Only she had said nothing wrong; she'd said something familiar. Something that reminded him of his mother. Her heart squeezed with warmth and sadness. "What else did she like to say?"

He looked up at the morning sky, as though considering, the ghost of a smile back in place, his lips so enticing, the warm feeling in her heart turned into a heat that stirred deep down in her abdomen. "*Petit a petit, l'oiseau fait son nid.*"

Little by little, the bird makes its nest.

"Not when I fell or scraped a knee, but when we lived here, and she was saving up for us to move."

Eden touched the small, white scar on the cleft of his chin. "I wish I could have met her."

"She would have liked you," he said, his hands

sliding to her waist. "She would have liked your choice of company, too."

"Her son?"

With a smile, Cassian shook his head. "Erik."

Eden quirked her eyebrow.

"She would have said the friendship meant something."

"Like what?"

"You don't care what other people think. You make your own choices. Form your own opinions." His thumb slipped beneath her sweatshirt and grazed the ridge of her hipbone.

Eden swallowed, the heat in her abdomen growing. She wanted him to kiss her. She physically ached for him to kiss her.

But before he could, a sharp pain sliced through her temple.

With a wince, her hand clapped over the spot.

Cassian stood—no longer relaxed, but alarmed. Vigilant. "What's wrong?"

Eden blinked several times in rapid succession, unsure what had just happened. Disturbed by how similar it was to the pain she'd felt on the rooftop. When Mordecai was controlling her. "I-I don't know."

The sound of squealing brakes interrupted her confusion.

Cassian turned.

Eden brought her hand away from her temple and exhaled shakily.

Far below, a large truck had pulled up to the fence. A man stepped out from the idling vehicle and slammed the door.

"What's that?" Eden asked.

"A delivery."

The man down below opened the back doors of the truck and started unloading large sacks of rice and stacking them against the fence.

Cassian sighed. "The reason Mona was so willing to let us stay."

Extra hands for tomorrow's load.

23

Eden quickly understood the need for extra hands.

Getting the food through the fence and into the basement of the silos required a lot of strength and maneuvering. She received several strange looks after her first load when she carried two sacks of rice instead of one. She dialed back after that, taking better care to blend in.

When the work was done, Eden and Cassian used the final square on their ration cards for a bowl of bland oatmeal, then spent the rest of the day planning.

Eden was going to attend the support group. They both agreed she had a better chance of getting information from Isabella Bryson than Cassian did. They weren't, however, comfortable with her retinas being scanned upon entrance. While Eden clung to her assumption that the Monarch didn't know about her, she didn't want to leave a trail should her existence be discovered. Nor did she want her parents driving to Wilmette if Jack pinpointed their whereabouts via retinal scan.

The plan was to sneak in.

Until they arrived in Wilmette at half past four and discovered the library—a large building made of gray brick—had surveillance cameras everywhere. There wasn't a single window or back door exit they could sneak into without being surveilled.

Which meant retinal scans it would have to be. They needed to follow this lead, and it was the best way they knew how. The one with the highest probability of getting the most information. Hopefully, Jack wasn't watching for her. Hopefully, nobody was.

"I can go in alone," she said.

Cass shook his head. Apparently, he didn't like the idea of sending her into the library by herself with a woman who may or may not be The Monarch. And since Eden's retinas were going to be scanned, there was no added risk in his being scanned, too. His identity would register in the same way it had at the Prosperity Ball—Cassian Ransom, an upstanding citizen without a record.

Eden pulled a baseball cap over her hair and matched Cassian's stride as they walked toward the front entrance.

"Remember the signal," Cass said.

Eden nodded.

Five clicks of the tongue with a quick break after the first two—an audible warning to get out of there in case something went sideways. An audible warning that would go unnoticed by library patrons. But not her. If she wanted to, she could hear it from across a football stadium. Her superhuman hearing, she was learning, worked similarly to a zoom lens on a camera.

"You okay?" Cass asked.

She nodded with a confidence that contradicted her nerves, then stepped inside and brought her eyes to the scanner. When Cass was through, he gave her elbow a squeeze, grabbed a random title from the nearest shelf, and settled into a cushy chair next to a drinking fountain while Eden made her way toward the meeting room.

The door was open.

Inside, a table had been pushed against the wall. It was filled with bottled waters, a variety of sodas, a pan of brownies, two bags of chips, plates, and napkins. Nearby, a pair of women spoke in hushed tones. One was small and mousy with red-rimmed eyes she dabbed with a crumpled tissue. The other was a head taller with long, bottle-blonde hair, dressed in a savvy-looking pant suit with cute boots. She held onto the mousy woman's elbows like letting go would result in the lady's collapse.

A man cleared his throat.

Eden moved out of the way as he stepped past her—as bald as an egg—and slogged toward the oblong circle of chairs. The blonde woman greeted him by name—Walter—then turned to Eden with a friendly smile.

"Are you here for the support group?"

Eden nodded in a way she hoped looked shy. All the while, her heart pounded in her ears. Because what if this woman recognized Eden as Subject 006? What if she had a device in her pocket like the device Mordecai had at the ball? A gun, too, which she would place in Eden's hand and command her to finish the job she'd resisted on the roof of The Sapphire. Eden swallowed, forcing the thoughts away. "I wasn't sure if you were meeting today."

"I thought we'd need the support today more than ever." The woman gave the mousy lady's elbow a squeeze, then stepped forward to introduce herself. "I'm Bella."

Short for Isabella.

Eden shook Bella's hand in the way her father taught her not to. A limp fish, he would call it. But it fit the role she needed to play—a sad, shy girl in a new city with no family. The kind of girl a woman running a support group might take under her wing.

"I'm Jen," Eden said.

"It's wonderful to meet you, Jen. I'm glad you're here." The woman followed the welcome with such a warm smile, it was impossible to imagine her hurting anyone. Certainly not to the point of requiring a glass eye.

Eden returned the smile timidly and took a seat across the circle from Walter, who stared straight ahead, tapping his knee. He wore wire-rimmed glasses, a khaki flight jacket unzipped over a buttoned shirt the color of this morning's oatmeal, a pair of tan trousers, and velcro walking shoes that matched his jacket. The man was very beige. He continued tapping his knee while the room filled and Eden felt increasingly conspicuous.

She was the youngest attendee by at least ten years.

When there was only one empty seat remaining, Bella checked the clock, closed the door, and turned to the circle with an encouraging, watery-eyed expression. She welcomed everyone with a warmth equal to her smile, then ran through a short list of reminders.

Everything said during the meeting was confidential.

Judgmental statements weren't allowed.

This space was safe and sacred.

Nobody in the room was alone.

"Why don't we go around and share with the group why we came today," Bella said.

The mousy woman with the crumpled tissue went first. Her name was Georgia. She managed two wobbly sentences before bursting into tears. She couldn't stop checking the list of confirmed casualties. So far, her son's name wasn't on any of them, but he wasn't answering his phone and while he hadn't won a ticket to the Prosperity Ball, how could she be certain he wasn't trapped somewhere beneath the rubble?

As soon as she finished sharing her worst fears, a flood of others followed.

Family estrangement was always hard, Bella said. But extra so in the middle of a crisis. Georgia wasn't the only one who cried. The tears flowed freely, occasionally interrupted by a bubble of laughter that would lighten the mood. It was a good mixture of sharing and listening. The group had chemistry. A culture that was almost certainly cultivated by their leader—Bella Bryson. An abusive foster mother.

When it was Eden's turn, she kept her story brief.

Her name was Jen. She was eighteen. New to town. She hadn't spoken to her parents in two years, so when she saw the flyer on the bulletin in the lobby, she decided to come. Everyone listened with dewy-eyed sympathy, and when she was done, Eden passed the tissue box to her left.

By the time the meeting ended, Eden knew Walter was estranged from his younger brother and Linda hadn't spoken to her sister in over a decade and Georgia blamed her ex-husband for poisoning their son against her. But Eden didn't know a thing about Bella other than how adept she was at leading the group. She knew when to pull people in and when to give them space. She knew how to steer the conversation back on track when it lost its way and how to tactfully interrupt when a member talked for too long.

Not once did she share her own heartache, whatever that might be.

As the room emptied, Eden wandered to the refreshment table and opened a bottle of water. She helped herself to a brownie she wasn't hungry for while Bella gave hugs and said goodbyes and arranged a special coffee date with Georgia. She munched on some chips and took sips of her water until it was just the two of them.

Bella joined Eden by the table. "So, what did you think?"

"Everyone was very nice," Eden said.

Bella smiled, her head tilting slightly. "Was this your first time attending a support group?"

"Was it that obvious?"

"No. Not at all. You're just very … young." Bella stared kindly—without any judgement—as though waiting for Eden to talk. She seemed so comfortable with the silence, Eden wondered if she wasn't a therapist in another life.

"Are you doing okay?" Bella finally asked. "In the midst of all that's happening."

"I think so." Eden twisted and untwisted the cap on her water. "What about you?"

"Oh, I'm hanging in there."

"That's good." Eden made a show of fidgeting, the water bottle crinkling in her grip, when another searing pain came in the same spot as before, so sharp Eden hissed.

Bella reached out and took her elbow. "Are you okay?"

Eden held her temple, unsure if she was. Momentarily distracted from the mission. The ruse. The role she was playing. This was the second time today. Three altogether. The first had been that night in the shower, when she was trying to scrub the smell of smoke from her hair.

Bella dipped her chin. "Jen?"

"Sorry." Eden released a nervous laugh. "I've been battling a headache. Ever since ... well, you know."

"It must be bad."

"Yeah. They can get pretty bad. So, who are you estranged from?" She cringed inwardly at the awful segue. "If you don't mind me asking."

Bella didn't seem to mind. In fact, she smiled a wistful smile. "My daughter."

Eden nearly choked.

Her daughter.

Cleo had mentioned nothing about a daughter.

"She's just a few years older than you," Bella said.

This explained why she kept gazing at Eden in such a motherly way. Eden probably reminded Bella of her daughter.

"What's her name?" Eden asked.

"Willow."

"That's pretty."

"It is." The moisture in Bella's eyes thickened. Then she took a deep breath and painted on another smile—one that looked more brave than genuine. She gave Eden's hand a squeeze. "I hope to see you next month, Jen."

Cass sat at the library table pretending to read the book open in front of him, peeking at the conference room door. Every person who entered after Eden had left, including an extra woman with bloodshot eyes, who must have been in the room before Eden went in. He didn't like this—not knowing who the enemy was. They no longer had a face or a name. Mordecai was dead and he hadn't been operating alone. More enemies were out there. One of them might be in that conference room with Eden right now.

He turned a page as a tall woman carrying a box of items appeared.

Eden exited behind her.

Cass sat up straighter, overcome by a strong swell of relief. He cupped his forehead, watching from beneath his palm as the two exchanged friendly words by the conference room door. Eden gave the woman a shy wave, then ducked into the ladies' room. The woman lingered, watching her go. The muscles in Cassian's shoulders tightened. He came to the edge of his chair like some altercation might go down right here in the Wilmette Library.

After a beat, the woman turned and exited through the front entrance. The second she was gone, Eden reappeared from the ladies' room and made a beeline for Cass, her expression bright and a little flustered.

She slid into the seat across from him. "She has a daughter. Her name is Willow. She's a few years older than me."

"Francesca's age."

Eden nodded.

Cass drummed his finger against the table and peered from the stacks to the study rooms to the computer bays. This wasn't the place to talk or do any of the searching they needed to do. They weren't going back to the silos, and he wasn't bringing Eden to his apartment. This wasn't the same as before—when Mordecai was still alive and Cass had been alone, trying to bait him.

Which only left one place he could think of.

Forty-five minutes later, Cass turned down the alley

behind Lou's training facility. He climbed off his bike. Told Eden to sit tight. Lou knew many people, and he heard a lot of things. He also had a loose tongue. If someone was out there looking for Eden, Cass didn't want to walk inside Lou's with her right next to him.

He punched in the code and let himself in the back.

Lou was in the main area, moving around behind the front desk.

"Hey," Cass said.

With a jump, Lou whirled around, then set his hand against his chest as fear gave way to relief. "Hey-a Cass. It's been a while. I was starting to think you mighta been downtown at the wrong time."

"I was, actually."

Lou's eyes went wide.

"I made it out just fine."

"Lucky guy," Lou said, wiping the sweat from his upper lip. "Crazy times right now."

Cass looked from him to the suitcase by the door. "You going somewhere?"

Lou patted his back pockets as though in search of a phone or wallet. "I, uh, gotta get out of town for a while."

Lou didn't leave town unless he was in trouble. Cass wondered which bookie had stepped in to fill Yukio's shoes. Yukio had always extended Lou some leniency. Perhaps the new bookie on the block wasn't as gracious.

"I can keep the place open while you're gone," Cass said.

Lou stopped patting his pockets.

"In exchange for room and board? If I have to take off before you're back, I'll lock up."

The training facility was a moneymaker. Closing up shop meant shutting down a lucrative stream of income. If Lou was in trouble, he would need that income to get out of it.

The heavyset man glanced at his watch, then dragged his hands along his pants. "That would be swell, Cass. And-uh, if anybody shows up lookin' for me, tell 'em I'm visiting my sister in Scottsdale."

As far as Cass knew, Lou had no sister in Scottsdale. As far as Cass knew, he had no sister, period.

Lou reached into the front pocket of his jacket and pulled out his keys. With a nervous nod at Cass, he picked up his suitcase and grabbed the door handle.

"Hey Lou?" Cass said.

Lou stopped.

"Mordecai's dead."

The man turned around, his face going sickly white. To Lou, Mordecai was a gambler. One of the biggest in Underground Fighting. If he was dead, it was because he didn't pay up.

"Did you ever hear talk of him being associated with Interitus?" Cass asked.

"Interitus?" Lou gave his head a rattle. "Why would Mordecai be wrapped up with terrorists?"

"What about The Monarch?"

"What's the Monarch?"

Cass considered. What was The Monarch? A gift could be given to a person. But a gift could also be given to a group or a cause or a place. He thought about the device in Dr. Norton's cabin—the image of the butterfly spinning into a three-dimensional holographic map. "Something or someone Mordecai was involved with."

Lou squinted, then shrugged. "I don't know, Cass. The circles we operate in aren't exactly legal. But Interitus? Whatever's goin' on, it doesn't sound like the kinda thing a person should get wrapped up in."

Too late.

Cass was inextricably wrapped.

And it wasn't his safety he cared about.

Lou shot him a goodbye salute, then headed out the door. Cass waited a few beats, then went to the back to let the girl he did care about inside.

24

Eden sat in a basement bedroom of a training facility owned by a man named Lou who needed to get out of town for a while. Cassian brought her here, then left to get something from his apartment, which wasn't far. He'd be back shortly. So here she was, trying not to crawl out of her skin as she watched Concordia on the small television perched on the dresser.

She was getting sharp pains in her head, and Isabella Bryson had a daughter. Her name was Willow. They were estranged. Eden itched for a phone, a computer—something that might allow her to research the girl or call Cleo so she could do the research for them.

But there was no computer or phone or metaverse headset. Just a bare desk and a chair. The television on the dresser. A monitor mounted in the far corner, recording the goings-on at the front door, which was nothing at the moment. And the full-sized bed she was currently sitting on.

Just one.

The implications left her feeling flustered and warm in the cold basement. A month and a half ago, she'd jumped on the back of a stranger's bike and showed up at Cleo Ransom's dorm room. Since that time—barring the seven-day stint he'd disappeared to track down Mordecai—Eden and Cassian had been together nearly twenty-four seven. And yet, it had never been just the two of them. At least, not at night.

First, there was Cleo. Then Dr. Norton and Jack Forrester and the famous neurosurgeon. Then her parents and Barrett Barr and Violet Winter and all those people living in the silos. Tonight, however, it would only be her. And him. And this one bed. Of all the things on Eden's mind, this shouldn't take precedence. But as Concordia's news anchor talked about the necessity of closing their borders, and with no way for Willow Bryson to distract her, Eden had a hard time thinking about anything else.

The hinges on the door squeaked.

Cassian had returned.

He set their backpack on the desk and pulled a laptop out from inside.

"Where'd you get that?" Eden asked.

"Behind a slab of drywall in my apartment closet. Or I guess, my former apartment closet. Everything else was cleaned out." He hung his jacket over the chair and sat down. He opened the computer, logged in, and pulled up the same strange browser Cleo used when they were researching Jack and Annette Forrester.

He typed Willow Bryson, Chicago into the search bar.

Three Perk accounts loaded at the top of the screen.

The government-approved social media site was back up and running.

Cassian clicked on the first account. It belonged to an acupuncturist living in Dayton, Ohio with three pet ferrets and a parakeet named Major Briggs. The second belonged to a retired schoolteacher who had only posted once, three years ago when she first created her account —a photograph of four toe-headed kids standing in front of an ice cream truck with the words living that grandma life joined in a hashtag.

The third Willow Bryson flipped off the camera in her profile picture. She had bleached hair streaked with faded pink, thick black eyeliner, and a dog collar choker.

"All alone in an F-Ed up world," Eden read.

The only line in Willow Bryson's bio.

Cassian scrolled through her account. She'd marked herself as "in a relationship" with Edgar Allan Poe. Most of her pictures featured a male cat named Morticia that liked to wrap himself around Willow's neck like a black scarf. Most of her posts were written in free verse poetry.

There wasn't a single photograph of Isabella Bryson or any mention at all of a family, which fit the story of estrangement. This had to be the right Willow—a hunch confirmed when Cassian reached the very first post on the account. A picture of a younger Willow with hair a more natural color, sitting between two similar aged girls atop a wooden sign that read The Orchard.

Francesca Burnoli stayed at The Orchard.

And here was Willow Bryson, sitting in front of The Orchard in a photograph without a caption.

"This has to be her," Eden said.

Cassian scrolled to the top and clicked on the most recent post, dated Thursday, October third. It was a close-up of Willow's face streaked with tears and black eyeliner, accompanied by the angstiest poem Eden had ever read.

There were only three likes and one comment—a fire emoji from someone who went by the handle @Love_Me_Pain. After looking at a few more posts, this seemed to be the only person who ever commented. Cassian followed the handle to @Love_Me_Pain's Perk profile. Her real name was Anastasia Blaire. She had long bangs and wore the rest of her black-dyed hair in two buns at the top of her head, similar in style to Cleo's Bantu knots. She had a tiny black heart tattooed beneath each of her eyes and owned a hole-in-the-wall coffee shop in Hyde Park.

Her most recent post was a picture of Willow. Dated Friday, the fourth of October at 8:26 pm. A half hour before The Sapphire exploded. In it, Willow sat on a stool in front of a microphone with her hands splayed, her face twisted in exaggerated sorrow, like she somehow knew what was coming.

Apparently, Anastasia Blaire invited artists to perform in her coffee shop every Friday night. Judging by Anastasia's posts, Willow was a regular. Which meant Willow had to live in Chicago.

Next, they looked up Willow's younger brother, Clay. According to Perk, he was a well-adjusted 16-year-old who played point guard for a traveling basketball team called the Glencoe Gladiators. He didn't post often, but when he did, he was almost always with people. Teammates from his basketball team. One or both of his parents. And a reoccurring girl named Charlotte. Cassian followed the handle to her account. In her profile picture, she wore Clay's jersey and held up her pointer finger in a number one sign and beamed at the camera with a scoreboard in the background showing a score of 73 to 68. Glencoe for the win.

Cassian returned to Clay's account and scrolled further into his past. Two years ago, he posted a picture with a dark-haired, dark-eyed man in his thirties. They stood side-by-side in front of a memorial that had been erected along I-95, right outside Washington D.C. It was as close as a person could get to the country's former capitol, as the area contained radioactive residue that made the city uninhabitable. In the caption, Clay wrote he was visiting his cousin Amir out east, then concluded with the words *never forget* in all caps.

Amir.

This was Isabella Bryson's nephew.

A young man who'd lost his mother when he was seventeen.

Cass searched his name but found nothing. Not a single Amir Kashif owned an account on Perk. Cassian took the search out of the social media site to the broader world wide web and discovered that Amir was a cybersecurity analyst for Under Armour in Baltimore. They also stumbled upon the same obituary Cleo had found yesterday for Amir's mother, Lillian.

Eden read the ending line over Cassian's shoulder. "She has gone from us, reunited with her beloved husband, Moshe, a man who died in service to his country."

They searched for an obituary for Moshe Kashif, but there wasn't one. They couldn't find any information on the man at all, not even his name on the veteran databases Cassian was able to access.

"Do you think he was alive when she got pregnant?" Eden asked.

Cass leaned back in his chair, as stumped as she was.

Lillian Kashif got pregnant in her forties, then died in labor. Along with the baby. There was no mention of the baby's father. Only her beloved Moshe, who was dead. Which seemed to imply that he was the father. Eden stared at the computer screen, trying to work out the mystery. What did these people have to do with The Monarch? And what did The Monarch have to do with her?

A buzzing sound filled the small room.

Cass looked at the monitor in the corner.

A young man stood outside, waiting to be let in.

Cassian left. Eden took his chair and started digging into The Orchard, jotting down a list of girls who would have stayed there at the same time as Willow and Francesca. When Cass returned, he accessed drone surveillance monitoring the Bryson's neighborhood and zoomed in on their home. The house looked like the kind Eden had lived in her whole life. Middle class America with neatly trimmed box bushes, two garden gnomes, and the American flag flapping in the wind.

They spent the evening toggling back and forth between the surveillance and the search bar, taking notes and watching joggers and dog walkers make their way through the quiet neighborhood. A few more of Lou's patrons came and went. Cass grabbed Chinese for dinner. They ate with chopsticks, discussing theories and possibilities until there was nothing left to say, and the training facility was closed and a yawn stretched Eden's mouth wide.

Cass stuffed the empty cartons into the plastic bag and tossed it toward the trash bin. It sailed straight through without hitting the rim. "It's late. I can take the floor."

His words caught her by surprise. She cast her attention to the floor in question, then swallowed and rubbed her earlobe. "We can share the bed."

It was big enough for both of them.

There was no reason for him to sleep on the cold, hard ground. Especially when there were no extra blankets that she could see. It didn't have to be a big deal. It wasn't a big deal. She was eighteen, for crying out loud. A girl who didn't embarrass easily. And yet, her cheeks had gone incriminatingly warm. Then even warmer as she registered the warmth.

"Eden," Cass said.

She forced herself to look at him.

His gaze was steady. He didn't look nervous or unsure as he studied her inquiringly. "I don't mind sleeping on the floor."

"And I don't mind sharing the bed," she replied, silently admonishing the tremble in her voice. She lifted her chin like a girl determined to mean what she said.

He studied her for a moment longer, then excused himself to check the locks and alarms. Eden found a half-empty tube of toothpaste in the basement bathroom. She used her finger to clean her teeth, splashed water on her face, and hurried to the room, where she quickly slipped beneath the covers and scooted as close to the wall as possible, her heart racing absurdly fast in her chest.

She stared at the ceiling, an intrusive image crowding her brain. The lithe and sensuous Ruby and the suggestive way she looked at Cassian in Angelica's apartment. A girl didn't look at a guy that way without a past. Without a history. Eden squeezed her eyes tight, willing the imagery away, her ears catching fire as Cassian returned and shut off the light.

The springs of the mattress squeaked as he stretched out beside her.

Never in her life had she been so aware of another human being. She could smell the mint of his breath, feel the heat radiating off his body as the invisible barrier between them crackled like a live wire. Eden could sense him waiting on the other side of it—this boy with so much more experience than she—and somehow, she knew he wouldn't make the first move. The fighter was a gentleman. He would wait on the other side of that crackling wire until she decided to cross it.

Eden's stomach fluttered.

Her breath went shallow.

Her fingers twitched.

She imagined reaching beneath the comforter to touch his hand. She curled hers into a fist and lay there in the dark—his nearness, his warmth, the slightly elevated but steady beat of his heart an intoxicating combination of torment and bliss, until she finally fell into a deep and dreamless sleep. For the first time since the horror that transpired on The Sapphire rooftop, she didn't have a single nightmare.

25

Jane sat cross-legged in the shade. On the edge of the tree line. Away from the others. Away from the television. Wishing someone would turn it off. For as far back as she could remember, Father had worked relentlessly to bring forth her powers. Jane had cooperated, desperate for them to come. Maybe then the pain would stop. But Father didn't tell her how exhausting those powers would be. He never explained what it might be like to hear every sound, register every smell, see every line and color in the sharpest detail. Combine that with the helpless panic radiating off Ruth and Alexander Pruitt—and now, even Barrett—and Jane felt like she might explode.

Rusted hinges groaned.

The screen door opened, then slapped shut as Barrett stepped outside, the sun reflecting off his dark, floppy hair. Even from this distance, she could clearly see the troubled look in his eye and the name he'd scrawled on the back of his hand. Eden. It kept slipping from his mind—the lone bug that refused to stick in his spiderweb of a brain.

Spotting her beneath the tree, Barrett headed in her direction. He glanced at the sack she hugged in her lap before ruffling his hair and meeting her eye with a gentle smile. "Hey."

He always greeted like this. As though she might greet him back.

She blinked up at him.

His shoulders lifted and fell with a deep breath. "Mind if I join you?"

Jane scooted over an inch or two—a nonverbal invitation of welcome.

Barrett sat down beside her. He leaned against the large trunk at their backs, planted his feet flat on the ground—slightly splayed—and rested his arms on his knees. She watched from the corner of her eye as he traced the four letters of Eden's name. "Do you think it could happen again?"

She looked at him more directly.

He narrowed his eyes. "I wish I knew how it happened, you know? I wish I knew what was going on. How can a name just … fall out of my brain?" He heaved a sigh. "It's not like I can look up answers on the web or consult a book. I mean, this isn't exactly like my grandfather's dementia."

Jane cocked her head. She didn't know that word. Dementia.

"You want to hear something crazy? Before we went to Maine, my mom and dad got into this big argument about nano-treatment. Mom wanted to look into it as a treatment plan for my grandpa, but my dad didn't like the idea. He was staunchly against it, actually. My mom got really pissed off when he objected and—" Barrett shook his head. "I don't know. Maybe I'm making it up in my mind, but I swear I remember her cutting this look my way, as if Dad wasn't just staunchly against nano-treatment, but staunchly against me. Because I guess they knew. They knew I had nanobots and my mom didn't like the idea of my dad being against anything that might be a part of me."

Barrett plucked a blade of grass from the ground and twirled it between his fingers.

Jane could picture his parents. His father's round face. His mother's kind eyes. By now, she'd seen them several times on Concordia National, the pair of them beseeching the camera with straight spines and crumpled expressions. Neither looked angry, like she imagined Father looking whenever his face flashed through her mind. They looked distraught. Like Mother used to look. Before Mother left.

"What if it happens again? What if I lose more names or what if I lose memories?"

Jane leaned closer. She enjoyed listening to Barrett talk. He did a lot of it and while it seemed to annoy some of the others, it never annoyed her. His voice gave her one singular sound to focus on. And often, he shared about his family—so opposite from hers, so foreign from any of her own experiences. The novelty of it seemed to shift something deep down inside of her. In the place her words were buried.

"Last night, I kept running every memory I could think of through my head. From as far back as I can remember. I even wrote some of them down. The really good ones I can't forget, you know?"

No, she didn't know.

Too often, Jane wished she could forget.

"Like my first day of kindergarten. I walked to school with Graham and Jameson, who weren't afraid of anything. At least, it never seemed like they were. Back then, I was afraid of everything. I mean it, too. If you can believe it, I was a super shy kid. I had to fight tears the whole first half of the day, I missed my mom so much. Then lunchtime came, and I found this note in my lunch box. Lots of kids had notes on the first day, but mine wasn't just a note. My mom drew this dinosaur on it. It was this cartoon she made up when Graham and Jameson were really little and this kid next to me—his name was Jordan—he sees it and he's amazed. Like, truly amazed. He could not believe my mom drew it. Plus, he loved dinosaurs. So I gave it to him and then we played Lava Monster at recess and he ended up being my best friend all the way through elementary school. When I got home, I told my mom all about it—my new friend Jordan and how much he loved the dinosaur and the next day at lunch, most of the notes stopped because it was the second day and most moms didn't write notes on the second day. But I had one. And this time, the dinosaur was on the toilet. Jordan laughed so hard milk shot out of his nose, which made me laugh so hard that I almost peed my pants. And I just … I wasn't nervous anymore." Barrett smiled—a wistful, far-off smile. "She put a note in my lunch box with a drawing of that dinosaur every day that year. She didn't miss a single one."

Jane was leaning closer now—impossibly riveted. She wanted Barrett to keep going. She wanted him to draw the picture of the dinosaur and tell her more and more stories about his mother.

Instead, his eyes went glossy. His face stretched long with sadness. "What if I forget about the dinosaur? What if I forget about my mom?"

Jane shook her head—a slight, subtle shake. She wanted to take Barrett's hand. Or maybe squeeze his shoulder. A gesture of comfort she sometimes saw Jack and Dr. Norton do with Alexander. She swallowed in an attempt to drum up the courage when the sound came—a horrible, screeching burst of noise that pounced so ferociously, she doubled over her crossed legs and threw her hands over her head.

When it ended, her heart thudded violently. Erratically. And Barrett had jumped to his feet.

After a moment of quiet uncertainty, he gently peeled her hands away from her ears, his eyes wide and filled with knowing as he crouched beside her.

"What happened?" he said. "Was it your hearing?"

She didn't have to nod for Barrett to know he'd guessed correctly.

Something was wrong.

With Barrett's brain.

With Jane's hearing.

She spent the rest of the day in her room, jumping at every sound, unsure when they might join together and scream in her ear. At lunchtime, Barrett lost another name—Cleo's—and began freaking out in earnest. He paced in the living room asking questions while Jack acted like a man in the throes of anaphylactic shock. The borders were closing. Annette and Ellery were waiting for a flight home. And he was an absolute mess. Studying Eden's network was his EpiPen.

Another reason Jane stayed in her room.

Jack had taken over Dr. Norton's living space, spreading the contents from their files across the floor along with all the images that had been taken over the years. Eden had the most, but there were images of Barrett and Violet, too. Images taken when they were babies and again more recently, before they woke up. Images that showed differences in Jane's network that were there now but weren't before. Differences that made her want to run before he could do any more testing.

Dr. Norton had told Jack to give her time.

But that was weeks ago.

That time had run out.

Jane had to go.

She hugged the sack of treasures to her chest and rocked on her bed.

She didn't want to go. Eden told them they needed to stay—she and Barrett both. That was their job. They were going to stay here and protect the others in case the bad guys came. Jane could not let anything bad happen to them. Not like Kitty. Not like the puppies. No matter how hard her heart pounded, no matter how frightened these tests made her, she had to be brave.

She had to stay.

A knock sounded on the door.

She squeaked and buried her face in her treasure sack.

"Jane?"

The voice belonged to Ruth. Earlier this morning, before her time with Barrett under the tree, Jane overheard her in the bedroom across the hall talking to Alexander about someone named Christopher. Then she burst into tears because she was so worried about Eden. Now Jane was adding to that worry by refusing to come out of her room. She crawled off the bed and opened the door with her hair hanging in her face.

"Ben made sandwiches for dinner. Would you like to join us?"

Jane took a deep breath.

It was time to be brave.

These people weren't like Father. She knew that by now. Not even Jack was like Father, and he scared her the most. Even so, her heart still raced.

She followed Ruth down the hall, her body trembling from head to toe.

In the living room, Jack was swiping through the holographic images projected from the device Jane had fixed. Alexander was doing weightlifting exercises in his wheelchair—something he'd resumed ever since Eden left, as if building his strength was no longer a choice but a necessity. Maybe he thought he could go after her once he was strong enough.

Dr. Norton sat at the kitchen table. There was a plate of sandwiches in the center, along with a bowl of carrots. Barrett paced in front of it, his hair sticking up in every direction, muttering as he looked down at his upturned palm, where he'd scrawled another name in blue ink—Cleo.

"I think I understand it," Jack said, holding his hands in such a way as to frame all the work spread on the floor in front of him.

Barrett stopped pacing.

Jack pulled up the holographic diagram with the different colored dots. He zoomed in and captured an image—a cluster of yellow markers gathered around the lymph nodes in Eden's neck. He walked to a printed image near the fireplace and held it up beside the projection. "These have been active since birth. They're the ones that interact with her immune system."

He scrolled up to the brain and captured a different image. Most of the markers were red. He picked up several printed images from the floor—cross-referencing. Back and forth, back and forth, his bloodshot eyes bright with discovery. "These were manually activated once she was connected to the host. They enhance her senses, her speed, her strength."

"Her memory," Barrett added.

Jack nodded and pointed out the blue markers—not gathered in any one specific place, but spread evenly through her body. "Then there's these. Nodes that have been pre-programmed to come online automatically at a specific time, based on predetermined signals. These markers brought her network online." He looked at Jane when he said this.

She ducked behind her hair.

"We already knew all of this," Alexander said, stretching his bad leg straight in front of him.

"In a vague sense, yes. But not with this amount of detail." Jack zoomed in on one of the blue markers. He was able to blow it up to one thousand times its size. He moved from blue marker to blue marker until he found one darker than the rest, with a fluorescent globule floating in its center. He'd been studying this one a lot. "It's master slave technology."

"What's that?" Ruth asked.

Jack zipped around the diagram, zooming in and out with such speed, Jane's stomach clenched. Then he returned to the dark blue. "This is the master. It's the only node with output capabilities. The others only have input."

"What does that mean?" Alexander said with a hint of frustration.

"Think of ears for input. Mouths for output. All the blue nodes have ears. But only this one has a mouth." He glanced at Jane again, then back at the image. He pointed at the dark blue marker. "This one is the Queen Bee. She's the one who sends the orders. She's got ears, too, but her input receives external communication. She interprets these external signals and relays them to the others as commands."

He swiped to a different projection.

He called it the command log.

Alexander stopped his exercises. He sat up straight in his chair. "If we isolate the Queen Bee, is it possible to disable it?"

"I think it might be," Jack said.

"What would that do?" Barrett asked.

"Eden's system would no longer have a commander. She couldn't be controlled."

The words settled in the room—potent, hopeful.

Jack went to his computer and tried pulling up the browser. When it didn't work, he dragged his hand down the length of his stubbled cheek, his expression tight with frustration.

"What's wrong?" Ruth asked.

"It's this laptop. It's been lagging all day. I think there must be some sort of glitch with the old system. I need to shut it down and run the updates." As soon as he finished saying it, his mouth went slack. Barrett's, too. As if realizing the same thing at the same time.

"Updates," Barrett said.

"Technology needs to be updated." Jack's eyes took on a manic glow. "Phones. Computers. Cars. All of it. They need regular updates, otherwise …"

"Things go wrong," Barrett finished.

Like his memory.

Like her hearing.

Their insides were teeming with technology.

Microscopic robots zooming through their veins. Microscopic robots that formed a cohesive system.

And those systems hadn't been updated for sixteen-and-a-half years.

26

Cass peeled off his shirt and grabbed the pull-up bar, his heart hammering against his sternum after a merciless run on the treadmill. He lifted himself—rep after rep—his lats burning, sweat trickling as he silently repeated the same refrain with every hoist.

She's eighteen.

She's eighteen.

She's eighteen.

As though enough repetition might sear that fact into his brain.

Eden Pruitt was eighteen years old. Practically still a minor. With a set of loving, involved parents who might not be physically present but were absolutely part of the picture. Which meant Eden Pruitt was entirely different from any of the girls he'd been with before.

He needed—no, he wanted—to tread carefully.

Cass let go of the pull-up bar and moved to the dip station, attacking his triceps as relentlessly as he attacked his lats, as if doing so might help him fall asleep faster come nightfall. Never mind the fact that this was his fifth day of unforgiving, rigorous exertion and physical exhaustion had yet to do the trick.

His attraction built like steam in a kettle. The accumulating unanswered questions on their quest for answers didn't help. If something didn't give soon, he might combust. He moved to an elevated glute machine, slid his ankles beneath a set of heel pads and began doing inverse sit-ups, targeting his lower back.

Tonight—finally—they would attempt to talk with Willow Bryson, who lived in a halfway house in North Lawndale. Between her Perk account and location tracking, her home address was simple to locate—a fact Eden had found disturbing. It shouldn't be so easy, she said. But it was. Especially with government-issued phones.

They didn't feel settled about approaching Willow on her home turf. It would be less intimidating if they arranged a run-in at the coffee shop in Hyde Park. So they'd waited. And waited. And waited.

On Monday, the search and rescue efforts in downtown Chicago shifted to search and recovery. The missing were no longer missing, but listed among the dead. One-thousand-fifty-two casualties, a number significantly less staggering than the number after The Attack but no less traumatic. Especially given the high-profile nature of so many of the deaths. The nation was triggered, grieving, and hypervigilant. That night, Eden had a sharp pain in her temple while running on the treadmill. So intense, she nearly fell off. It rattled her. It rattled Cass.

On Tuesday, they found a girl who stayed at The Orchard the same time as Francesca and Willow. A living, breathing girl who wasn't in prison or rehab or six feet under. But working in the city as a nail technician, which was how they ended up in Kenwood, loitering outside a salon called Cute-Icles. Eden went inside and requested the technician named Dezi, who was opinionated and chatty until Eden mentioned The Orchard and Dezi turned into a clamshell. If she remembered Francesca or Willow, she refused to say.

On Wednesday, they followed Clay, hoping for an opportunity to interact with him. No such opportunity presented itself. The kid was sixteen, but his parents treated him like he was eight. His dad took him to school on his way to work. His mom picked him up, then gave him a ride to and from basketball practice in the evening. Eden believed this was because of their estrangement from Willow. After losing their daughter, they went overboard with their son. She spoke the words like one speaking from experience. Cass suspected she was thinking of Christopher and her own parents.

On Thursday, they watched drone surveillance as twelve girls came to the Bryson's home at dinnertime.

"Do you think it's a study group?" Eden asked.

"Why are there only girls?" Cass replied.

Neither of them had an answer.

The girls didn't leave until ten.

Now it was Friday. They had gathered information like a pile of puzzle pieces without a picture to guide them. Hopefully tonight that would change. Hopefully tonight, they would get some answers and the pieces would start clicking into place.

As Cass swung his torso upward, he spotted Eden in the hallway that led to the back entrance. She wore a light gray racerback tank top with black leggings, her hair pulled back into a ponytail as she peeked into the gym.

Cass stopped his inverted sit-ups and grabbed a towel to wipe his face as she came all the way inside, her attention flitting to his bare upper half. To the fresh scar on his side, where broken glass had sliced him open. An injury she mended while he lay unconscious in the back of Norton's truck. She looked away and moved toward Lou's boxing ring—one he'd spent a significant amount of time in over the last decade.

She quirked an eyebrow. "Want to spar?"

He had nothing left to teach her. The student had long surpassed the instructor. She could easily best him. And yet, she had energy to burn, too. She was leery of the treadmill after the mishap and the weights didn't challenge her. Apparently, Cass still did.

He tossed aside the towel and stalked to the ring, feeling every inch the hungry lion. Knowing he'd have to exercise more restraint.

They went through a few warm-ups even though he was already warm and she didn't need the lead-in. Slowly, the drilling increased in speed and intensity until both of them were breathing hard. Cass knew she was stronger and quicker and more agile than any opponent he'd faced in a fight, but today, she was distracted. Today, he was keeping up with her. When she pivoted to throw him over her hip, he hooked her arm and brought her with.

He landed flat on his back with Eden straddling his waist, their chests rising and falling in unison, her face so close to his, the tips of their noses nearly touched.

Desire slammed through him.

But Cass didn't move. He lay very still. Like the slightest movement might scare her away.

A lock of hair had slipped from its tie and fell toward him as her attention dipped to his lips. And then, with exquisite slowness, she kissed him. A featherlight touch, like dipping her toes into a pool to check the temperature. And when she was done, she pulled back, her green-gray-blue eyes searching his.

For a fevered breath.

For a hungry beat.

Until simultaneously, they dove.

Their mouths collided.

A week's worth of restraint blown to pieces as Cass grabbed her waist and flipped her onto her back. When she curled her fingers into his hair and arched into him, he lost his mind. With his blood pounding, he slid his arm beneath her—pulling her closer, unable to get enough, his lips moving down her jaw, to her neck …

When a familiar refrain screamed in his head.

She's eighteen!

And he would not lose control inside a ring.

Not again.

Not with her.

He stopped—pulled back.

Out of breath.

His desire magnified by affection and fondness and a deep and abiding respect for this girl who would lay down her life in a heartbeat if it meant protecting another. This girl who could still smile, even when the world had been turned upside down and inside out. This girl who was steadfast and true and absolutely, unequivocally too good for him.

He pressed his forehead to hers, knowing he was ruined for anyone else. Knowing he would spend the rest of his life trying to deserve her.

27

The Coffee Hound was dimly lit with a haziness that gave the impression of employees smoking after hours. It was nothing like The Roast in Eagle Bend, where she first encountered Cassian Gray. A boy who threw her off kilter then. A boy who was still throwing her off kilter now. Her skin flushed at the recollection of their make-out session inside Lou's boxing ring. She shook the memory away. Now was not the time to daydream about Cassian's hands or lips or chiseled physique. Now was the time to focus on their objective.

Find and speak with Willow Bryson.

On a small stage perpendicular to the counter, a young man wearing moccasins stood behind the mic, strumming a guitar, singing a melancholy song about death and the end of love. Eden grabbed a chair at a table that hugged the far wall as Cassian ordered two decaf coffees at the counter. She discreetly but thoroughly scanned the room for Willow, her stomach twisting when the scan returned empty.

They'd been waiting for this moment all week.

Every sign pointed at her being here.

But there was no girl with bleached hair streaked with pink.

A smattering of applause skittered around the coffeehouse as the man finished his song.

He strummed his guitar and began another.

Cassian sat across from her, noticing the same thing she had.

Willow wasn't here.

Anastasia Blaire, Perk handle @Love_Me_Pain, was. In fact, she brought them their coffee. In an attempt not to stare, Eden took a sip much too quickly. The drink scalded her tongue but only for a fraction of a second, a reminder of what she was. Of what was inside her.

The liquid soured in her knotted stomach.

She stared at the door, willing Willow to walk through, when suddenly, it swung open and there she was. Willow stepped inside with a gust of chilly wind, wearing a lime green peacoat and deep purple lipstick and a black leather choker with spikes. She blinked dully as her retinas were scanned, then removed her coat and hung it over a chair next to their table. She sat down and crossed one army boot over the other—close enough for

Eden to touch as she stared at the man on the stage with an expressionless face. When he finished, she clapped twice—slowly, almost sardonically—then stood up and tromped to the stage. She gave the guitar strummer a fist bump, stepped up to the mic, and stared at the crowd—silently waiting until every last patron was quiet.

No more nonchalant listening. No more whispering across tables.

Once Willow had a rapt audience, she clutched the microphone in this sensual, almost erotic way and began reciting a poem with so much passion, Eden felt embarrassed. It was an awkward performance—aggressive and high-strung. And yet, the moment she finished, The Coffee Hound broke into an applause much more heartfelt than any they'd given the crooner.

Willow didn't bow or smile.

She didn't begin another poem.

Her face returned to its expressionless mask as she traipsed off the stage and into the ladies' room.

Eden blinked at Cass as the ovation stuttered to its end. Then she stood and went after her.

Willow wasn't inside a stall, but leaning over the one and only sink, gripping both sides of the dingy porcelain like she was having a panic attack. Eden stopped in the doorway. Willow took a loud, gasping breath and looked up, her thick black eyeliner smudged with tears as her attention snagged Eden's in the mirror.

"Are you okay?" Eden asked uncertainly.

Willow glowered.

Eden stepped all the way inside. "That performance was ... really great."

"You lie." Willow spoke in the same way she arranged her face—devoid of all inflection.

"I'm not lying." She was, actually. The performance had been painful. But now was not the time for candor. "It reminded me of ... Poe."

Willow's expressionless mask slipped. She looked at Eden, not in happy surprise, like one discovering a commonality with a stranger. But with dubious suspicion. "I love Poe," she said.

"What's not to love?" Eden replied.

Willow dragged her fingers beneath her eyes, making the smudged eyeliner worse. Eden stepped closer to the dirty mirror and pretended to search her face for pimples that weren't there.

Their attention caught once, twice. On the third time, Eden took a calculated risk. "You don't remember me, do you?"

"Should I?" Willow said.

"We used to live together."

Willow narrowed her raccoon eyes.

"At The Orchard. It must have been twelve, maybe thirteen years ago."

"You lived at The Orchard?"

"Yeah."

"And you recognized my face?"

"I'm good with faces. It's an odd quirk, but I never forget a face. No matter how long it's been. As soon as you walked on the stage, I knew who you were."

"I don't remember you."

"I'll try not to take that personally." Eden reached into the pocket of her hoodie and uncapped a lip balm. "So, did you ever end up with a family?"

"No." The answer was so blunt, it almost felt like a slap.

Eden cleared her throat. "Me either."

Willow stared openly now—in this unblinking, disconcerting way—as she pumped soap into her palm and worked it into a lather.

Eden applied the lip balm to her bottom lip and tried not to squirm. "I'm not surprised you don't remember me. I was painfully shy back then. Kept to myself, mostly. I was always on the outside looking in. I remember wishing for a friendship like the one you had with that girl. What was her name?" She capped her lip balm, then snapped her fingers. "Francesca! That's it. I remember being jealous of your friendship with Francesca."

If Eden was hoping the not-so-subtle transition would defrost Willow's demeanor, it didn't work. The second she spoke Francesca's name, the girl's suspicion went glacial.

"The two of you left at the same time. Everyone said you were placed together. I'm sorry to hear you never got a family. I was hoping it would work out for you. Are you still close—you and Francesca?"

Willow didn't answer.

Eden pressed valiantly onward. "It's weird, what a small world we live in. I actually ran into her a month ago. Here I am in this giant city, and I run into two people I lived with once upon a time."

Willow turned off the water. "You ran into Francesca?"

"Crazy, right?"

"Where?" Willow said, demanding. Almost hostile.

Eden pulled back her chin.

"Where did you run into her?"

"Downtown. Before downtown was … well. I was walking to work, and she walked past me. I thought I recognized her, like you. But it took me a bit because something was different about one of her eyes."

Without drying her hands, with no warning at all, Willow turned around and walked out the door. Eden blinked, then walked out after her. Out into the warm entryway as a different artist beat boxed on the stage.

"Wait," she called.

Willow spun around. "Who are you really?"

"What?"

"I don't remember you from the girl's home and I remember all the girls. Also, there's no way you saw Francesca here in the city."

"Why not?"

"Did my mother send you?"

"Your mother? I thought you said—"

"Isabella Bryson. Did she hire you to follow me or something?"

"No," Eden said.

Willow narrowed her eyes into slits, then she turned around like she was going to walk away.

"I'm trying to find The Monarch," Eden blurted, cringing as soon as the words escaped.

Willow stopped.

She froze with her back to Eden, the beat boxing from the stage wrapping around them like an insulated bubble.

"You're right," Eden muttered, taking a step closer. "I didn't live in The Orchard."

Willow turned around. "What's your connection with Francesca?"

"A friend of mine knew her. Ten or so years ago. She had a glass eye. When my friend asked about it, Francesca said The Monarch gave it to her."

Willow crossed her arms.

"Does that mean anything to you?" Eden asked.

For a moment—a blip of a second—sadness blossomed beneath her hostility. But then her expression snapped shut, closing like a Venus flytrap.

"I'm sorry, but I can't help you," she said before turning around and marching to the table where she collected her lime green peacoat and let herself out the door.

———

Eden returned to the table where Cassian sat staring hard at the door Willow had just walked through. She slid into her seat while the beatboxer finished; hardly anyone clapped at all. She set her elbows on the table, wrapped her hands around the coffee mug, and began relaying the entire strange interaction that transpired in the ladies' room.

"She thought I was working for Isabella Bryson."

Cassian drummed his thumb against the table.

"She seemed so convinced that I couldn't have run into Francesca here in the city. Which must mean she doesn't live in the city. But couldn't she have been visiting?"

"Maybe she wouldn't have without Willow knowing."

"Which would mean they keep in touch."

Another poet stepped on the stage—a Black man wearing a beanie over long dreadlocks.

Eden slumped in her chair, trying to combat the hopeless disappointment crawling through her chest. They'd come here looking for answers. They hadn't found a single one.

"Wanna get out of here?" Cass asked.

Her stomach dipped.

She imagined returning to Lou's with no more information to occupy them. Just the memory of their make-out session and the single, full-size bed. With a nervous swallow, she nodded.

He tossed a tip on the table and snagged his jacket from the back of his chair. He motioned for Eden to go ahead and followed her out into the night. As they turned toward his bike, she could feel someone behind her.

"Excuse me, miss?"

Cassian spun around like one prepared to throw a punch.

A young man stopped short and held up his hands. "Relax, man. I'm just a messenger." He reached into his pocket, which hardly encouraged Cassian to relax. His entire body tensed beside her like he was expecting the guy to pull a gun. Instead, he removed a folded slip of paper.

"What's that?" Eden asked.

"A note. Some girl paid me to pass it to the pretty blonde in the sweater. You're a pretty blonde. And you're wearing a sweater."

Eden's attention flitted about like the girl was hiding somewhere in the dark.

The messenger lifted his eyebrows.

She reached for the note, but he pulled it back. "A messengers gotta get paid, yeah?"

He'd already been paid.

With a glower, Cassian pulled a twenty from his back pocket and handed it over.

The guy exchanged the note for the bill. He nodded at them both, clapped Cass on the shoulder, then slipped inside The Coffee Hound.

A gust of wind blew, crinkling the paper.

Eden's pulse raced as she unfolded it.

Two lines had been scrawled in blue ink.

You'll find answers in the Bryson's safe. Basement.

Willow had underlined the last word.

Eden looked up at Cassian, her hope restored.

They wanted answers. Willow had given them a map.

Their treasure awaited in the Bryson's basement.

28

As soon as they reached Lou's, they began to plan.

First, they needed to identify the best time to get in and out of the Bryson's home, preferably without the family knowing anyone had paid a visit. They pulled up archived surveillance to establish a routine.

Every weekday, Gage and Clay left together for work and school. Bella came and went with no reliable consistency. In the evenings, she brought Clay to practice. A half hour later, Gage would arrive home from work. An hour or two after that, Bella and Clay would return and remain until the next morning when the routine restarted itself.

On Thursday evenings, the group of girls would come.

If Cassian and Eden were going to sneak in, the weekends were their best chance.

For the past several Saturdays, Gage would leave at noon. Bella and Clay would follow an hour later. Both vehicles would roll into the driveway around four. For the past several Sundays, the three of them left together at exactly nine in the morning. Eden guessed they were going to church—an unsettling thought.

Looks could be so deceiving.

She was proof. Barrett, Violet, and Ellery were proof, too.

So were the Brysons—from the outside looking in, an all-American family. The father, a guidance counselor at the local high school. The mother, a volunteer at a crisis pregnancy center and a support group leader. The son, the starting point guard for his traveling basketball team. Eden pictured the three of them sitting in a church pew, nicely dressed with hymnals in their laps while somewhere out there, a girl named Francesca Burnoli lived with only one functional eye.

Cassian tapped the sticky note marked Saturday. "This is our best bet."

It was the longest, most dependable stretch of time.

Three hours to get in, find the safe, break into the safe, get whatever answers were hiding inside the safe, then get out.

It should be plenty of time.

It was also tomorrow—a fact that both terrified and exhilarated her. Breaking and entering was a serious felony, but Eden was beyond ready for answers. As far as they could see, this was the only way to get them.

"She drives away before she closes the garage," he said, rewinding and watching as Bella reversed out of the driveway and onto the road. The garage door didn't start closing until she shifted into drive. "I bet we could sneak in through the garage without her noticing."

The biggest hurdle would be the safe itself.

After a few basic searches, they discovered that there were many kinds of safes. They had no idea what kind the Brysons owned. Thankfully, it seemed the most foolproof method of breaking into a safe without a code or key was the same across the board, regardless of the type. Not so thankfully, the method required a powerful earth magnet called neodymium, which was no longer sold commercially.

Cassian pulled two familiar, small discs from the inside pocket of his jacket. "What about these?"

Eden leaned away, surprised to see them.

The discs were magnetic. Powerful enough to shut down electronics. Powerful enough to shut down Eden and Barrett and Violet. Were they powerful enough to shut down the locking mechanism in the Bryson's safe? Jack had attempted to learn their composition. He'd ruled out iron and nickel. Might it be neodymium or something just as strong?

"They have surveillance cameras," Cassian said. "Even if these don't work for the safe, we'll be able to use them to disable the security system."

At 1:02 pm the next day, the Bryson's garage rumbled open. Bella reversed from the driveway with her son riding shotgun.

Blood thrummed through Eden's veins.

They had parked Cass's bike a few streets away, then crept through yards like stealthy ninjas. Now they were crouched along the side of the Bryson's home, behind a row of bushes, Eden's ear cocked as the tires of the SUV rolled over the curb and a gear shifted.

Bella drove away as the garage began rumbling shut.

Eden leaned forward, ready to move, but Cassian held up his hand. He waited until the last possible moment, when Bella's car was much further down the road, then slid his backpack through the shrinking gap between the closing garage door and the ground—triggering the sensor.

The door stopped and reversed course.

Up ahead, the Bryson's SUV turned out of sight.

Cassian peeked around the corner, then threw the

small disc. It zipped through the air and clinked against its target—a security camera mounted above a set of storage shelves made of plywood. The red blinking light above the lens went black. Cassian stepped out from behind the bushes and gestured for Eden to follow. Once inside, she jabbed the button and the garage door rolled shut with a resounding clatter.

They'd done it.

They'd gotten inside.

Cass climbed the three stairs to the door leading into the home. There was a keypad above the handle. He removed the second disc from his pocket and held it over the lock. He pulled his thumb and forefinger apart. The disc clamped onto the metal and a mechanism clicked.

He twisted the handle and eased the door open—just a sliver. Inside was a tidy mud room with a washer and a dryer and on the opposite wall, the home security control panel. Cass removed the disc from the keypad and threw it with a flick of his wrist. It sliced through the air and landed with a soft but decisive clack.

They had reason to believe that this would disable the entire system. To test the theory, Eden stepped out of the camera's view as Cassian climbed the storage shelves and confiscated the first disc. They waited to see whether the red light would return.

When it didn't, Eden stepped inside the home, her body humming with adrenaline. She was committing a crime that could easily result in another mug shot. The normal emotions in such a situation had to be fear and unease. Instead, she felt the same feeling she'd felt when she took part in that idiotic senior prank—invigorated. Like someone stepping out into the fresh air after living in a windowless basement for far too long. Like she was designed for this kind of adrenaline. A disconcerting thought as she beheld the Bryson's life in still form.

A gym bag sat half-zipped on a wooden bench with a pair of basketball shoes tucked underneath. A sign that read Happy Fall Y'all hung above the washer. There was a bowl of kitty chow and a bowl of water and beside the disabled security panel, a key holder designed to look like five cats, their tails curved into hooks, with a set of spare keys hanging on one of them.

A dishwasher ran in the next room and a cat meowed as Cass stepped inside behind her.

A fluffy white feline slinked into view.

It blinked at them, intruders in the entryway. Then it crept closer with its head low to the ground. With another meow, it wound itself around Cassian's leg, rubbing up against his calf. He scratched behind its ear with one hand, pulled his gun with the other, and peeked into the kitchen.

The camera mounted above the pantry didn't blink red. Further proof that their theory was valid.

The kitchen was clean and orderly except for a stray

bowl in the sink. A vase of flowers had been set on the table—red and orange and yellow mums. A candle on the counter scented Radiant Red Maple sat next to a stack of mail. Eden thumbed through it. Bills, mostly. Along with an already opened thank-you card from someone named Jules.

They tiptoed into a sunny living room with a fireplace. Fake fall leaves lined the mantle, along with an assortment of small pumpkins and gourds. Orange pillows accented a matching sofa set and above the couch was a large metal cut-out of the United States painted with rustic blues and reds in the design of the American flag. Framed photographs hung on the walls to their left in a darkened hallway. Willow Bryson wasn't in any of them.

To their right, a door. Slightly ajar.

Cassian pushed it.

The hinges let loose a slow, ominous groan.

On the other side, a set of rickety wooden stairs led into a basement.

The cat followed them down, meowing curiously as the temperature dropped and the steps creaked. When they reached the bottom, Cassian pulled on a hanging string and the space flooded with light. There was a refrigerator and a chest freezer and a dusty foosball table with a litter box underneath.

They walked through the room, into another that

seemed to be half storage, half workspace, with the furnace and water heater and shelves and boxes on one side, a workbench with an assortment of tools on the others. There were also two doors across from one another. One had a heavy-duty bolt.

Cassian unlocked it and opened the door.

Eden hoped to find a safe on the other side.

Instead, they found a room with no windows. Just a cement floor and padded walls and a naked twin mattress with no frame.

A shiver crawled across her skin. "What is this?"

"Evidence that the Brysons aren't who they pretend to be." Cass closed the door and locked the bolt.

Eden tried not to imagine Willow or Francesca trapped inside.

With a shudder, she moved to the other door.

It led to an oddly shaped closet. And in the back stood the Bryson's safe. Tall and black with a five spoke handle. Eden's heart leapt as Cassian stuck the disc to the upper left corner and slowly dragged it toward the handle in the center.

Nothing happened.

He tried again.

And again.

And again.

On the fifth attempt, there was a click.

Cassian twisted the handle and opened the safe.

The first thing Eden noticed was an array of firearms and two bulletproof vests. Then—a significant amount of cash, a folder of birth certificates, social security cards, a will, and passports. Cassian thumbed through them as Eden spotted a cigar box on the safe floor. She reached behind one of the hanging Rifles and pulled it out into the open. She lifted the lid and found photographs and postcards and pamphlets inside. She scooped the stack into her hand, her knuckle skimming something beneath.

A miniature, glass blown sculpture of a Monarch Butterfly.

Her body broke out into goosebumps.

With her breath hovering in her throat, she picked it up. Turned it over. Positive it had to mean something.

"Celebrating *Sanctus Diem*," Cassian read.

It was the title of the pamphlet on top of the stack.

"That's Latin," she said.

They looked at one another meaningfully.

The name of her network was Latin.

Ellery and Violet and Barrett's were Latin, too.

"Do you know what it means?" he asked.

"Sanctus means holy and Diem means day. So … Holy Day?"

"Look at the date," he said.

Eden gaped.

October the fourth.

The day of The Attack.

The one for which Interitus was responsible.

She turned the pamphlet over and found more Latin on the backside.

"*Magnes Matres*," she read. "That means ... Great Mothers."

The strange heading was followed by a long list of names in tiny font. With a quick computation, Eden registered that there were ninety-three of them.

It was an odd number.

Cassian pointed to a name halfway down the list.

Lillian Kashif.

Bella Bryson's sister.

She flipped to the next item. A photograph of a younger Clay standing between Willow and another girl Willow's age.

"That's Francesca," Cassian said.

With both of her eyes intact.

Eden flipped the photograph to the back. The next was a picture of six women, one of whom she recognized immediately, and her goosebumps multiplied. "This is Prudence Dvorak."

"Prudence Dvorak," he repeated, as though trying to place it.

"She's a fugitive. A member of Interitus."

Her name and her face had been on the news.

She was a known follower of Karik Volkova.

And here she was, inside the Bryson's safe, along

with five other women. All six of them stared somberly at the camera, reminding Eden of painted portraits from centuries past wherein the subjects never smiled. What was Prudence doing in this picture, and who were the rest of these women? Eden checked the back of the pamphlet to see if Dvorak's name was listed, so wrapped up in the onslaught of questions spinning in her mind she didn't hear the sound. She didn't register it at all until it stopped.

It was the sound's absence that caught her attention.

A garage door going silent.

Then a car door slamming shut.

A third door opening in the mudroom above them.

Beside her, Cassian froze.

He'd heard it too.

"Should I call the police?" came Bella Bryson's voice from up above, so clear it was as if she were inside the strangely shaped closet with them.

"Not yet," came Gage's low reply.

Overhead, a set of heavy footsteps tromped across the kitchen and into the living room. Eden didn't move. She stood beside Cassian, unmoving in front of the opened safe. Her mind flitted to Willow Bryson and for a moment, she wondered if the girl had set them up. Did she contact her mother? Tell her some random girl came to The Coffee Hound and started asking about The Monarch?

"Glory?" a male voice called down the stairs.

The cat meowed at their feet.

Eden's chest went tight as the feline darted away.

"Gage, come look at this," Bella called.

"What is it?"

"Some sort of ... magnet. On our security panel."

The basement door clicked shut.

Eden's blood went cold.

More clomping feet.

A long pause.

She pictured the Brysons, huddled together around the security panel, examining the disc Cassian had thrown. If they were in league with Mordecai, did they know what it was? Did they have a collection of their own? The footsteps moved across the living room again and stopped at the top of the stairs.

The door opened.

A few seconds later, something bounced and rolled down the steps. Something that made a sharp hiss as soon as it hit the ground. Eden looked outside the closet and saw a plume of smoke gathering through the opened doorway.

With a curse, Cassian stuffed the file and the cigar box into his bag. He grabbed a gun and handed it to Eden, but she recoiled. The last time she held a gun, she almost killed him. She almost killed her mother. Cassian shut the safe and pocketed the disc. They stepped out of the closet, where the smoke was thickening.

He covered his mouth and nose with the hem of his shirt.

Eden glanced from the heavy-duty door with the bolt to the basement windows on the perpendicular wall. It was their best chance for escape. Cassian lifted her easily. She wrenched the window open and crawled out into the fresh air. Cassian lifted himself after her.

"They're out here!"

The shout came from nearby.

It belonged to Clay Bryson, who was backpedaling with wide, frightened eyes, not more than several yards away, watching the basement windows.

Eden and Cassian didn't stick around to shut him up. They took off, hopping over the fence, sprinting through the backyard as Gage came tearing around the house, yelling at them to stop. To freeze.

A gun fired.

A bullet whizzed past Eden's ear.

She and Cass jumped into another yard and sprinted out onto the road as another shot exploded. They didn't stop until they reached his bike. Eden climbed on behind him as he revved the engine and tore away.

29

The fifty-minute drive from Glencoe to Lou's doubled as Cass wove in and out of suburbs, checking his mirrors for a tail. He saw no one following, but that didn't mean nobody was. By the time he pulled into the back alley, his hammering heart had calmed into something less like cardiac arrest.

He pocketed his keys. They let themselves downstairs, where they spread the items they'd taken across the bed. Like actual puzzle pieces ready for assembly. The small glass butterfly, the pamphlet, the photographs, and the postcards.

Eden picked up the pamphlet. She ran her finger over the words *Sanctus Diem* and the date underneath. She turned it over to the list of names. Then she opened it and scanned the contents inside, slowly sitting on the edge of the bed.

Cass sat beside her.

There was a strange poem about fallen empires, an invitation to join *Invictus* and the promise of some future Utopia. Below the call to action was a PostScript written in more Latin. If this was Interitus propaganda, then America was the empire in need of falling. But something didn't fit. The tone of the poem didn't suggest a desire for the empire to topple. It read more like a cautionary tale, as though the author wanted the empire to stand.

Eden opened Cass's laptop and began translating the Latin phrases.

Caelum In Terra.

Ad Astra per Aspera.

And beneath that, *Salvo Impetum*.

The first meant Heaven on Earth.

The second was a saying—through hardship to the stars.

The third translated to mean saving blow.

Cass thought about Francesca and her eye—an injury sustained under the care and supervision of the Brysons. A family with a disturbing room in their basement. Was this 'saving blow' some sick and twisted ideology to which they subscribed? Was this what Francesca meant when she said the glass eye was courtesy of The Monarch even though her foster parents had technically done it? Whoever or whatever this Monarch was, the

Brysons were obviously followers. Devoted believers. And Francesca, the girl in need of saving.

His stomach rolled.

The whole thing was redolent of his father.

Cass hadn't known the man—not really—and yet his most formative memories revolved around him. The first was Cass's earliest. The night before they fled—he and his mom. The night his father turned his violence on Cass, who had the audacity to cry over the death of their neighbor's dog. His father saw the tears as a sign of weakness. The lashing would make him stronger. Cass didn't see him again for seven and a half years and when he finally did, the bastard made up for lost time. He beat Cass to within an inch of his life and, in a sick and twisted way, it *had* made him stronger.

It had made him lethal.

Eden typed the phrases into the search bar along with The Monarch, Karik Volkova, Prudence Dvorak. The only connection they could find was the one they already knew. Dvorak was a follower of Volkova. And the Brysons had a picture of Dvorak, along with this pamphlet glorifying the darkest day in American history.

Cass set the pamphlet beside his laptop, backside up. He placed one hand on the back of Eden's chair, the other on the edge of the desk. "Try running a search on one of these names."

She plugged in the first.

Melody Aigner.

An obituary loaded at the top of the page.

Eden clicked on it.

Melody Aigner died on the fourth of October, not during The Attack, but exactly four years later. The cause of death wasn't listed.

Eden tried the next.

Rosalyn Berkovich.

Links to three different Perk accounts appeared. And below them, another obituary. Eden clicked, then leaned back in her chair. Rosalyn Berkovich also died on the fourth of October, four years after The Attack. And this time, a cause of death was listed.

"Childbirth," Cass read.

It was the same way Lillian Kashif had died.

On the fourth of October.

Four years after The Attack.

Cleo had mentioned the date when she relayed the information she'd found on the Brysons. He'd written it off as an unfortunate, insignificant coincidence. Now, however? Lillian Kashif was on this list, too.

Eden searched the third name.

Ingrid Breen

Another obituary.

The fourth of October.

Four years after The Attack.

Cause of death—childbirth.

She moved down the list, plugging names into the browser with fingers that visibly trembled until they'd gone through all ninety-three of them. Each one died on the fourth of October, four years after The Attack, and any time a cause of death was listed, it was the same.

Childbirth.

According to the obituaries, the babies died too.

Eden flipped the pamphlet to the front side and searched the Latin phrase again, this time with the date. October 4th. *Sanctus Diem*. Not a single relevant result loaded on the screen. "Why did all these women die in childbirth exactly four years after The Attack?"

Cass shook his head, trying to make sense of it himself.

Sanctus Diem.

Holy Day.

The Attack.

These dead women and their dead babies.

Through hardship to the stars.

Heaven on Earth.

He swallowed an acidic taste in his mouth. "Do you think it was some sort of sacrifice?" A sick ritual to commemorate the sacred day? Some twisted attempt to usher in this promised Utopia?

Eden clasped her head between her hands as though to keep it from spinning off her neck. Cass turned to the bed where the confusing pieces were spread. He picked up a postcard with a photograph of a statue carved from white marble—a naked woman with two equally naked children, one at the woman's side, the other draped across her lap. He turned it over to the note on the other side.

"Dearest Bella," he read aloud, "thinking of you and your great sister, a true martyr for the cause. May her sacrifice be known and forever honored. Always, M."

By the time he finished reading, Eden stood by his side.

He flipped the postcard to its front.

"I know that sculpture," she said, taking it from him. "It's in Pemberley."

"Pemberley?"

"Mr. Darcy's estate. From Pride and Prejudice? It's not actually Pemberley. It's Chatsworth House."

Cass blinked at her, wondering how she knew this.

"My mom is enamored with anything having to do with Jane Austen. We've watched every rendition of Pride and Prejudice ever made. Her favorite is the version that uses Chatsworth as the Pemberley Estate. We took a virtual tour, and I saw this statue. The woman is Leto—the mother of Apollo and Artemis. In Greek mythology, she's the goddess of motherhood."

Motherhood.

Magnes Matres.

A true martyr for the cause.

"What cause?" Cass said.

Eden's face turned a concerning shade of white.

"What is it?" he asked.

She sat at the desk, where she picked up a pencil and jotted two dates on a sticky note. July 10th. October 4th. Then she wrote the word babies and tapped it with the pencil's point. "We were born on July tenth, if born is the right word for it. Me and Barrett and Violet and Ellery. That was the date in Dr. Norton's files. Almost three months later, ninety-three women went into labor and died. The babies died, too."

She wasn't talking to Cass. She was thinking out loud.

"Volkova wanted weaponized humans. He experimented with adults. They all died. Then he tried with frozen embryos. And it worked." Her brow furrowed. "But if these ninety-three women were some sort of failed experiment like the adults, wouldn't that experiment come before us—the successful ones?" She narrowed her eyes at the sticky note. "It doesn't fit."

Cass set his hand on the crown of his head and fisted his hair, every bit as stumped as she was. Somehow, all of this was connected. The Attack. *Sanctus Diem*. Prudence Dvorak. Karik Volkova. Eden and Barrett and Violet and Ellery. Gifts for The Monarch. Isabella Bryson. Her sister, Lillian Kashif, and the other ninety-three women. Each one dead, along with their ninety-three babies.

Cass picked up the glass figurine—an orange and black butterfly.

He turned it over between his fingers. On the third turn, he noticed something on the underside of the monarch's wing.

"Look at this," he said, showing what he'd found to Eden.

A minuscule chip fixed to the glass. The same size and shape as the chip inside the device Mordecai had used to control Eden. The chip Violet had fixed back in Dr. Norton's cabin. And beneath the other wing? A button so small, it was nearly microscopic.

He pressed it, and a projection flickered to life.

"Whoa," Eden said.

It was a database with more names, along with ages and locations. Some were highlighted in yellow, like Clay Bryson's girlfriend. Some were highlighted in pink, like Willow Bryson, Isabella's estranged daughter. A few others were struck through with a straight, decisive line, like Francesca Burnoli.

Cass tapped on her name, and the projection changed to an individual profile.

A picture of Francesca. Along with a small bio, a birth date, and below that, in all caps, a single word. One Eden read aloud.

"Deceased," she said. "That explains Willow's reaction when I told her I saw Francesca. She told me there was no way I could have seen her in Chicago. This is why."

Eden couldn't have seen her in Chicago.

Francesca Burnoli was dead.

Cass swiped back to the database and tapped another name.

Another picture. Another bio. Another birth date.

No death. Which meant this girl was still living.

Cass scrolled to the very bottom. The most recent entry.

Eden came out of her chair.

It was her name. Her first and last name. And in parentheses, the fake name she'd given at the support group. Jen. A feeling of dread knotted in Cassian's chest as he tapped on her name to see what else they knew.

They had her age. Her birthdate. Her photograph. Her parents' names. Her run-in with the San Diego Police Department.

"How did they get all this?" Eden asked, her voice filled with alarm.

"The retinal scans." They must have accessed the retinal scans at the library to learn more about this support group newcomer named Jen. Only Isabella Bryson didn't find a Jen. She found an Eden Pruitt. The rest would be easy enough to find. Cass knew only too well. Which made him a fool. A complete idiot. They never should have risked scanning Eden's retinas.

"Do you think they know what I am?" Eden said.

Cass rubbed his jaw, the dread in his chest tightening. Before he could hypothesize, his phone rang.

Cleo's number lit the screen.

He couldn't even get out a hello. The second he answered, Cleo greeted him with a frazzled, "What happened?"

"What do you mean?" he answered.

"Are you watching the news?"

"Should I be?"

"Turn on the television."

Eden grabbed the remote to the small set on Lou's dresser.

As soon as she turned it on, Cass's face and Eden's face filled the screen. They stood side-by-side in the photograph, wearing the same clothes they were wearing now.

"You're on Concordia-Chicago," Cleo said.

Cass turned the call to speaker and set the phone on the desk.

"I don't understand." Eden sank onto the bed. "We shut down the security system. We made sure the cameras were disabled."

He tilted his head. "It was taken from inside the safe."

There must have been a camera. One that took a picture automatically as soon as the safe was opened. A camera that was its own separate device, so it continued to work despite the disc. One that must have been completely silent, otherwise Eden would have heard it.

"Has this made national news?" she said, her cheeks going pale.

"No," Cleo quickly replied. "Just Chicago. My mom called me as soon as it broke. The police want her to come in for questioning. She's meeting her attorney at the station now."

Cass cursed under his breath as the news anchor continued, alerting the public that the burglars were still at large and possibly armed. Considering everything that had happened in Chicago, it was a footnote of a story—small script at the bottom of a page. Very few would pay attention to it. But it was enough to get their faces on television. Her face on television. And no doubt, the Brysons would be digging. That digging would lead them to Alexander and Ruth Pruitt, which could very well lead them to the same information Cass and Eden had found when searching for answers in Cleo's dorm. Alexander was once Alaric Taylor, a man who worked for the CIA. A man who was sent to destroy Karik Volkova's prized experiment.

Cass dragged his hand along his jaw.

"She wants me to disappear until she knows how this is going to play out," Cleo said. "I'm headed to Mona's."

He glanced at the monitor in the corner of the room. They'd been here for nearly a week. Cass had been letting people in, making reluctant small talk with wannabe fighters and up-and-coming trainers. Not to mention the people who recognized them from the library, the nail salon, The Coffee Hound, Cleo's dorm.

They couldn't stay here.

It wasn't safe.

Cass spun into motion—so sudden and decisive Eden just sat there with her mouth slightly ajar, looking increasingly alarmed. He gathered the items on the bed. He stuffed their clothes into the backpack. He snagged his gun from the dresser and tucked it into his waist belt, all the while eying the monitor in the corner of the room like a SWAT team might materialize outside Lou's gym. He snapped his laptop shut and slid it into the bag.

"We'll meet you there," he said.

As much as he didn't want to go back, it was the only place they could hide in the city. The only place that wouldn't be buzzing with surveillance drones programmed with facial recognition software. They would collect themselves at the silos, and then they would get out of Chicago.

30

"Are we safe here?" Eden asked, her body trembling from the electrifying ride, wherein she had wrapped her arms tight around his torso and buried her face in his shoulder, positive they were going to be stopped and apprehended as the unsettling sound of drones whirred overhead. Thankfully, there weren't any here—this lonely spot in the middle of Chicago between an industrial train yard and a ship canal.

Cassian peered through the waning light toward the silos. He'd seemed so sure in the basement of Lou's—getting them here with speed and decisiveness. But now, lingering outside the fence as the sunlight faded, he didn't seem nearly as confident.

Were they safe here?

Were they safe anywhere?

"It's our best option," he finally said.

More accurately, their *only* option.

Cass grabbed the backpack and took a seat on the ground.

"We're not going inside?" Eden said.

"Mona is expecting Cleo. We'll receive a warmer welcome if we arrive with the person she's expecting."

Eden sat beside him and leaned against the fence. The past few hours had brought an onslaught of intense emotion. Exhilaration. Fear. Confusion. Frustration. Shock. She stared at the bag in Cassian's lap, their clothes stuffed inside. The cigar box, too. A part of her wanted to avoid that box. Keep it shut. Stop pressing forward, because pressing forward only seemed to suck them deeper into whatever this was.

They'd gone to the Prosperity Ball hoping for a specific outcome—the end of a nightmare. They'd broken into the Bryson's home hoping for a specific outcome—answers to their questions. Both times, they'd only fallen further into the rabbit hole. Would they ever find the bottom or would they forever be falling deeper and deeper?

Eden took a dogged breath. Gathering her resolve, she unzipped the front pouch of the backpack and removed the box. When she lifted the lid—there it was. The pamphlet with the word *Invictus* on top. So close to Interitus, but with an entirely different meaning. On the inside, the strange poem about fallen empires and the promise of a future utopia. *Caelum In Terra*. Heaven on Earth. A reality that would only come to fruition through sacrifice. She scooped up the glass butterfly and pushed the button. The same projection Cass discovered in Lou's basement shined in front of them.

"They must be recruiters," Cassian said, his words chasing a shiver up her spine.

"Recruiters?"

"For whatever cult this is."

She thought about the twelve girls who came to the Bryson's home every Thursday evening. Gage, a guidance counselor. Isabella, a volunteer at a crisis pregnancy center. Leader of a support group. They were both in positions of trusted leadership and confidential support.

Eden wasn't an expert on cults, but thanks to Erik, she knew the basics. Two summers ago, he'd watched a documentary about The People's Temple and their leader, Jim Jones, who convinced over nine hundred of his followers to drink cyanide-laced Kool-Aid in a mass suicide.

"Parents gave it to their children," he'd said, unable to let it go. Unable to get over it.

That documentary had propelled him into a short-lived obsession with cults. Erik wanted to understand what kind of people could become so brainwashed, so mind-bogglingly suggestible, that they would move to some remote country in South America, remain in deplorable conditions, then poison their own children. In the end, he reached a disturbing conclusion. A humbling conclusion.

It could happen to anyone.

Given the right circumstances.

Or rather, the wrong ones.

The Brysons were surrounded by young people, lonely people, hurting people. They were preying on the vulnerable. Individuals without a support system. Individuals who could be easily swayed. Foster kids. High school students in need of counseling. Pregnant women in crisis. People estranged from their families. All of it fit. Cassian was right. The Brysons were recruiters.

The question was—for what?

How did this Invictus fit with Interitus and Prudence Dvorak?

They clicked on each of the names in the database, reading the bios the couple had culled together amidst the occasional haunting call from a train or barge. They searched for connections, patterns, breadcrumbs until Eden's eyes crossed. The more bios they read, the more convinced she became that this was leading nowhere. Certainly not to the Monarch.

They'd lost the plot.

She pressed the small button and the projection

vanished. She placed the glass butterfly into the cigar box as two bright beams sliced through the dark.

Headlights.

Cleo's Tesla stopped behind Cassian's bike.

Cleo stepped outside. "What are you guys doing out here?"

"Waiting for you," Cassian said. "How's your mom?"

"Exercising her right to remain silent, I'm sure." Cleo pocketed her keys. "I haven't been able to talk to her since I left Milwaukee. I ditched my phone and my computer. They're way too easy to trace."

At the worried look on Eden's face, Cleo continued. "Hakuna matata, Six. Both devices have been wiped clean. I can't have authorities stumbling upon The People's Press now, can I? Everything has been transferred, and it's all right here, safe and sound." Cleo patted the front pocket of her corduroy jacket as she took a seat on Cassian's other side. "So, what the hell happened?"

They'd kept in touch with her throughout the week. She knew about Willow Bryson. She knew they'd been planning to break into the home to find answers in the safe. She didn't know about any of the things they'd found. Eden filled her in, and when she finished, Cleo opened the cigar box. She reached past the butterfly and the pamphlet to the photograph beneath of the six women.

"RIP Lillian Kashif," she muttered.

"What?" Eden said.

Cleo pointed to the woman standing to Dvorak's left. "Lillian Kashif. Bella Bryson's dead sister."

Eden leaned over Cass to get a better look. She'd been so distracted by Prudence Dvorak she hadn't closely examined the others. When they researched the ninety-three Magnes Matres, they didn't bother pulling up Lillian's obituary. They already knew how and when she died. Eden had only seen her face once in passing, when they researched her son, Amir. Now that Eden looked closer, she could see that Cleo was right. Lillian Kashif was in this photograph. And now, thanks to Eden's photographic memory and the research they'd done in Lou's basement, she recognized the other four, too.

Eden made quick cross-references in her mind.

"Sasha Farooq," she said, pointing at the woman on the far right. "Cordelia Gill. Felicia Humboldt. And Janice McMillan."

"Say what?" Cleo said.

"These women. They're all on the back of the pamphlet." She snagged it from the box and handed it to Cleo. As she and Cassian scanned the list of Magnes Matres, pinpointing each one, Eden stared hard at the girl in the middle of the photograph. "Except for Dvorak."

"Dvorak?" Cleo said with the same hint of familiarity Cass had when they were in the Bryson's basement.

"Prudence Dvorak," Eden said.

Cleo's expression stretched with recognition.

Unlike these women, Dvorak was alive. At least according to authorities. She was at-large. A member of the terrorist regime that tried its best to bring America down. In a photograph with Lillian Kashif.

"Amir," Cass said.

Eden looked at him.

"He has to know something." He ran a search for Amir Kashif on his phone. Unlike Cleo's, his wasn't issued by the government and thus, wasn't easy to trace. Cass found the same information they'd found before. He was alive and well. Working in Baltimore but living in—

"Bethesda?" Cleo said, like the name was gum stuck to the bottom of her shoe. "Why in the world would he be living in Bethesda?"

It was a very unusual place to live, given its proximity to Washington D.C. After The Attack, survivors in the surrounding metropolis left in droves, turning the once thriving suburbs into quasi ghost towns, Bethesda chief among them. Once home to over sixty thousand, a favorite hotspot for foodies and clubbers, Bethesda's population had dwindled to eight hundred. And apparently, one of them was Amir, who hadn't just stayed in town but moved to town. A Chicago transplant who arrived twelve years ago.

Before they could work out the oddity, a flashlight bobbed through the night.

Cassian snapped his laptop shut and came to his feet, shielding his eyes as a skinny kid shone the light in their faces. He stopped on the other side of the fence—the same boy they met the first time they visited.

"Mona's waiting," he said.

Inside, it became quickly apparent that this wasn't Cleo's first time in the silos. She knew people. And when they reached Mona's room, she received a greeting much warmer than the one Cassian had. Not affectionate per se, but not so matter of fact either.

According to Cleo, Mona was a pacifist. Once Cassian decided to fight, he was no longer welcome to stay. Not that he'd wanted to stay if she'd let him. Maybe Mona took his career choice personally. Hence, the coldness between them. None of that coldness existed between Cleo and the older woman. Only a familiarity that turned Mona's face into something less hard.

Eden tried to imagine Mona conducting hypnotherapy with a younger Cleo—a little girl plagued with pain after a car accident left her fatherless and injured. Maybe their sessions together had cracked Mona's reticence. Or maybe the welcome had nothing to do with Cleo and everything to do with her mother, a woman who risked her livelihood to help the people living beneath these very silos.

Like Francesca and her glass eye.

Like Cassian and his broken body.

Now Cleo's mother was being detained and interrogated at a police station because of her association with them.

"We need to get to Bethesda," Cleo said after the pleasantries were exchanged.

"We?" Cass crooked his eyebrow.

Cleo ignored him. "Or anywhere close by. Like Baltimore. Is there a community there? Or a safe house?"

"Sure Cleo," Cass cut in sardonically. "You can come with us."

"Hey, I'm not a criminal on the run. My mother is simply a person of interest. If we're getting anywhere safely, you need a front man. I don't see anyone else volunteering."

Cass glanced at Eden.

Eden shrugged.

Cleo's attention slid to the virtual reality headset on Mona's desk—her brown eyes aglow with anticipation. "Can I check the map?"

"I thought your mother wanted you to lie low," Mona said.

"Think of how low we could lay hundreds of miles away from Chicago."

Mona stared at Cleo for a beat, then stepped aside as if to say *be my guest.*

Cleo didn't hesitate. She scooped up the headset like a hungry diner grabbing a fork.

Eden watched as Cleo slipped the headset over her eyes and powered it on. "What map?"

"Off-the-grid communities and safe houses." Cleo extended her arm to press some invisible button in front of her. A virtual button.

"Safe houses?" Eden said.

"Safe homes for people who live off the grid. There's a network of them, all across the country. There has been ever since the government started requiring retinal registration and mandatory fingerprinting. It's part of the Amber Highway."

"The what?" Eden said.

"An off-the-grid metaverse. Created by some guy who calls himself Gollum. It's run by a select group of people called the Teutonic Knights. All of it is highly encrypted and elusive." Cleo continued to interact with the space in front of her—pushing, swiping, zooming in like Jack did with the device in Dr. Norton's cabin. Only Eden couldn't see anything she was interacting with. "It's how *America Underground* is circulated. It's how off-the-grid communities communicate with one another."

"It's also how you get one of these," Cassian cut in, holding up his phone.

So this was where the black-market existed.

The Amber Highway.

Cleo set her hands on her hips and leaned back on her heels, her head subtly moving as though examining a large image in front of her. "There's a community in Alexandria. That's really close. And ... holy crud." She tapped the air, then peeled off the headset, her expression alight with excitement. "There's a safe house *in* Bethesda."

31

Eden awoke to a warm hand on her shoulder.

Her eyes fluttered open.

Cassian stood above her—his gorgeous face riddled with unease.

Last night, after discussing how they would get to Bethesda, after a dinner of soggy mac and cheese—they'd each found a spare bed in an attempt to get some sleep. Eden couldn't believe she'd fallen so deeply in this underground maze of noise. But fall deeply she must have, for Cassian was already up and dressed and ready for the day.

"What is it?" she asked, running her fingers through her tousled hair.

"The Brysons are dead."

Eden sat upright. "What?"

"Someone broke into their home last night and killed them. A single bullet through each of their heads."

Alarm shot through her veins as she processed Cassian's words. A single bullet through each of their heads. Like Yukio. Like the security guards at SafePad Elite. "H-how do you know this?"

"It's all over Concordia."

"Chicago?"

"National."

She tried to swallow, but her throat had gone bone dry. "Are they saying who did it?" she asked, knowing the answer, hoping she might be wrong.

But the look in Cassian's eyes all-too-quickly vanquished that hope. "Authorities have set up checkpoints at all major highways and interstates going in and out of the city. They're urging travelers to cooperate. They set up a tip line. Any tips that lead in the right direction will be generously rewarded."

Eden's heart sank, her entire body swimming with dread.

"They're linking us to the attack in Chicago and the break-in at SafePad."

Her fingers closed around the blanket over her legs. She shook her head, wanting him to stop. Surely, it couldn't get any worse. But Cassian had one more thing to say.

"They're showing pictures of your parents."

On Concordia *National* News.

How long until the government connected the dots?

How long until they realized what she was?

Jane stood on the threshold of the bad room, her pulse beating faster than the wings of a hummingbird. She could hear Barrett's heartbeat beside her, Alexander and Ruth and Dr. Norton's upstairs. All of them much slower than her own. She could also hear the television. The squeak of a couch spring. The tapping of Alexander's cane. The scuffling of two chipmunks on the deck. The groan of wood as the house settled. The chirping of birds. The lapping of the lake.

There were no sounds from Jack.

Last night, he left for the airport to meet his wife and daughter. Now they were reunited and settling in at home, somewhere in the city of Milwaukee. Jack refused to bring his daughter here. He acted like Jane and Barrett might accidentally kill her. Her name was Ellery, and her superpowers remained locked away. Unlike Father, Jack didn't want them to come out. Maybe because once they did, she might start glitching like Barrett's memory and Jane's hearing.

Exactly one week had passed since they realized why

it was happening. One week since Jane decided to be brave. She was taking it in increments—first standing at the top of the steps, then working her way further down each day. Fear screamed at her to run, to take flight. But she pressed it down, forced herself to remain, motivated to help Barrett, who'd forgotten another name, and Ruth, who had barely eaten since Eden left them a note and rode away on Cassian's motorcycle.

Jack slept as much as Ruth ate, obsessed with his discovery. The Queen Bee. The master node. And how to disable it. As if doing so would keep his daughter's superpowers locked away forever. He took more images of Barrett, all the while looking eagerly at Jane. But he didn't force her. She didn't think Dr. Norton would let him. She didn't think Ruth would let him, either. Now Jack was gone, and Jane was so close—standing in the basement, outside the bad room with Barrett beside her.

He didn't fill up the space with words like he normally did. Instead, he was unusually quiet, like he knew she needed to concentrate.

She was safe, she told herself.

She was safe.

She was safe.

She was safe!

With a squeak, she snatched Barrett's hand.

He gave her palm a squeeze and didn't let go. "Are you sure?"

Her pulse thrummed faster. And faster. And faster. So fast she thought she was going to die. But she wasn't. She wouldn't. *She was safe!*

With a terrified breath, she took a precarious step inside.

Barrett led her to the scanner.

Jane lay on the table and squeezed her eyes shut, trying to block out thoughts of another room. A very bad room. All too similar to this one. Her earliest memories weren't horrible. When she was little and Mother hadn't yet left, the tests weren't so bad. Just cuts on her arms. Then Father would start the timer to see how fast the cuts would heal. But the longer her powers stayed locked away, the worse the tests became. Until Mother left and he wasn't just cutting her skin but breaking her bones and injecting lethal poisons. Once, he mutilated her eardrum. Father used technology more advanced than the scanner Barrett was preparing now. He studied her for hours on end, year after year, always exploring. Always tinkering. Then he built the machine.

Her toes curled at the memory.

Sixteen years of learning her system, understanding her system, manipulating her system. As if he were one step away from unlocking the potential that so stubbornly refused to break free.

It never worked.

As hard as Jane tried, the powers didn't come. Self-healing was the best she could do. Father thought it was a matter of motivation. Pain was no longer doing the trick. So one day, he brought Kitty home. A soft little kitten, so tiny Jane could cup the animal in her palms. For an entire glorious year, as Kitty grew into a gray, fluffy cat who licked Jane's nose and nuzzled in her lap, Father didn't do any tests at all. And just when Jane was beginning to think the tests were over, they resumed in full force.

Kitty was the new motivation.

But Jane still failed. No matter how desperately she wanted the powers to come, they refused. Then one day, Father got so angry, Kitty died.

Violet's words left.

And Violet did, too.

Her nostrils quivered.

She wasn't Violet anymore.

She was Jane.

And this room was not Father's.

It was Dr. Norton's.

And these tests weren't really tests at all. Not the kind she could fail, anyway. They were just pictures. A series of images that might help them unlock a new key. A key that would keep them safe from the bad people.

"All done," Barrett said.

Jane's eyes flew open.

He sat at the computer.

A printer hummed to life.

Jane jumped at the sound, then fled from the room.

She raced up the stairs like a monster was nipping at her heel and collapsed in the foyer, scooting back on all fours until her shoulders pressed against the closet door.

It was over.

She was safe.

Dr. Norton and Ruth and Alexander stared at her as the printer stopped and papers crinkled. Barrett came up the stairs with a stack of images in his hand. He shot Jane a thumbs up and handed the stack to Dr. Norton, who shuffled through them over his cup of coffee. "Are these—?"

"She did it," Barrett said, beaming proudly.

A loud beep filled the house.

Jane clapped her hands over her ears as everyone else turned to the television, which had made the noise.

Ruth gasped as her daughter's face filled the screen.

"Eden Pruitt and Cassian Ransom, both armed and highly dangerous, are believed to still be in Chicago," the news anchor reported.

The lady inside the television called her a terrorist.

Cassian, too.

The lady said they were at large. In Chicago. Members of Interitus. Responsible for the most recent attack on the city. A series of short videos played. Cassian and Eden entering a coffee shop. Cassian and

Eden walking through a public library. Police officers inside a salon called Cute-Icles, questioning the nail technicians. All the while, a hotline number scrolled across the bottom of the screen.

Dr. Norton turned up the volume.

Ruth grabbed his phone and tried calling Cleo, something she'd given up on a few days ago because Cleo never answered. This time, the phone didn't ring. It made a funny noise similar to the late-breaking news, followed by an automated voice that said the number was no longer in service.

As if on cue, Cleo Ransom's face filled the screen, too.

Not a terrorist, but a person of interest.

The footage cut to a giant house, where reporters swarmed a tall, smartly dressed Black woman as she made her way inside.

"Dr. Ransom," one of them shouted. "Did you really not know your nephew was a terrorist?"

She made no comment.

And then, more photographs appeared on the television. This time, of Alexander and Ruth Pruitt.

Alexander sank into a nearby chair.

Ruth pressed her fingers against her mouth. "Oh my goodness, what are we going to do?"

Nobody had an answer.

A reporter was interviewing a guest who survived the Prosperity Ball. He claimed to have conversed with

Cassian and Eden that night in The Sapphire's ballroom. "I'm not really that surprised," he said. "Something about him felt dangerous. I simply dismissed it because of his connection to Beverly."

Ruth kept shaking her head. "Someone will recognize us. They're going to make the connection. They'll know why we disappeared. They'll know who Eden is—"

"Ruth," Dr. Norton said—calmly, reassuringly. As though trying to mitigate the hysteria in her voice.

"Our faces are on Concordia National News! And we disappeared. We just … disappeared. And now here we are, with different names and an 18-year-old daughter who is being touted as armed and highly dangerous. With ties to *Interitus*."

Barrett's face had gone off-white.

Alexander seemed to have lost his words altogether.

Maybe they were hiding with Jane's.

Tears welled in Ruth's eyes. Frightened, helpless tears as she sank onto the armrest of the sofa. "If they find her …"

The unfinished statement hung in the air.

If they found her, they would finish the job the former CIA agent couldn't.

They would destroy Karik Volkova's weapon.

32

Eden stood between Cassian and Cleo, ready to come out of her skin. They were inside Mona's office—room, whatever it was with the bed and the desk and the bins—in immediate need of getting out of Chicago. But there was no safe way of leaving. Eden ached to speak with her parents, but she couldn't take even the tiniest risk of jeopardizing their location.

"I'm sure by now there's an APB on my car," Cleo said. "And even if there isn't, we won't make it past the checkpoints."

Which meant last night's naïve and simple plans were a bust.

"Train and bus stations will be crawling with cops," Cass said.

"Airports are obviously out of the question," Cleo added.

"Doesn't your mom have a private jet?" Eden quipped.

"Yeah, but how are we supposed to use it? I guarantee the government is monitoring her phone calls, her internet activity. We have no way of getting in touch with her."

Which left … what? Walking was out of the question. Even if they could traipse halfway across the country, they were bound to be detected at some point. Eden bit her bottom lip. How in the world were they going to escape Chicago and make it all the way to the east coast undetected with the entire country on high-alert and drone surveillance and facial recognition and retinal scans everywhere?

"There's the train yard," Mona said flatly.

The train yard.

Cleo's posture straightened. "Train hopping. Finn did it this past summer. He traveled with a group of hobos for two weeks, all the way from Lincoln to Boise."

"Why?" Cass said.

"He plans to write an article about it. The lost art of anonymous travel. According to him, train hopping is the way to go. If you're patient and careful enough, you can get almost anywhere in the U.S. without a single retinal scan. Without paying anything either."

"Chicago to Baltimore is a common route," Mona said. "And there are several train hoppers living here who would be willing to help you along with a little incentive. Zeb is the most experienced."

"Can we trust him?" Eden asked.

"Trust him to *what*," Mona replied, "lead you in the right direction?"

"There's a bounty on our heads."

"Zeb hasn't watched Concordia News since it debuted twenty years ago. Nor is he the type to trust hotlines. Or phones." Mona arched her thin eyebrows, waiting for them to make their decision.

Cleo broke the silence first. "What are we going to do with our vehicles? We can't leave them outside the fence. Eventually, they're going to draw attention."

"I can take them off your hands," Mona said. "If you're train hopping, you'll need the right supplies. And that will cost you money." She shuffled to her desk, unlocked the bottom drawer, and pulled out a small safe. She removed a stack of well-worn twenties, licked her middle finger, and counted out a hundred of them.

Two thousand dollars.

Cassian's bike alone was probably worth more than that. Never mind Cleo's Tesla. Mona was going to make out like a bandit. But like Cleo said, what other choice did they have?

He took the stack of bills.

"I'll go find Zeb." With a nod, Mona exited the room.

When she was gone, Eden turned to Cassian. "This doesn't feel right."

Judging by the look on his face, he agreed with her instincts.

"Of course it doesn't feel right," Cleo said. "Nothing about this *is* right. But it's the only way we're going to get out of here."

Eden squeezed her eyes shut and pinched the bridge of her nose. "This safe house in Bethesda—Elmer and Eloise Miller. You think they're trustworthy?"

"They wouldn't be listed as a safe house if they weren't."

"But we aren't just people living off the grid, Cleo. According to Concordia, we're fugitives who blew up Chicago."

"Safe houses don't subscribe to Concordia."

But that didn't mean they weren't tempted by money.

Eden's mind spun, her nerves a tangle.

Nowhere felt safe, and this underground world kept getting crazier and crazier. Fighters and gamblers and illegal newspapers and off-the-grid communities and safe houses and this illicit metaverse called the Amber Highway. Was this really happening? She and Cass and Cleo were going to hop on a train and make their way east, then stay in some random couple's home, trusting that they wouldn't at least be tempted to call the hotline?

"We should probably disguise ourselves," Cleo

continued. "I wonder if Enez is still here. She's fabulous with braids. We should also try to get the authorities off our scent. Get them thinking we're headed west instead of east."

"How do you propose we do that?" Cassian asked.

"A phony call to the hotline?"

He shook his head. "They'll be tracing every call that comes in."

"So we need someone to call for us. Someone who won't rouse suspicion or get into trouble if the call is traced."

Cassian blinked at her. "Do you have someone in mind?"

Cleo didn't.

But Eden did. "My friend Erik. He lives in San Diego."

Cleo smiled. "That's definitely west."

Cassian made quick work of finding his number, then handed Eden his phone. "Keep it brief in case they look into his phone records. The shorter the call, the less likely they can trace it. We'll ditch this phone before we leave."

Eden took a shaky breath.

She hadn't spoken with Erik since the day before her house was ransacked in Eagle Bend. Her best friend since the sixth grade. And now, suddenly—after dropping off the face of the planet, with her face on Concordia National News—she was going to call him, and she couldn't stay on the line long enough to explain any of it.

He didn't answer the first call.

He didn't answer the second.

When Eden dialed the third time, he picked up halfway through the first ring, his greeting soaked in wariness.

"Erik?" she said.

Silence followed.

A long, pregnant pause.

Cleo tapped her wrist like she was wearing a watch.

"Erik?" Eden said again. "Are you there?"

"Eden?" he finally replied, his voice even higher than usual. There was another brief silence, and then, like a popped cork, the questions spewed. "What's going on? Where have you been? Why haven't you called? And why are reporters saying you had something to do with the bombings in Chicago?"

Eden closed her eyes, missing him terribly. She ached to answer him. To go somewhere private and tell him everything. The whole crazy story. But she couldn't without putting too many people in jeopardy. "Listen, Erik, I need you to call the hotline."

"What?"

"The hotline. I need you to call it. Tell them I contacted you. Tell them I'm coming to San Diego."

"Eden—"

"Please." With that, she ended the call.

With heartbreaking gentleness, Cassian took his phone.

"Think he'll do it?" Cleo asked.

"I know he will," Eden said.

The makeshift door swung open.

Mona returned, followed by a sallow-skinned man with a scraggly beard and stooped shoulders. He reeked of alcohol. He smiled at them, revealing a missing front tooth. And when he shook their hands, his was trembling slightly.

"So," Zeb said, his voice like gravel. "I hear you're wanting to get to Baltimore."

33

They spent the rest of the morning holed away in Mona's room, listening to Zeb share his wandering expertise on the craft of train hopping. For this was what it was to Zeb—an artistic skill. One that could be honed with practice and study. One that lit his jaundiced eyes the longer he talked. He drew them a map with his trembling scrawl. He wrote them a list of items they would need for the journey. He told them what to expect and how to know which trains to catch—which rides were safe, which rides would be challenging, and which rides were impossible. He told them about the many dangers, including a collection of gruesome stories about train-hoppers who had lost life and limb. He told them how to evade the yard bulls, a name he used for railroad cops, and when Eden asked how long the trip would take and he responded, "not more than a week", she tried not to choke on her rubbery eggs.

All the while, the malnourished boy rounded up the items on Zeb's list—a difficult task, as most retail stores required retinal scans. They sent him off with a substantial chunk of their cash, another exercise in trust, for how could they know he wouldn't take the money and run, or see their faces on the front of Concordia Times and turn them in?

Cassian destroyed his phone and tossed it into the canal.

Cleo found the woman named Enez to do her hair, a process that took several laborious hours. By the time she was done, Cleo's regular style of Bantu knots had morphed into a headful of tiny braids that hung long down her back. Eden's hair went in the opposite direction. Enez tied it into a low ponytail and cut off twelve inches, resulting in a choppy, shoulder-length style much shorter than she was used to. And much easier to tuck beneath her new army green beanie. Cleo had found it in one of Mona's bins. She'd also found a baseball hat for Cassian and a pair of Buddy Holly glasses for herself. Between the new hairstyle and the glasses and the removal of her snake bite lip piercing, Cleo's appearance was so different, Eden wasn't sure she'd recognize her if they were to pass one another on the street.

The boy didn't return until early evening, heavy

laden with three bulging backpacks attached to three rolled up sleeping bags. They waited until nightfall before sneaking off to the train yard, the swirling gray clouds overhead an ominous sign. They hunkered in the hiding spot Zeb had shown them for five whole hours, two of which involved rainfall, before a train with ridable cars rolled to a stop. They hopped into a well and ducked low, Eden's heart crashing as a flashlight cut through the drizzling night. Another uncomfortable hour passed before the train started moving and when it did, the sound was deafening—a thunderous, ear-splitting racket as the behemoth machine picked up speed and the city lights sped past in a blur.

They were going, going, gone.

Out of Chicago.

No longer in the center of the bullseye.

The rain clouds cleared. An expanse of star-strewn sky stretched overhead. Their clothes dried out. And as cornfields whipped past at seventy miles per hour, Eden understood the fond look on Zeb's face. Because, for one bright and breathtaking moment, she felt like she was riding on the back of a steel dragon.

Time became a blur, like the passing scenery.

Zeb had warned them that train travel was an unpredictable, often-frustrating mode of transportation. But he had done so like an indulgent grandfather, watching his grandson's naughty behavior with an amused twinkle in his eye. Train travel was more than frustrating. It was maddening, with stops occurring for no rhyme or reason. One minute, they were zipping along in a rush of inescapable noise. The next, they were hiding from the bulls as floodlights rolled over their backs. Then there was the unpredictable nature of how long the train would remain stationary. Should they hop off and try to catch another or should they stick it out and wait? There was no way of knowing. Never mind the constant, nagging concern that they could be headed in the wrong direction.

Somewhere halfway through Ohio, they made their second transfer.

They crept along the periphery of a new train yard—sleep-deprived but glad to be on solid ground. After three days of this taxing mode of travel, without phones or Concordia News or any other human beings other than the occasional conductor or yard bull sweeping the grounds with a flashlight, Eden felt cut-off from the world. Like there was no witch hunt. Like there was no Monarch. It was just her and Cleo and Cassian and this massive system of steel and freight.

They hid behind a cluster of bushes while Cassian snuck closer to get a better sense of their surroundings. Eden sat cross-legged on the ground and wrapped herself in her sleeping bag, wishing her superhuman powers would keep away the night's chill.

Cleo did the same, her teeth chattering as she stared from Cassian's shrinking backside to Eden. Back and forth, back and forth, like the pendulum of a grandfather clock.

"What?" Eden said after the third swing.

"Nothing. It's just ... intense."

"What is?"

"The way he looks at you. The way you look at him."

A flush crept up Eden's cheeks. "What do you mean?"

"Oh, come on," Cleo said. "If sexual tension could be measured, yours would be off the charts."

Eden flushed hotter.

"I understand now why Cass was so reluctant to let me be the tag-along. I am the pernicious third wheel, completely ruining what could have otherwise been a romantic trip of a lifetime."

"Right. Because running for our lives is so romantic."

"Emotions are heightened by life-or-death situations. Not diminished."

With a roll of her eyes, Eden pulled a protein bar from her pack and tore it open.

"You two were alone together for an entire week. In Lou's basement."

Eden took a bite and chewed.

Cleo gave her a wide-eyed, exasperated look. "So, has there been ...?"

"Has there been what?" Eden said around the mouthful.

"Hanky panky."

"*Hanky panky*? What are you—eighty?"

"Well, has there?"

"No!" Eden's ears had gone mortifyingly hot.

Cleo smiled impishly. "Do you want there to be?"

Eden slugged her in the arm.

"Ouch!" She clutched her shoulder. "Superhuman strength, remember?"

"Sorry," Eden muttered.

Cleo rubbed the spot. "In all seriousness, I've never seen Cass like this. Ever."

Eden tried to imagine what she meant. "Serious and brooding?"

"Attentive and protective. Which is kind of ironic if you think about it. If he's going to worry about anyone falling off a railcar, it should be me. Or him. The people who would meet an untimely death. You would just dust yourself off and jump back on."

Eden ate the rest of her bar as a bullfrog chirped behind them.

"It's probably comforting," Cleo said.

"What is?"

"Your indestructibility. Given what happened to his mom."

Eden considered the offhanded remark, even after Cassian returned.

He didn't want to stay. There were too many bulls afoot. So they crept onward, through the trainyard, and huddled out of site in an outcropping of trees. For seven agonizing hours. Until finally, another train rumbled toward them—a parade of graffiti-plastered boxcars.

Zeb would call this an easy ride.

Cleo went first, using a rusty foothold to climb aboard. Eden and Cass followed right behind when two things happened simultaneously.

The rusted perch snapped and a piercing pain sliced through Eden's temple.

Her stomach dropped.

Before she could fall, Cassian's arm was around her. He pulled her up into the boxcar, their bodies pressed together, their hearts beating in unison.

He was there. Always.

Attentive and protective.

Just like Cleo said.

"It happened again," he said, his golden eyes boring into hers like the pain was Mordecai and they were back on the rooftop of The Sapphire.

She rubbed her temple and released a shaky breath.

Eden understood his concern. She felt it herself. These flashes of pain were disconcerting, coming and going with the same rhyme and reason as the trains.

"All good?" Cleo asked, rolling out her sleeping bag in the empty car, no doubt eager to catch up on some much-needed sleep without fear of falling off or losing their packs.

Hesitantly—and without breaking eye contact—Cass let Eden go.

The train picked up speed.

Eden rolled out her sleeping bag, too, and with the train rumbling east, she fell fast and hard. When she awoke, Cleo was next to her, buried inside her sleeping bag, snoring softly. Across the boxcar, Cassian was awake, watching her through the dark.

She joined him.

"What time is it?" she asked with a yawn.

"Closer to morning than midnight. I think we're somewhere in Pennsylvania."

"Haven't you slept?"

"A little."

The train released a long blast of noise—a warning call that carried through the night as the boxcar rocked and rumbled.

Eden took a deep breath and gave voice to her accumulating worry. "What if this is a wild goose chase?"

Cassian looked at her.

"What if Amir Kashif doesn't know anything? What if someone calls the hotline with information that leads to my parents and Dr. Norton?"

"Your dad was in the CIA."

"I know. And now his face is on national news."

Cassian rubbed his jaw, his palm scratching against several days' worth of stubble. "He knows how to protect himself better than most. Your parents are smart. They're going to be okay."

He couldn't know that.

Yet he spoke with such steady certainty, her tangled nerves loosened a bit.

"And even if Amir doesn't know anything, we still had to get out of Chicago." He folded his hands in his lap. Eden studied them. Cassian had great hands. The kind that were equipped to handle a great many things. Her skin tingled as she recalled the feel of them in her hair. On her hips. Sliding up her ribcage. Heat swirled in her chest. Maybe Cleo was right. She was the pernicious third wheel. For if she were not snoring a few feet away, Eden felt sure that she and Cassian would repeat what had transpired inside Lou's boxing ring.

As much as they would have liked to ride this train all the way to their destination, they had to hop off when they reached Maryland. Their final ride was brutal—a train pulling trailer cars. The trailers were too small to share, which meant they rode isolated from one another, exposed to the wind, with no way of getting comfortable. Whenever they rolled through a yard, they had to wedge themselves on top of the axles to avoid being seen. On the whole, it was a miserable, ear-piercing experience that made Eden curse Jeb. But then they would zoom through a mountain pass and a view would open up—so breathtakingly beautiful—she would forgive him a little.

On the fifth day, as they rumbled over a bridge with a highway beneath them, Eden saw the first sign for Washington D.C. An exit overlaid with a blood-red X and NO ENTRY in bold, capital letters. The next time the train slowed to a stop, Cassian got their attention and motioned for them to hop off board. Eden did so happily, eager to feel solid ground beneath her feet.

Cleo looked bone-weary.

Eden gave her elbow a squeeze.

They were close now, almost to their destination.

This would be the most dangerous leg of the journey.

After five days of isolation, headlights made her unease hurl into tumult. The barking of dogs had her suppressing squeaks like Violet. Beneath a moonless sky, they scuttled through the shadows with their hoods up and their heads down, propelled by a sense of urgency. None of them spoke until they wound their way past a string of dives that made up Bethesda's downtown.

"Why would he want to live here?" Cleo whispered.

Eden didn't have an answer.

Neither did Cassian.

Amir was a cybersecurity analyst, an occupation that brought in an annual income substantially higher than the national average. He could absolutely afford a home in Baltimore, and yet he lived here, in this dump of a town that seemed almost inhospitable.

At half-past nine, they reached the address Mona had given them. A two-story home in a derelict neighborhood, the only house on the block that didn't look on the verge of collapse. Several wind chimes hung on the front porch, their bamboo reeds tapping together in the breeze. After twenty-four hours inside the belly of a freight, the tinkling peal felt like balm to Eden's ears.

Smoke curled from the chimney.

A yellow glow peeked through the cracks in the blinds.

The residents were home and awake.

They were here, feet away from this safe house that belonged to an elderly couple named Elmer and Eloise Miller. But what if it wasn't safe? They decided Cleo should go first, as she was the least conspicuous. She crept through the yard and onto the front porch while Eden's heart bruised her sternum.

Cleo knocked three times. Waited. Then knocked three more.

A few moments later, the door opened. Its hinges released a loud groan.

An old woman stood framed in the half-opened doorway—tiny and frail. She took one look at Cleo, dusty and travel-worn, and opened the door wider. Eden blocked out the chimes and focused on the conversation as the woman peered out into the night.

Cleo waved at them to come.

And suddenly, the three of them were standing inside the foyer of a warm house that smelled like chili. The elderly woman had thin, white hair, a face full of winkles, and veiny hands covered in age spots. As she shut the door behind them, Eden held her breath, waiting for the moment when her wizened eyes would go wide with recognition.

"Who is it?" a deep voice said from the next room.

A man appeared in the foyer entryway. Much closer in age to Dr. Norton, at least twenty years younger than the woman. Which meant this wasn't the woman's husband. Eden's stomach clenched as the man took them in and the recognition she'd been bracing for slid into place.

But he was familiar, too.

Cleo dropped her bag.

It fell to the floor with a heavy clunk.

The man smiled at her reaction.

An invisible valve in Eden's chest opened wide and all the pressure whooshed away.

They were safe.

The Elmers would not turn them in.

For the man standing in the entryway was a fugitive, too. Had been for the past twenty-one years. Cleo had a picture of him hanging in the top corner of her dorm room mirror. Dayne Johnson, one of America's most infamous media moguls. A controversial figure before The Attack. A wanted criminal after. With a bounty on his head every bit as enticing as the bounty on theirs.

34

Eden awoke with a start, sitting upright on the bedroll Eloise Miller had given her.

Cassian and Cleo's bedrolls were empty.

Sunlight poured through the basement windows. Above the drone of a television, Cleo's voice filtered down the stairs. Dayne Johnson's, too. Along with a voice she didn't recognize. The elderly man of the house—Elmer Miller.

When they arrived last night, he was already asleep. Cleo's knock had interrupted a game of chess between Dayne and Eloise. She said it kept her mind sharp and it would do her husband good to learn how to play. The game was abandoned in lieu of their new guests. Eloise served them heaping bowls of chili she'd reheated in the microwave as they took turns taking hot showers. Then she gave them each a bedroll, a pillow, a blanket, and asked Dayne to show them downstairs for an uninterrupted night's rest.

Eden hurried to her feet, then let herself into the unfinished basement bathroom, the cement floor cold as she rinsed her face and gargled mouthwash, then spit it down the rust-stained drain, all while listening for the voice she had yet to hear.

Cassian's.

When she finished, she made her way up the creaky staircase and found Cleo, Dayne, and the elderly couple sitting together at the kitchen table, drinking from steaming mugs of coffee. Dayne's elbow rested atop a copy of *America Underground*. Elmer selected a bagel from the assortment arranged on a plate in the center of the table. He had more hair in his large ears than he had on his bald head. He wore bifocals and a tan cardigan and blinked at her from soupy eyes as Eden stood in the kitchen entryway.

"Where's Cassian?" she asked, scolding her thumping heart. There was no reason for this edge of panic. He was probably in the next room. Never mind that she couldn't hear his heartbeat. Or his breathing.

"He left," Cleo said.

"What do you mean, he *left*?"

"He went to Baltimore." Cleo gave her a meaningful look. It was Friday. Amir Kashif would be in Baltimore for work. "To get us phones. And take care of ... some other things."

"How did he get there?" Eden asked, the growing sense of panic now ringing in her ears.

"We let him use our car, dear," Eloise answered, taking the bagel from her husband as if he were a small child who'd just taken an extra cookie without permission. "We don't drive it much anymore."

The ringing intensified.

Cassian left.

Without so much as a goodbye.

He was driving to Baltimore in a car in broad daylight. With drones and police officers and a hefty reward on their heads. What if he got pulled over? What if he was recognized?

"Don't worry, Six," Cleo said calmly. Reassuringly. "It's Cass. He knows what he's doing."

Eden was far from reassured.

She felt frightened.

And angry.

How could he have left without telling her first?

"I'd like to introduce you to my husband," Eloise said. "I'm afraid it won't be the first time I will have to do so. Elmer, this is Eden. Eden, this is Elmer."

Elmer started to stand.

Dayne helped him to his feet.

He shuffled across the kitchen on slippers with argyle

socks showing beneath his slacks, followed closely by his wife. When they reached Eden, Elmer took her hand between his, his thin skin like paper.

Eloise patted him on the back. "He's going to have a rest. And I'm going to watch my show in the sewing room so you can watch television in the living room. Please help yourself to coffee and bagels. There's fresh fruit in the refrigerator."

Eden watched them go—Eloise and Elmer. An adorable couple who reminded her of the retirement facility she and Erik used to visit in San Diego. It felt like a different life. Like a movie she'd watched a long time ago, featuring a naive girl who had swallowed all the rhetoric. People living off the grid were criminals. Illegal newspapers were dangerous. Surveillance was a necessary part of a safe and secure life. In that alternate universe, her biggest concern had been how the world treated people like Eloise and Elmer, as though they were a bother. An inconvenience. Sometimes, like they didn't even exist.

It was the way Eden had treated them just now.

She hadn't even smiled.

But how could she smile when her stomach was in knots?

Cassian was gone.

On his way to Baltimore.

"You know," Dayne said, his chair creaking as he

returned to his seat. "That show she watches? It's a little scandalous."

Cleo smirked. "Scandalous, huh?"

"Let's just say it's not Wheel of Fortune." He smiled fondly, then took a sip of his coffee. "They are wonderful people. Truly wonderful. I owe them everything."

"Have you been living here this whole time?" Cleo asked, spreading cream cheese on her bagel.

Dayne nodded. "My house is across the street, but I haven't set foot inside it for twenty-one years. Before The Attack, the Millers were no more than neighbors I saw occasionally, whenever we took our trash out at the same time."

Eden bypassed the coffee. She didn't think it would help calm her racing heart. She served herself a glass of orange juice instead and sat across from Dayne.

"I was in L.A. during The Attack. Otherwise, I would have been in the heart of D.C. By the time I found my way home, the witch hunts had begun. Everyone who was anyone in the media had to go underground."

A story was spun; the media was to blame.

Reporters and journalists and their dangerous agendas were held responsible for the country's rapid decline. Because of them and the proliferation of fake news on social media, America was in a state of chaos. National security was so preoccupied with the internal fighting, they didn't see The Attack coming.

Media moguls were labeled enemies and insurrectionists.

Dayne Johnson, chief among them.

They were rounded up and arrested in droves. But not Dayne, who had vanished into thin air. All this time, he'd been hiding across the street.

"Little did I know, the Millers had a secret room in their basement. A hidden room. When authorities raided the neighborhood, that's where I was. Right under their noses."

"Two decades is a long time to hide." Cleo licked a dollop of cream cheese from her thumb. "How does a guy like you not go mad with boredom?

"I haven't been bored. I've been busy."

"With what?"

He tapped yesterday's edition of *America Underground*. "Who do you think publishes this?"

Cleo gaped.

Dayne chuckled.

Then humored her by answering each one of her rapid-fire questions. How did he start it? How did he run it? Who were his writers? Eden's mind flitted to Cassian's mother. She'd been one of his writers, once upon a time—in the small apartment she'd rented for her and her son. Would Dayne Johnson remember her ten years later? Eden might have asked if not for Cleo and her inquisitive assault. Apparently, the community in

Alexandria wasn't just your standard, run-of-the-mill, off-the-grid community. It was the hub of *America Underground*.

"Wouldn't it be easier if you lived there?" Cleo asked.

"Eloise needs help caring for Elmer. And I prefer a quieter space. I'm able to communicate with my team just fine via the Amber Highway."

At this, Cleo's eyes took on an orb-like glow. "Are you Gollum?"

"No."

"Do you know his identity?"

Dayne winked good-naturedly. "If I did, it's not something I would share now, is it?"

Cleo pressed him for a short while, but the man remained stalwart. Eventually, she moved on to different questions. What was it like before Concordia? Were the networks really spreading false information for the sake of ratings?

"There were a few bad eggs," Dayne said. "But you'll find that in any industry. On the whole, we cared deeply about the truth. America simply needed a scapegoat."

Eden was too distracted to pay attention.

She excused herself into the living room, where she remained glued to Concordia, waiting with bated breath, bracing for the late-breaking news that would surely announce the capture of Cassian Ransom.

35

The directions Dayne had given Cass led to a shady neighborhood in Baltimore. Nondescript shops lined the streets, their windows boarded. He followed the directions on the paper precisely—parking two blocks away, then knocking seven times slowly when he reached the correct door, which was marked with the faded amber outline of a lotus leaf—a trademark of The Amber Highway, one that branded every black-market shop operating within its realm.

Cass pulled his hat low and counted down from thirty. When he reached zero, he would knock seven more times. The sun behind him glinted off the glass door front, giving him a good view of his reflection. He'd opted not to shave completely but had used Dayne's clippers to clean up his neck. Now he was a guy with a close-cut, neatly trimmed beard. As good of a disguise as he was going to get.

As he reached fifteen, he tried not to think about Eden, who would be furious with him. He left without telling her. But what good would have come from waking her when she'd been sleeping so soundly? Cass needed to do something. He needed to move. To act. And so he had. And now here he was, taking a substantial, but necessary risk. If they were going to get answers from Amir, they would need the right equipment.

He lifted his fist and knocked seven times more.

There was a moment—an extended pause—then the turning of a bolt.

A man with a body like Lou's opened the door halfway. He wore a mask and sunglasses, obscuring most of his face. "Yeah?"

Cass handed him the slip of paper on which Dayne had written, with an outline of a yellow lotus leaf that matched the outline on the door, identifying him as friend, not foe. The guy looked at it, then back up. Cass couldn't see his eyes. Couldn't read his face. He had no idea what the man was thinking. Finally, he opened the door the rest of the way—an invitation inside. Cass was patted down in an empty front room. Checked for wires and bugs. The man took Cass's gun. Then he took the crisp, clean bills folded inside a money clip in Cass's back pocket. He thumbed through them while Cass ground his teeth. When the guy finished counting, he returned the money but kept the gun.

"Just for now," he said.

Cass followed the man through a sliding panel that disguised itself as a wall, into a storage room that wasn't empty at all, but lined with occupied shelves.

"What are you looking for?" the man asked.

"Two phones. A couple of trackers. Ghost glasses, if you have any."

Phones and trackers were sold legally, with the right permits. Ghost glasses, however, weren't sold legally at all. They existed solely in the black-market, as they obscured facial recognition software. Any citizen caught wearing them once would pay a hefty fine. Twice and off to jail they would go.

"You're in luck," the man said. "I had a pair come in last week." He unlocked a large safe and removed a pair of the coveted glasses stowed on the top shelf. He set them on the counter and motioned toward a row of nearby shelves stocked with phones. "Cheapest on the left, most expensive on the right." Then he nodded across the room to another shelf. "Trackers are over there."

Over a thousand dollars later, he was reunited with his gun and back in the car sporting his newly acquired glasses, heading to Under Armour headquarters in a much nicer part of the city. Employees parked in a garage that required retinal scans. Cass found an empty side street and made several calls, trying to confirm that Amir Kashif was in the office today. He couldn't find his extension in any of the directories and reaching a human operator who could help him was proving impossible. He booted up his laptop and spent two frustrating hours trying to access one of the many available networks. When he was finally in, he confirmed Amir's place of employment but found no extension. All the while, Concordia played on the radio. The footnote of a story that was a local Chicago break-in had become a national, flashing headline. His name and Eden's name were mentioned every other sentence, making Cass's train-traveled muscles all the sorer.

With a terse exhale, he dialed the number again.

This time—miraculously—a bored-sounding woman answered.

"I'm trying to reach Amir Kashif," Cass said, working hard to keep the frustrated bite from his tone.

"Who?" the lady responded.

"Amir Kashif," he repeated.

"How do you spell that?"

Cass spelled the name.

The typing of computer keys sounded on the other

end. And then, "I'm sorry, but nobody by that name works here."

He blinked several times.

"Are you sure you have the right name?"

Cass looked down at his opened laptop, where he'd pulled up Amir's public profile. Cybersecurity analyst for Under Armour in Baltimore.

"Sir? Are you still there?"

"Yes," he said. "I am. And yes, I'm sure."

He could hear more typing. When the woman finished, her answer was the same. Amir Kashif wasn't in the employee database, which was why Amir Kashif didn't have an extension. Cass disconnected from the call. He rubbed the stubble on his cheek and peered at the large building. He pushed his thumb across his bottom lip, then dropped the phone into the cup holder in the console, set his laptop in the passenger seat, shifted into drive and headed back to Bethesda.

An hour later, Cass drove down Amir's street. There was no garage, and the driveway was empty. So, he parked along the curb, half a block away, and waited. At quarter past seven—after the sun had set and darkness had rolled down the mostly deserted street—Amir returned home.

Cass sank lower in his seat while the man parked his car and stepped out into the night. He strolled up his walk and let himself inside, unaware he had an audience. A light went on in the house. A shadow moved on the other side of the drawn blinds. Cass grabbed one of the trackers and slinked through the dark. He attached the device underneath Amir's rear bumper, safely out of view, then quickly returned to his vehicle.

It was late.

And he was eager to get back to Eden.

As soon as he stepped inside the Miller's home, she was right there. Waiting for him.

And for what felt like the first time since he left this morning, Cass exhaled. Before she could speak, before she could even glower, he pulled her to his chest and wrapped her in a hug.

She melted into him. "Don't do that again."

"I won't," he said, setting his chin on the crown of her head.

They stayed that way for a while, their hearts beating in unison, and when she pulled back, he kept his arms around her as she looked into his face. "Nice glasses."

He crooked an eyebrow. "You like them?"

"I like you."

To that, he kissed her. Without thinking, like it was the most natural thing in the world.

Her lips were soft and unsuspecting.

And then, she wrapped her arms around his neck

and kissed him back. The kind of kiss that would have kept going—a slow burn that built in heat and fervor until the clearing of a throat popped the intoxicating moment.

With his hat askew, he looked over Eden's shoulder.

Cleo stood behind them, smirking. Then her eyes went wide. "Are those ghosts?"

Cass took off the glasses and handed them over to a greedy Cleo, eager to inspect them. While she did, he told them everything—about the masked man and his black-market shop, about Amir not working for Under Armour, about the tracker Cass put on his car, which would enable them to monitor Amir remotely. Before they could decide on their next move, they needed to establish his routine.

Tracking, like train-hopping, required patience.

Only this was far from miserable.

There wasn't much to observe over the weekend. Nothing consistent, anyway. Amir stayed close to home—running the occasional commonplace errand. Which meant they spent Saturday and Sunday making themselves at home with Elmer and Eloise Miller, who were sweet, and Dayne Johnson, who was only slightly pompous and naturally inquisitive. An expected trait for someone who had dedicated most of his life to journalism. At first, Cass was hesitant to tell him anything. But reason won in the end. A guy like Dayne might have a piece of the puzzle they were trying so hard to put together. They told him handpicked pieces of their story, off the record. He'd never heard of The Monarch or this group called Invictus that seemed to be another name for Interitus. But he was very interested in the pamphlet and the recruitment database they'd found in the Bryson's safe.

All the while, Cleo was in heaven, learning the ins and outs of the illegal newspaper trade. And the kiss between Eden and Cass had breached some sort of dam. Gone was the torturous self-restraint that had marked their time at Lou's, replaced by the most rousing combination of deep affection and tantalizing desire. They spent plenty of time alone and Cass found himself relaxing, knowing things couldn't get too carried away with Eloise humming in the next room.

On Monday, Amir didn't go to Baltimore.

He drove to Fort Meade.

When his car was parked, they pulled up his exact location.

"No way!" Cleo practically hollered.

It was a warranted reaction. For the location was that of the NSA.

Cass had stared, deeply unsettled. They were wanted fugitives with a growing bounty on their heads, tracking a man who worked for a powerful government agency. A man who had connections to Prudence Dvorak, who was linked to Karik Volkova.

His car didn't move again until 5:10 PM, when he exited the parking lot.

He merged onto the highway without making any pit stops.

When the blinking dot that was Amir's vehicle reached Bethesda, it didn't wind its way to Amir's home address, but stopped along the town's derelict thoroughfare. This time, Cleo donned the ghost glasses and left to see if she could find out where he was. Cass and Eden stayed behind as she reported everything via phone. Amir was inside a diner, sitting alone at a table in the window. The waitress brought him food. He gave her a polite nod and dug in. When he finished, he paid and left. Then pulled into his driveway at quarter after seven.

The next day, the same routine unfurled. At exactly ten after seven, he left for work. His car remained at NSA headquarters until ten after five. He didn't tarry in Fort Meade, but headed straight to Bethesda, where he would grab dinner at the diner—a Reuben and a house salad with French dressing. This time, Eden left to watch him—the only place they could as his blinds remained drawn at his house.

At 7 PM, he paid his bill, nodded politely at the waitress, gathered up his belongings and went home.

This was his routine on Monday.

On Tuesday.

And on Wednesday.

Cass was beginning to think this *was* a wild goose chase. A euphoric, perfect wild goose chase. One that could happily go on for days. Weeks. Months.

But then Thursday came and Amir deviated from his routine.

36

Nineteen days had passed since Eden rode away on Cassian's bike. Twelve since their faces became headline news, and Jane decided to be brave.

Ever since, the adults had become obsessed. They studied the print-outs from Barrett and they studied those same images on Dr. Norton's computer, where they could zoom in and zoom out of Jane's system at will. Every day, Jack made the commute from his home in Milwaukee to Dr. Norton's cabin to study them.

There'd been one tip that led authorities to San Diego but didn't pan out. And then, nothing but an entire nation on the lookout with no promising leads.

The world was in a holding pattern.

Jane and Barrett, too.

He hadn't forgotten any more names, and she hadn't

experienced any more blasts of sound. But a relapse felt inevitable. They had diagnosed the problem, but they had no clue how to fix it. The days were long, and Barrett was going stir crazy. He had read and memorized all of Dr. Norton's books, everything in their files, and every random fact and figure he cared to research online. With nothing left to do, they took to raiding Dr. Norton's game cupboard.

They sat in the center of Jane's bed, whiling away the hours playing mancala, backgammon, dominoes, and Gin Rummy 500. Barrett filled the quiet with stories of his childhood, of his family—so absolutely opposite from Jane's experience that they might as well have been fairytales from a book.

Currently, he was talking to her about the time his brothers tried to sneak their pet guinea pig to school in Jameson's backpack when, outside, Jack's car tires came to a stop on the gravel. They abandoned their half-played game of mancala. Jane grabbed her sack of treasures and hurried outside with Barrett.

Jack gave them a curt nod as he strode toward the front porch.

Barrett launched into an idea he had—a potential new angle—as the two went inside.

Jane remained where she was, enjoying the cool breeze on her face. The sound of rustling leaves that had changed into vibrant shades of yellow and orange. The scampering of squirrels. The beating of insect wings. And …

She tilted her head, registering the familiar thump-thump, thump-thump of a human heart. Not from the cabin, but from inside Jack's car.

The back door opened.

With a gasp, Jane took a lurching step away as a girl crawled out into the open.

A human girl with long auburn hair and bright green eyes and a fierce expression. She came to her feet, looking from Jane to the bulging pillowcase hugged tight to her chest, to the cabin behind her.

"Who are you?" she demanded.

With a squeak, Jane hid behind her hair.

"What is my father doing here? And was that …" The girl narrowed her eyes at the house. "Was that *Barrett Barr*, the kid who's been missing since the summer?"

Jane took another step away.

The girl looked at her strangely, then noticed a curtain fluttering inside the opened kitchen window.

She crept closer, hunching between the window and the front door as the conversation swirled out into the open, so loud a person didn't need superhuman senses to hear it.

"There's no Queen Bee," Jack said. "Her system doesn't have one."

His excited declaration was met with silence.

"It's why her signal is so much weaker than Eden's and Barrett's. It's not there. She doesn't have a master node."

"Does that mean …?" Ruth's question trailed off into nothing.

"She can't be controlled."

Jane slapped her hand over her mouth.

Inside, Jack paced. She could hear his footsteps. "Now we just need to figure out how. How did she do it? And how can we do the same thing to Eden and Barrett and Ellery?"

The girl beside Jane shifted.

Jane could feel her voice—her words—burrowing deeper and deeper. To a place that could never be reached.

"Will she let us take more images?" Jack asked.

"I don't know," Barrett said. "It was really hard for her to take the ones she did. I mean, you should have seen her. She was legitimately terrified. I think something traumatic must have happened to her that makes the setup downstairs really triggering."

"Well, she's going to have to get over it."

"Jack," Ruth admonished.

"Your daughter's life depends on it. *My* daughter's life depends on it."

The girl shifted again—her body coiled and alert.

"How would more imaging even be helpful?" Barrett asked.

"I don't know. But I do know something that *would* be helpful. Jane *talking*. She knows. She has to know."

Jane buried her face in the pillowcase.

She did know.

As hard as she tried to forget, she would always know.

"You can't force her to talk," Dr. Norton said.

Silence ensued.

A long, tension-filled silence with nothing but the drone of Concordia News in the background.

And then, "Why are you still messing with that? Surely you have the whole thing memorized by now."

"Nervous habit," Barrett said apologetically.

Jack was talking about the device. The projections. Barrett had a habit of mindlessly scrolling through them like a person flipping through channels on the television.

"Can we please turn that off?" Jack barked.

"It's the only way we'll know if Eden and Cassian are caught," Alexander said.

With those words, the girl spun into action.

She marched up the porch steps and shoved through the front door.

Jane followed skittishly.

"Eden and Cassian? As in, *Eden Pruitt* and *Cassian Ransom*?" The girl looked around the room, from Dr.

Norton to Alexander and Ruth Pruitt, both of whom had been on the news, to Jack, who had gone an alarming shade of gray, to Barrett Barr and the holographic projection that had come to a stop on the map with the five glitching dots. "And you're the missing kid, Barrett Barr. Dad, what in the world is going on?"

"How did you get here?" Jack said, his voice a low, ominous rumble that made Jane want to flee.

But the girl—Ellery—didn't cower. She folded her arms defiantly and lifted her chin. "I hid in your trunk."

Jack swore.

"You wouldn't tell me anything! Mom and I run off to Rome with zero explanation. Chicago blows up. We come home and you've lost about twenty pounds you didn't need to lose. You reek like cigarettes, which means you're smoking again, and you keep leaving without saying where you're going."

Jack took Ellery's arm and stepped toward the door. "I'm taking you home."

She jerked her arm free, then strode to the nearest armchair, where she parked herself obstinately. "I'm not leaving."

"Then I guess I'll have to drag you."

"Jack," Ruth said. "I think you should tell her."

Jack threw daggers with his eyes.

"She has the right to know," Barrett agreed.

The room erupted.

Everyone jumped in.

And in the midst of all that arguing, something strange occurred. Not another glitch. But another dot. On the map. Only this one wasn't jumping around. It was steady and very suddenly … there. Nobody but Jane noticed. They were too busy arguing. And before she could find a way to notify them, a seventh dot appeared.

She squeaked.

Barrett looked at her.

Then he looked at the map, where an eighth dot materialized.

37

Eden was beginning to suspect that Amir Kashif was a dead end. He moved from Chicago to Bethesda because he worked for the NSA and while that surprising discovery had been a high note of intrigue, his actual life turned out to be quite boring. Not to mention lonely.

Their search had come to a standstill. They would have to find another lead, like one of the twelve girls who went to the Bryson's home every Thursday. The thought of returning to Chicago carved a deep pit in Eden's stomach. The trip itself felt like an impossibility. The city, a hostile danger zone. Not to mention, she was growing quite fond of Eloise and Elmer. She liked being here. She especially liked being here with Cassian.

When she was with him, she could ignore everything else.

Her worried parents in Wisconsin.

The mysterious pain in her temple that came and went without warning.

The national manhunt unfolding outside these walls.

Even the nanobots inside her; they could still be controlled.

None of that had changed. And yet, their time at the Miller residence was a reprieve from the insanity that had marked Eden's life ever since she came home to a ransacked house in Eagle Bend. But reprieves couldn't last forever. Leaving felt inevitable. When it came to Amir Kashif, there was nothing to see.

Until 5:12 pm on Thursday, the twenty-fourth of October, when he departed from his routine.

Eden sat up straighter, watching the flashing dot that was Amir's car bypass the highway that would take him to Bethesda and head north instead.

Cassian sat up, too.

They were in the Miller's basement. Cassian's laptop, on a rickety table they were using as a makeshift desk. Upstairs, Cleo was in the living room with Dayne, chatting about the most recent edition of *America Underground*. Eloise was making dinner in the kitchen, humming along to Frank Sinatra while Elmer sat at the table, his pencil scratching against paper. Eloise gave him a Word Search every evening. To keep his brain sharp. Which was, when it came to Elmer, a losing battle.

"Where's he going?" she asked.

Cassian didn't answer. Cassian didn't know.

They watched—transfixed by the moving dot—for forty minutes. Until it stopped and stayed in a residential neighborhood in Baltimore.

Cassian zoomed in on the location and jotted the address.

It was a large, gated home owned by—

"Aigner," Eden said, coming out of her chair.

It was a name she knew. She hurried to the cigar box they kept tucked in Cassian's pack and pulled out the pamphlet.

There it was.

Melody Aigner.

The very first name on the back.

One of ninety-three Magnes Matres.

And here Amir was, inside a home that belonged to Jason and Veronica Aigner, surviving parents listed in Melody's obituary.

The inevitability of leaving vanished.

This wasn't a dead end.

Whatever was going on, Amir was involved.

Amir, with the NSA.

Cassian pulled up drone surveillance, but they couldn't see anything beyond the large trees covering the property. Amir's car remained. Dinner was prepared. They brought Cassian's laptop upstairs, where they filled Cleo in and ate Eloise's chicken casserole.

Amir's car didn't move until 8 pm.

The property gates opened. His car exited. Followed by a parade of eight more.

"It's Thursday," Cassian said meaningfully.

The same night the Brysons hosted a meeting of their own. One in which twelve girls attended, all of them on a holographic database stored in what was quite literally a monarch butterfly.

The bird's-eye view prevented them from collecting license plate numbers.

They would have to collect them next Thursday, assuming the meeting was a regular event. One of them would have to drive into Baltimore. The only time they drove anywhere was in the evenings to watch Amir in the diner. They took turns, leaving through the garage, driving the Miller's car, always under the cover of dark. Always right here, in the ghost town that was Bethesda. The trips lasted an hour and a half altogether and came with little risk. Going into Baltimore would be something else entirely.

Eden pushed the unnerving possibility away. They had an entire week until then.

But then Friday came and Amir went off script again.

Instead of heading to the diner when he reached Bethesda, his car stopped along an unfamiliar side street.

Eden wasted no time.

She grabbed the glasses and her beanie, stuffed her shoulder-length hair out of sight, took one of the phones, the Miller's keys, and made a beeline for the door.

Cassian snagged her arm.

"Be careful," he said, his eyes brimming with intensity.

When she reached Amir's car—which was dark and empty—she parked a half-block away and slipped out into the drizzle, with her hood up. She tried to see into the storefront windows, but almost all of them were boarded. The ones that weren't were as dark and empty as Amir's car.

Where had he gone? And what was he doing?

She looked up and down the street, noting the number of cars parked along the curb. Not just hers and Amir's, but several. Where were the owners? She looked at the windows above the stores. None of them were lit. They weren't apartments. So why were so many cars parked on this abandoned street?

Eden tried a door.

It was locked.

She tried another.

Locked.

As she approached the next, she could hear the distinct sound of voices. Not a specific conversation, but the low, quiet chatter of many.

The door swooshed open.

Eden ducked into the shadows, her heart lurching into her throat as Amir opened an umbrella and stepped out into the rain.

She caught a glimpse inside before the door shut all the way. There was a bar. And tables. And people. Inside a nameless store with boarded-up windows. It reminded Eden of a speakeasy. Only this wasn't the prohibition. Drinking was perfectly legal, so why the cover-up?

Amir crossed the street to his vehicle.

Eden's phone rang—loud and disruptive.

She forgot to silence the ringer.

She answered quickly with fumbling fingers, eager to silence the sound. Thankfully, Amir was already in his car, driving away.

"He's on the move," Cass said.

"I know. He just came out of a ... private drinking lounge."

"Private drinking lounge?" Cass repeated. "Was he meeting someone?"

"I don't know." Eden stared at the door, wishing she could go inside. Knowing it would be too conspicuous if she did.

"He just parked at the diner," Cleo said in the background.

Eden climbed into the car and made her way to the usual looking spot. Sure enough, Amir sat at his table in the window as the waitress brought him a Reuben and a side salad. Eden sunk lower in her seat with her hood up, her attention so zeroed in on Amir it was a wonder he couldn't feel it.

And then it happened.

Something so discreet, she might have imagined it.

But no. She'd seen him do it—so imperceptibly, she would have missed it had she not been watching with such unwavering ferocity. Amir Kashif had reached inside the pocket of his shirt and removed something. Then he'd wiped his hands and left that something inside a crumpled napkin.

He paid his bill.

He nodded politely at the waitress.

Then he left.

Eden sunk deeper into her seat, her eyes glued to the napkin on the table.

Amir drove away.

Eden remained.

She watched as the waitress picked up the napkin and slipped it into the front pocket of her waist apron.

Eden's pulse quickened.

Why would someone put a crumpled napkin in their pocket, especially when the crumpled napkin belonged to another person?

The waitress moved out of sight.

Eden slipped out of the car and darted beneath an

awning, hoping a different angle might provide a view of the young woman. She needed to see what happened to that napkin.

A hulking figure on a scooter drove past, tires splashing up rainwater, then pulled into the diner's alleyway. Eden pressed herself further into shadow as the side door opened and the waitress appeared, holding a to-go order.

She handed the bag to the hooded figure.

Eden stared hard at the waitress's pocket, trying to figure out if the crumpled napkin was still inside. Was it there, or had she put it in the bag and handed it off to the mystery person on the bike? Eden's heart raced, adrenaline coursing as the hooded figure drove away and the waitress went back inside.

She wasn't sure what to do.

Stay here and watch the waitress or follow the bike?

She could always find the waitress. She'd worked the same shift at the diner every night this week. But the person on the bike? Eden might never have this opportunity again. And so, she made her decision. She didn't get back in the car. That would be too visible, especially on these empty streets. Instead, she ran, the rain soaking through her hooded sweatshirt—stopping whenever she got too close, waiting to see which way the person would turn. Further and further, to a wooded park on the outskirts of town.

Eden breathed heavily and crept forward as her target hid the scooter in a bramble of bushes, then trudged over wet leaves. She followed from afar, her eyesight like a high-powered night-vision zoom lens. She watched as the tall, broad figure neared a terrace of wooden planks raised above the ground—a sun deck in the middle of nature. A place for park-goers to stop and rest and enjoy their surroundings when it was warm, and the sun was shining. Not a place to go at night in the dark in the rain.

The person looked around, then kicked through a pile of leaves at the base of the terrace. Eden hid behind a tree as the figure got down on all fours, stuffed the to-go bag underneath the wooden planks, and slithered in after it. Then the leaves re-accumulated, like the person on the other side was shifting them to hide his or her tracks.

Eden leaned against the tree, stumped.

Intrigued.

Excited.

Something was going on.

She stared at the deck.

Was the person homeless? Living off the grid?

She waited to see if the figure would reappear. She waited until she was soaking wet and shivering, too. Then she ran back to the car, returned to the Millers, and relayed the entire bizarre scenario to Cassian and Cleo.

38

Eden stood behind a tree, staring at Cassian as he made his way toward the bramble of bushes where the scooter hid. Cleo sat on the limb above her, a pair of binoculars in hand. It was early morning. A thin layer of ice frosted the ground. Fog hovered in patches as pink sunbeams crested the horizon.

Last night, Eden had asked Dayne about the existence of a local speakeasy. Was there one in Bethesda? If there was, the infamous media mogul didn't know about it. Eden had spent the rest of the night hardly sleeping, her mind a beehive of buzzing thoughts.

She could have imagined the whole thing. Amir reaching into his pocket. Placing something into the crumpled tissue. There was a very real chance that her mind had played a trick. There was a very real chance the three of them were spying on a homeless person who'd found a warm, dry place to sleep on a rainy night.

Her uncertainty rose with the sun.

And now her heart was pounding out of her chest, her attention zipping from Cassian to the terrace, positive the person sleeping beneath would choose this moment to wake up and crawl out into the open.

"Are you sure he's still under there?" Cleo asked.

"The bike's still there," Eden replied, her attention returning to the bramble of bushes.

Cassian had reached his target.

Eden silently urged him to hurry as he bent down and attached the tracking device beneath the left foot pedal. In the distance, a lady with a Great Dane wound her way up the path.

The muscles in Eden's shoulders went taut. She hissed at Cass, who spotted the woman and ducked out of sight.

The lady stopped on the deck. Sat on a bench. Unleashed her dog.

The giant canine lifted its nose into the air and sniffed.

Cleo muttered an expletive.

Eden's entire body coiled. What if the dog caught their scent? What if it raced toward her and Cleo, or Cass, with sharp barks and raised hackles? What if it blew their cover and despite Cassian's facial hair and

Eden's beanie and Cleo's new style, the owner immediately recognized them? They shouldn't have done this. Not together. No matter how badly all of them wanted to go, only one of them should have. Time had made them foolish. They were much too exposed.

The dog caught a scent.

Thankfully, not theirs.

Eden watched as it ambled off the deck, its tail wagging as the lady made a phone call. Eden imagined the mystery guy underneath, listening to the footsteps overhead. The dog sniffing around the leaves that hid the entrance to his sleeping quarters.

Its tail wagged faster, then it let loose a deep bark and started to dig.

"Charlie," the lady beckoned, pulling a ball from her pocket while still on the phone.

The dog looked up with a leaf stuck to its muzzle.

"Go get it!" The lady tossed the ball toward a line of trees. Charlie abandoned the scent to make chase. After several rounds of fetch, a jogger came up the path. The lady ended her phone call, pocketed the ball, and leashed Charlie. She nodded a friendly hello at the passing jogger, and a few minutes later, the path was empty again.

A pair of squirrels scampered along the bench, then skittered up a tree. Birds twittered in branches, hiding in leaves that had turned with the fall.

Cassian joined her.

The person under the deck didn't appear.

She couldn't imagine he was still sleeping. Not after that lady and her dog. She also couldn't imagine staying under there for much longer. Eventually, he would have to stretch his legs. But time ticked by with no signs of movement, and Eden could no longer bear the wait.

With her eyes closed, she imagined extending her ears like they were on a fishing line that she had cast toward the deck. She registered nothing. No heartbeat. No breath. But perhaps she was too far away, even for her. She had to get closer and there was nothing suspicious about running in the park. She crept out from the trees onto the path and jogged. If someone came up the path, she would look down. Thankfully, the path remained empty. She stopped when she reached the deck. Pretended to stretch, her ears on high alert. But there was nothing to hear, which meant the guy was dead or no longer there.

She sat on the edge of the deck, near the disrupted pile of leaves. She pretended to tie her shoe, then finished the work Charlie had started—all the while listening. Just in case she'd missed it before. When she cleared the leaves away, she looked around—up and down the path—then went for it. Eden got on all fours and shimmied inside as Cassian and Cleo approached behind her.

"Holy crap," she muttered.

"What?" Cleo said.

"It's a ... den." This wasn't just dry space under some slats of wood. This was cozy, dug to a depth a person of average height could stand in. There was a large tarp lining the ground, a sleeping bag and a pillow, and a makeshift table created by a broken, upturned barrel. There was no empty to-go bag or empty container or crumpled napkin, which meant the guy who lived here had taken it with him.

Eden crawled all the way inside. The tarp crinkled beneath her shoes as Cleo came in behind her, then Cassian.

"This is wild." Cleo said each word like it was its own sentence.

It was wild.

And mysterious.

The guy had obviously left. But why was the scooter still in the thicket?

Cleo set her binoculars on the upturned barrel, then lost her footing.

"What the—?" She stumbled, the tarp giving way beneath her. Once she recovered, she tapped the spot with her shoe. When it didn't connect with solid ground, she grabbed the corner of the tarp and yanked it up.

There was a tunnel.

An actual tunnel.

Big enough for a person to crawl into.

Eden stared—wide-eyed, dumbstruck—as Cassian turned on his phone's flashlight and shined it inside.

The opening was narrow, the tunnel itself significantly bigger. A person wouldn't have to slither through it like a snake or even crawl on all fours. It was big enough to walk. Perhaps not fully upright but walk all the same.

"Where do you think it leads?" Cassian asked.

There was only one way to find out.

As if reading her mind, Cleo moved toward the tunnel.

Cassian grabbed her shoulder before she could wriggle inside.

"Come on, Cass," Cleo said. "We have to see where this goes."

"We have to be smart."

"Seeing where this goes *is* smart."

"And if we encounter this mystery person along the way?"

"Eden's superhuman. She can knock him out and we'll run."

"And when he comes to? What then? Say goodbye to getting answers. Amir will know we're here. He'll know we're looking. We'd be a lot smarter to track the bike and see where this guy goes. See who he is."

Cleo took a breath. "You and Eden have a bounty on

your heads. If we wait until next Friday to see if this happens again—to try and establish some routine—that bounty is going to be in the millions."

Cass shoved his hand toward the tunnel's mouth. "That's better than crawling into something completely blind."

Cleo heaved a sigh and looked at Eden like she had the final say.

Eden twisted her mouth to the side. She saw Cassian's point. She understood his hesitancy. But she couldn't look away from that tunnel. Nor could she quench the curiosity thrumming through her veins.

"I think we should check it out," she said.

A muscle ticked in Cassian's jaw.

"You don't have to come."

He rolled his eyes. "If you're going, I'm going."

Cleo let loose a quiet whoop and grabbed her binoculars.

With a thrill of anticipation, Eden crawled inside.

The tunnel veered south at a downward angle, descending deeper underground.

Cassian led the way with the light from his phone.

Eden kept her ears perked for any signs of danger.

And Cleo kept muttering about the wildness of it all. About drug cartels and underground tunnels and a documentary she watched once upon a time. Eden wondered how long it had taken to dig something like this. They walked a mile at least, and then the tunnel came to a stop. Eden could see its end up ahead. A wall of roots and compact soil. Without a trace of the hooded figure anywhere. Confusion bubbled inside her, but then she felt it. A cold draft.

Another tunnel—one that led straight down.

Cass shined his light.

Whoever had created this had dug through the cement beneath and added a ladder.

After a moment's hesitation, Cass climbed down.

Eden followed.

She landed on a set of rusted train tracks inside a massive tunnel that went in both directions. Eden had been expecting a sewer system. Instead, they were in—

"This is the DC Metro," Cass said.

The DC Metro.

Goosebumps marched across Eden's skin.

She swallowed the dryness in her throat as Cassian walked one way, studying the ground beneath him. Then he turned around and went the other way, stopping to examine a small pile of debris. "Tire tracks," he said, bending into a crouch.

"Tire tracks," Eden repeated.

Cass straightened and wiped his hands. "Judging by the tracks, it was a three-wheeler. Like an ATV. And he went that way." He nodded toward Washington D.C.

The three of them stood in the silence—bloated with

implication—until Eden shook her head. "How can he have gone toward D.C.?" It made no sense. The place was a radioactive graveyard. Completely off limits, unless someone wanted to grow a third arm.

Neither Cassian nor Cleo had an answer.

"Could it be an off-the-grid community?" Eden asked.

"It would have been on the map," Cass replied.

"Unless this one has gone rogue," Cleo said. So rogue, they were disconnected from all the others. Maybe Concordia reporters were partially right. Maybe this one was harboring members of Interitus. Maybe this one was home to The Monarch.

As Cleo hypothesized aloud, Eden heard something.

The grumble of a motor in the distance.

She shushed them quickly, then gestured for Cass to turn off the light.

The tunnel went black.

The sound of the motor drew nearer.

Cassian grabbed her arm. Eden grabbed Cleo's. The three of them hurried in the opposite direction, around a bend, and flattened themselves against the wall as a beam of light sliced through the dark.

An ATV rumbled toward them.

They ducked lower—beneath the beam of light—as the driver pulled to a stop beneath the ladder. Immediately, Eden knew this wasn't the same person from last night. That guy had been hulking—too big for the moped he rode on. This person was noticeably smaller. When he pulled to a stop, Eden could make out his features and his approximate age. A middle-aged man with thinning, blonde hair. He didn't notice them at all—didn't even think to look—as he cut the engine and the darkness returned.

Eden could hear him climbing the ladder, then slowly disappearing overhead.

Nobody moved.

They stayed in their crouched positions until Cleo released a long, shaky breath.

Cassian turned on his light.

"That wasn't the guy from last night," Eden said.

Cleo made a beeline for the ATV, her fingers stopping on the key in the ignition. The man hadn't taken it with him. Probably because he didn't need to worry about theft down here in a secret tunnel.

"We could take this," Cleo suggested, gripping the handlebar. "Follow the tunnel. See where it goes."

Cass could get on behind her. Eden could run beside them. It would be much quicker than walking, but the sound of the motor was loud, and they couldn't be loud. They had to move slowly, with the utmost caution. If they were headed into Interitus headquarters, there would be surveillance. Besides, if that guy returned and saw the ATV missing, they'd be in serious trouble.

They followed the tracks on foot, Eden's ears focused in front, their eyes peeled for cameras, motion sensors. Old-fashioned booby traps. They reached an abandoned rail car with a wooden ramp that would allow an ATV to ride up and through. Cass drew his gun as they crept inside.

The railcar was abandoned.

Rusted over.

Its rear half in the tunnel. Its front half out, where the tunnel opened into a station with a platform and a sign that said Tenleytown. They stayed hidden in the railcar as Cassian reached into his front pocket and removed the small disc they'd used inside the Bryson's home—its twin no longer in their possession, as they had to leave it behind when they escaped through the basement window and ran for their lives. He nodded toward a camera mounted at the far end of the station.

Eden's stomach dipped.

Cassian was right.

This stretch of underground was being monitored.

He threw the disc with a decisive flick of his wrist. It sailed through the air, connected with the camera's lens, and the tiny red light went dark. After a quick beat, the three of them crept through the open door onto the platform. Eden shuffled to the escalators and looked up to the blocked-off entrance above. They hurried down the length of the platform and once they were out of sight, Cassian removed the disc.

They continued on in this way.

Mile after mile.

Station after station.

Until they reached one that didn't have an obstructed entrance at the top of the escalator.

Eden followed it up, creeping carefully, her senses on high alert. When she stepped out into the open, she gaped. She'd seen pictures. Most of them taken months after The Attack. But pictures on a screen weren't the same as seeing something up close and personal.

They were standing in Washington D.C.—a once-thriving hub of history and politics and tourism and architecture. Now, a ruin—decimated and abandoned and left in nature's indomitable grip. Toppled buildings and upturned cars overrun with vines and weeds. There was no sign of life other than the squirrels and chipmunks and birds that had built their nests in the rubble. According to the government, nuclear activity remained prevalent in the area. Both here and in New York. Breathing this air could be deadly. They shouldn't be here. But the squirrels and birds looked fine. And Eden couldn't help herself. An insatiable curiosity drew her.

She crept down the length of the block, then stopped in the middle of a plaza with a fountain in its center. It was made of white marble, double-tiered and adorned with three sculptures. A female figure with long hair holding a boat in her right hand while caressing a seagull with her left, her foot mounted on a dolphin. The other two figures were nude. A female with long hair, holding a globe in her left hand. And a male wrapped in a ship's sail, holding a conch shell.

"This is Dupont Circle," Cleo said.

They took it in, probably longer than they should have before finally returning underground.

At Farragut North, the entrance was collapsed. Part of the tunnel, too, but a path had been cleared, with ATV tracks in the rubble.

They walked faster, propelled by a growing sense of urgency.

The next stop was Metro Center in the heart of Washington DC. As they came out into the station, Eden heard the rumble of an approaching vehicle. They hurried up the escalator, above ground to hide from view while a utility vehicle zoomed past below them, the driver speaking into a walkie-talkie. "I'm heading there now. Must be a short circuit. Over."

"Figure it out, please," came the reply. "We need our surveillance working."

They'd noticed.

The surveillance system was cutting in and out because of the disc.

Not until the utility vehicle was long gone did they continue onward.

Eden knew where they were headed. She'd seen and studied plenty of maps over the course of her schooling. Their next stop was Union Station. Just north of Ground Zero, where the Library of Congress and the Capitol Building once stood.

When they reached it, they held back as two men loaded supplies from the back of a trailer and stacked them next to an escalator. Once the trailer was unloaded, they carried the supplies up the stairs. Eden's heart thundered as she and Cassian and Cleo crept up a different escalator to the mezzanine, where there was a crumbling marble staircase, piles of rubble, and the haunting whispers of screams silenced long ago.

But Eden could hear their echoes—the din of terror and confusion as this gargantuan building shook and all the glass exploded and the ceiling fell and impossible heat engulfed everything, turning one of the country's architectural gems into something straight off the set of an apocalypse.

One man's walkie-talkie squawked.

"The security cameras are down again. Over."

The man unclipped it from his belt. "Yeah, we know. Xavier's checking them out now. Over."

Eden was so absorbed—so dialed into the conversation ahead of her—she wasn't listening for anything behind. Until she heard the sharp intake of breath.

"Don't move."

She whirled around.

A woman was holding a knife to Cleo's neck.

39

"Hands in the air. Now!" A manic spark gleamed in the woman's dark, familiar eyes, like she would like nothing more than to carry out the threat pressed against Cleo's throat.

Regret slammed through Eden. So did recognition.

Here was Prudence Dvorak, in the flesh.

And they never should have come.

Cassian put his hands up, a muscle ticking in his jaw while Eden's mind raced. Could her speed and strength get them out of this situation she'd led them into? She stared hard at the blade poised against Cleo's carotid artery. Eden might be superhuman, but that didn't mean she could get to Cleo before that blade did irreparable damage.

"Did you come for the asset?" Prudence wrapped one arm tightly around Cleo's waist, her attention darting from Cassian to Eden, her dark hair in a long braid that tumbled over her shoulder.

Eden blinked dumbly. *The asset?*

"Are you spies for Swarm?"

"Swarm?" Eden said.

"I'm not a fool. And neither are you. So stop playing dumb." Dvorak pressed the knife harder, making Cleo drop her binoculars with a wince. "Or so help me, I will send a message to dear Pater written in her blood."

Pater.

Swarm.

The asset.

Prudence Dvorak was speaking a different language.

"We're not playing dumb," Eden blurted, her voice a tremble. "We don't know what you're talking about."

Dvorak glared, the manic gleam in her eyes still very much alight. "Eden Pruitt, an eighteen-year-old fugitive. Cassian *Gray*, the Underground Fighter."

"How do you know that?" Cassian asked in a low, ominous tone. To authorities and reporters, he was Cassian *Ransom* with no connection to fighting.

"You think we wouldn't do our research? Your faces have been all over the news. Wanted, with ties to *Interitus*." Prudence spat the word like it was bitter gall on her tongue. "And then you show up in Bethesda."

"How do you know we were in Bethesda?" Eden asked, alarm spiking through her chest.

Prudence didn't answer.

Footfalls sounded behind them.

Someone was coming. But Eden couldn't look away from the knife at Cleo's neck. Cleo's eyelids fluttered, then opened wide with shock and confusion at the sight of whoever this someone was. "Francesca?"

The name was so jarring, Eden couldn't help herself. She looked.

And there, coming to an abrupt halt, was a girl every bit as familiar as Prudence Dvorak. She had the same pixie haircut. The same androgynous face. The same glass eye.

But it made no sense.

Francesca was dead. Her name struck through and marked deceased on the database they'd found in the Bryson's safe. And yet, here she was. Very much alive. With Prudence Dvorak. Another jarring, confounding fact. Dvorak and the Brysons were in league with one another. Francesca had run away from the Bryson's. Then—supposedly—she died. So why was she here, with Dvorak, staring suspiciously at Cleo?

"You two know each other?" Prudence demanded.

"She's the doctor's daughter," Francesca replied. "The one who helped me with this." Francesca gestured to her eye.

"We thought you were dead," Eden said.

"Death was the only way I'd ever be free."

"Free from what?"

Cassian didn't wait for an answer. He pulled his gun and aimed it at Dvorak. Francesca pulled a semi-automatic and aimed it at Cassian. Eden's heart leapt into her throat, her muscles coiling like a snake, ready to strike Francesca before she could pull that trigger.

Cassian cocked his gun. "Drop the knife or you'll get a bullet through your head."

"You put a bullet through her head, and I'll put several bullets through yours," Francesca said.

Cleo clutched Prudence's forearm, as though trying to create enough space between the knife and her neck so she could catch a breath.

The woman didn't relent. "Tell me who sent you."

"We sent ourselves," Eden answered. And when the knife drew blood, she threw up her hands and blurted, "We're looking for the Monarch."

Prudence narrowed her eyes. *"Looking for?"*

"Yes."

"We're supposed to believe you aren't one of his disciples?"

His. The Monarch was a man.

"Wouldn't you know if we were?" Cassian said.

"Why would I know?" Prudence replied.

"Because he's your boss."

Prudence smirked. "You think The Monarch is my superior?"

Eden thought about the tattooed man who took the cyanide pill. She thought about his dying words. She thought about Mordecai on the roof. *A gift for the Monarch.* They served him. Followed him. If Dvorak wasn't The Monarch, then The Monarch was in a higher position than she. "Did he take over for Karik Volkova? Is he the new leader of Interitus?"

Prudence scoffed. "Interitus doesn't exist, you silly little girl."

Doesn't exist?

Before she could process the words, a cold barrel pressed against the base of her skull.

"Drop the gun." The deep words were pointed at Cassian.

But the weapon was pointed at her.

Cassian's attention shifted from Eden to the male figure behind her, anger and fear flashing in his eyes. But she wasn't afraid. She was curious. What would happen if this man pulled the trigger? How fast would her nanobots repair such damage, and what would Dvorak do when they did? Apparently, Cassian didn't want to find out.

He set his weapon down.

Eden was shoved against a wall, her hands gruffly yanked behind her back as the giant-of-a-guy with the deep voice grabbed Cassian and did the same. He was six foot five at least, with broad shoulders and light brown skin and tightly curled hair that was buzzed on the sides and long on top. He wore the same hoodie as the guy on the moped.

He was the guy on the moped.

Eden had to restrain herself. Squash the instinct to spin around and break the guy's nose.

The knife was no longer at Cleo's neck.

Eden could make her move. Go on the offensive.

She knew she would come out the victor.

But these people had assault rifles. What if they used them against Cleo or Cassian? What if one of them was shot like her father had been shot? It was a risk she wasn't willing to take. And so, she cooperated with the manhandling, pretending to be at their mercy while they bound their hands with zip ties.

Dvorak commanded the guy to escort them to the interrogation room. They were pushed inside a vault-like prison. The door closed with a resounding boom.

A bolt slid into place.

Cassian craned his neck to look out the door's small window. "They don't know who you are. They wouldn't have left us alone in here if they did."

Eden looked at Cleo. A trickle of blood ran between her collarbones and her skin had gone an ashy gray. "Are you okay?"

"Nothing like the threat of imminent death to get a person's heart pumping." Cleo tilted her head one way, then the other, as though stretching a kink from her neck. Eden had a feeling Cleo would rub it if her hands weren't zip-tied behind her back. "What in the world is Francesca doing here? And what did Dvorak mean when she said Interitus doesn't exist?"

This was only the tip of the iceberg when it came to the tumult of questions tumbling through Eden's mind. Swarm. Pater. The asset? Francesca's fake death? The only way she could be free? Eden shook her head. "If Interitus doesn't exist, then who was responsible for the attack on Chicago?"

"Whatever cult the Brysons are a part of," Cassian suggested, still peering out the window.

But wasn't it all the same? The pamphlet. The Magnes Matres. Sanctus Diem. Interitus. Invictus. The Bryson's. Dvorak. The Monarch. They'd assumed they were all one and the same. But the dots didn't connect. Dvorak thought The Monarch had sent them. Dvorak thought they were his spies. All of which pointed to one obvious but puzzling conclusion. Prudence Dvorak and The Monarch were on opposite sides.

"They're coming." Cassian stepped away from the door just as it swung open.

Prudence, Francesca, and the hulking young man in the hoodie appeared, carrying three metal chairs in one hand, his semi-automatic in the other. He unfolded the chairs, then gestured at the three of them to sit.

Obedience was their ammunition.

If they continued to cooperate, they might glean more answers. Already, they'd discovered The Monarch was a man. Dvorak wasn't working with him. And the most intriguing of all—Interitus didn't exist.

"What did you do to our security system?" Prudence asked, fire crackling in her eyes. Fear, too. It was a dangerous combination.

Eden held her tongue.

So did Cassian and Cleo.

Dvorak unclipped her walkie-talkie and pressed the button. "What did you find, Xavier?"

"Nothing's wrong with the mainframe," a staticky voice replied. "I'm checking the individual cameras now. Over."

"Make it quick," Dvorak said, her unwavering attention boring into Eden like a laser beam. "We cannot afford to be blind right now."

With a *copy that* from Xavier, Prudence returned her walkie-talkie to her belt and glared. "How did you find us?"

"We followed Amir Kashif," Eden said.

Dvorak's cheeks went pale. "Amir doesn't come here."

"No, but he passed information to a waitress, who passed it along to him." Eden nodded at the hulking young man wielding the semi-automatic.

Dvorak's attention slid to the guy before returning to Eden. "What do you want with The Monarch?"

Eden stared back at her. She could bluff. Make something up. Or she could continue with her method of truth-telling to see how Prudence responded. She weighed the two options, then went with the latter. "I want to kill him."

At this, Dvorak leaned back on her heels, exchanging a suspicious look with her two comrades. "What reason do you have for wanting him dead?" she finally asked.

"The same reason she faked her death." Eden tipped her chin at Francesca. "Freedom." To live her life without the constant threat of being controlled. Of being hunted down. Of being used. As a gift. As a weapon. In whatever terrorist turf war was unfolding now.

Prudence removed the knife from her belt. She brought the tip of her finger to the tip of the blade and turned the hilt in a slow circle. "And how will killing The Monarch get you this freedom?"

Eden could feel Cassian's tension mounting beside her. He didn't like this game of truth-telling. "He's after her father," he cut in, before Eden could answer otherwise.

Prudence stopped twirling the knife. "Why?"

"Because he brought down Volkova."

Dvorak chuckled, like Cassian was a silly little boy, like Eden was a silly little girl.

"Did I say something funny?" he asked.

"Her father brought down the wrong man."

Eden straightened. "What do you mean?"

"Volkova was nothing more than a puppet. An overeager disciple."

The words were ludicrous.

Preposterous.

Impossible.

Karik Volkova was responsible for the death of millions. He was the leader of a terrorist regime that almost brought down America. Calling him an overeager disciple was akin to calling a devastating tsunami a harmless wave.

"Then who created them?" Cleo blurted.

Her question snatched Dvorak's interest like a Venus flytrap. "Created who?"

Cassian shot Cleo a look that could kill.

Cleo shut her mouth.

Eden opened hers. "A group of weaponized humans."

Dvorak's attention jerked to Eden. "You know about the Electus?"

The *Electus*? It was another foreign term. Like *Swarm* and *Pater*. Eden ground her teeth—so sick of the confusion—when the walkie-talkie at Prudence's waist beeped.

"I found something," came Xavier's voice.

Dvorak slid the device free and brought it to her lips, her attention glued to Eden. "Where are you?"

"Metro Center. There's some kind of ... magnet on the camera."

Without moving, giving nothing away, Eden loosened the zip tie around her wrists.

"Do you want me to remove it?" Xavier asked.

"Yes," Dvorak said. "But carefully."

There was a pause.

A crackling silence.

And then, the loud blast of a siren. So sudden and alarming, a jolt of electricity charged through Eden's veins. Dvorak's eyes went round and wide, fear morphing into terror in the expanding black of her pupils as she turned to Eden with a look of murderous accusation. As though she had set off the alarm.

"It's a raid!" Xavier shouted. "It's a—"

Gunfire silenced his cry as all three walkie-talkies squawked to life. The guy's. Francesca's. Dvorak's. A commotion of beeps. A flurry of voices as the siren continued to blare and footsteps and gunfire sounded outside.

Cleo ducked, like the bullets were whizzing into the room.

"Secure the asset!" Dvorak shouted at the guy. "Get them to the tunnel," she commanded Francesca. Then she flung open the door and raced out into the fray.

"Follow me," Francesca shouted.

Eden broke the zip tie as they ran through the cacophony, toward an escalator as soldiers poured into Union Station from the same tunnel Eden, Cassian, and Cleo had come, guns ablaze.

Francesca ran for the marble stairs. They followed her up to the ground floor, where Union Station stood like a monstrosity of toppled marble and granite. Sunlight poured through rips and holes and broken skylights in what remained of the arched ceiling high above, landing on piles of debris—dust and rubble, chunks of concrete, shards of glass, crumbling centurion statues, and collapsed support beams. They raced out into the open as helicopters circled in the sky and the staccato sound of gunfire rent the air.

People screamed and scattered as an explosion blasted the remains of a fountain, throwing Eden off her feet.

She landed hard on her back, her head cracking against the pavement. For a second, her ears rang. The world spun and darkened at the edges. But then it stopped, and the pain quickly receded. Francesca pulled her to her feet. Cleo was down in the rubble and smoke —unconscious, her hands still bound behind her back, a shard of marble lodged in her thigh. Eden pulled it out and the wound gushed crimson. She yelled Cassian's name, but he didn't answer. He didn't come.

Smoke and chaos and flames grew all around. Francesca tugged Eden's hand, demanding her to follow. Cleo was bleeding. Heavily. Screaming Cassian's name again, Eden gathered Cleo in her arms, then draped her over her shoulder like she weighed nothing at all. If Francesca wondered about Eden's strength, there was no time to question it.

Another blast rocked the ground.

Francesca ran.

Eden followed, desperately searching for the boy she couldn't leave behind. The boy who hadn't wanted to come. They were here because of her blasted curiosity.

But helicopters circled.

Guns fired.

And Eden couldn't stay.

With her heart cleaving in two, she raced after Francesca. Away from the fray—hoping and praying with every fiber of her being that Cassian was okay.

40

Eden felt exposed—too out in the open as she followed Francesca away from Cassian. Away from the sounds of helicopters and gunfire concentrated at Union Station. They reached Constitution Avenue, an annihilated remnant of a bygone era. When the country was led by a president and students took field trips to the White House—now charred black and partially standing as though somebody had doused it with gasoline, lit it on fire, and didn't hurry to extinguish the flames.

They crept past the Washington Monument, a gargantuan shaft toppled on its side. They ducked beneath partially collapsed support beams as Eden bore the weight of an unconscious Cleo with one thought forefront in her mind...safety. Before she could go back for

Cassian—and she would go back—she needed to get Cleo to safety.

She tailed Francesca until they'd wound their way deep into the bowels of the White House. The young woman walked with confidence, like a person who knew where she was going, then stopped in front of a stainless-steel keypad. She entered a password and a pair of giant steel doors slid open in front of them. Once they entered, the doors closed with a loud and definitive hiss.

They hurried along a tiled corridor, where pipes hung from the ceiling and into a room with wood paneling and a large conference table. There were television monitors and old-fashioned telephones and digital clocks and maps, and America's presidential seal mounted on the wall.

Eden broke the zip tie that held Cleo's hands behind her back and lay her gently on the floor.

She mumbled something incoherent, a line of sweat beading above her lip. The left side of her face was scratched and scraped. A deep gash cut through her right eyebrow. Eden tore Cleo's pant leg, where she'd been stabbed with a knife-like chunk of marble shrapnel. Blood gushed from the wound.

"We need bandages," Eden said.

"You're going to have to get creative," Francesca replied, turning on the televisions and unclipping her walkie-talkie. "Pru, are you there? Over."

Eden yanked off her sweatshirt and tore it into strips. She tied a tourniquet around Cleo's upper thigh, then stuffed the wound like Dr. Beverly Randall-Ransom had stuffed her father's.

The television monitors played footage of other rooms with people hiding inside. Along with ground surveillance where the battle unfolded. All the while, Francesca spoke into the choppy static of her walkie-talkie, trying to reach Prudence.

A line of military trucks rolled to a stop outside Union Station, where fires blazed, and smoke poured into the sky.

"I need to go," Eden said, applying pressure to Cleo's wound.

"If you leave, your friend will die. And I won't even have to lift a finger to do it."

Francesca was right.

If Eden left, Cleo would bleed out.

Her femoral artery had been punctured.

"Please, help. Until I come back. I swear I'll come back as soon as I find Cassian."

"Over her dead body." Francesca turned away from the screens—one eye glassy, one eye mutinous. "You have done enough damage. I will not let you cause any more. We are following emergency protocol."

Eden's heart raged.

She could easily overpower Francesca Burnoli. But

then what would happen to Cleo? She looked at the screens in a desperate search for Cassian, but she couldn't find him anywhere.

Cass's ears rang and beyond the ringing came the muffled sounds of warfare. His shoulder throbbed. He squeezed his eyes tight, then opened them wide—smoke and fire and soldiers in fatigues all around. He coughed, the pain in his shoulder searing, the pain in his head splitting, as he lay awkwardly on his side with his hands bound behind his back.

"Eden," he groaned.

He had to find her.

She wasn't safe.

They'd been ambushed by the government of the United States. The same government that had ordered Eden's destruction seventeen years ago. If they captured her, he knew they would order her destruction again.

Gritting his teeth, Cass scooted toward what remained of a retaining wall. He used the jagged stone to cut his ties. He pushed himself up, his left arm dangling like a limp fish by his side. He clutched his injured shoulder, grappling for the strength to force it back into place. With his molars clamped tight, he braced himself against the wall and used his good arm to pull his elbow up until the joint popped and the blinding pain abated.

His chest heaved.

Sweat beaded along his brow.

He wiped a smear of blood and grime along his forehead, then got to his feet when a rifle pressed against his temple. "On your knees."

Cass glared at his captor—not much older than himself. Then—lightning quick—he brought up his good arm, shoving the rifle up and away. Bullets sprayed the air as Cass swept the soldier's legs, bringing him down hard on his back as he seized the rifle for himself. He turned it on his captor, eliciting loud shouts all around as three soldiers aimed their semi-automatics at his head—fingers curled around their triggers.

He couldn't fight them all.

There were too many of them.

And Cass was no help to Eden dead.

He dropped the rifle and held up his uninjured arm.

The fallen soldier shoved him to the ground and jammed his knee into Cass's neck. He yanked Cass's hands behind his back. His shoulder screamed. Fuming, he ground his teeth against the pain as the soldier bound his wrists and pulled him to his knees.

When the smoke cleared, he saw Prudence Dvorak kneeling, too, on the other side of the decimated fountain. Along with several others.

But no Eden. Which meant she hadn't been caught.

The soldier forced Cass to his feet and shoved him forward, toward a line of military trucks, past bodies on the ground laying in pools of blood. Eden couldn't be among them. Eden couldn't die. He had to remind himself of this every time he looked at a new face. But Cleo? She wasn't immune to death.

A trickle of blood ran into Cass's eye. He blinked, trying to focus. But his head throbbed. His stomach roiled. The blast that knocked him out and separated his shoulder had no doubt concussed him, too. He swallowed his nausea as his captor forced him into the back of a truck.

By the time it was loaded, there were eight in all.

Eden wasn't among them.

Neither was Cleo.

Prudence Dvorak, however, sat across from him, glaring murderously as the truck rumbled to life and drove them away like prisoners of war.

41

Eden watched with horrifying dread as Cassian was loaded into the back of a truck, her short-lived relief at the sight of him alive quickly replaced by a cold and sickening panic. He had been captured. By soldiers who thought he was a member of Interitus. Prudence Dvorak might not believe in its existence, but the government sure did.

Francesca kicked the chair in front of her and cursed loudly.

Eden pressed harder against Cleo's wound, all of it too familiar—the blood on her hands, the horror stretching wide in her chest. Only this time, she wasn't in the back of Dr. Norton's truck and Cassian Gray wasn't behind the wheel. She looked at the truck where he'd been loaded, willing Cleo's bleeding to stop. Willing herself to wake up.

Wake up, Eden. Wake up.

She just needed to open her eyes and Cassian would be there—solid and steady and warm—like he always was. Her buoy in this storm-tossed sea. But Eden didn't wake up. And the buoy had been taken.

He'd been taken because of *her* recklessness. Once again, she'd been unable to resist. She made an idiotic decision. Only these repercussions were so much worse than a mug shot.

Francesca slammed her hands onto the table. "Seventeen years! We have been here—building our numbers, carefully organizing—for seventeen years and you show up and ruin it in a single day!"

"Organizing what?" Eden asked.

"The Resistance," Francesca spat.

The answer settled between them—as jarring as Francesca's appearance at Union Station.

"The Resistance," Eden repeated, her voice an unsteady whisper. She gave her head a small shake. "What are you resisting?"

"The man you came here to kill."

"The Monarch."

"And his followers. They call themselves Invictus. We call them Swarm." Francesca dug her fingers into her short hair, then slid them down her cheeks, pulling her face long as she stared at the monitors. "Seventeen years. He's been hunting her for seventeen years. Always searching for the one who got away. And now, thanks to you, he has her!"

"The government has her."

Francesca shot Eden a scathing eye roll.

Eden blinked, then looked down at her unconscious friend. Cleo the Conspiracy Theorist. If Interitus never existed, then Interitus wasn't responsible for The Attack. Had Cleo been right all along? "Is The Monarch someone in our government?"

"He's bigger than the government." Francesca studied the screens. Some soldiers were climbing into the trucks. Others were searching the bodies on the ground. With a despairing exhale, Francesca picked up her walkie-talkie and pressed the button. "Pru has been taken. Over."

There was no reply but the lonely sound of static.

"Asher, come in." Francesca twisted the knob on the two-way radio. "Asher, do you copy?"

Several squawks broke through the white noise.

Then the walkie-talkie beeped. "I didn't make it to the asset."

The deep voice belonged to the guy in the hoodie.

Asher.

"What's your 20?" Francesca asked.

"Bunker Four," Asher said.

Francesca pointed a remote at the television monitors. The surveillance switched from above ground to below.

Asher was crouched inside one screen, bent over a man who looked worse off than Cleo. The second screen was empty. In the third, a solitary young man sat slumped in one corner. And in the fourth, a group of survivors huddled together, all of them intact.

"Is the asset secure?" Asher asked.

"For now," Francesca replied.

"What do you want me to do?"

"Stay where you are. Follow emergency protocol. And stand by."

"Copy that."

Francesca set the two-way radio on the table and sank into the seat she had kicked—a gesture of defeat as she gazed forlornly at the monitors. "We were fifty strong. And now we're only ten." She pushed a button on the remote. The monitors returned to the scene unfolding above. A war zone. A graveyard as the soldiers combed through the dead.

Eden looked away. But she could never unsee it.

Cleo moaned.

Eden wanted to scream. She wanted to rant and rail. Tear the nanobots from her veins and inject them into Cleo's. The human body was so frustratingly fragile. So utterly at risk of incurring damage. First her father. Now Cleo. The bleeding had stopped, but what about infection? Eden had stuffed dirty bits of sweatshirt into her wound. How long until sepsis set in?

She grit her teeth. All of this because of The Monarch. Someone bigger than the government. But how was that even possible? "Who is he?" she asked.

Francesca looked at her.

"The Monarch. He's a man. *Who?*"

With her good eye, Francesca pinned Eden beneath a contemptuous stare. "America's favorite hero."

America's Favorite Hero?

There was only one person Eden could think of that fit such a description. But it couldn't be. He helped rebuild their country after it hit rock bottom. He started a foundation that served those who suffered from chronic health issues after The Attack. He loved America. He called himself a true patriot. And even if all of that was an act, why would he bomb his own hotel? Eden shook her head trying to collect her thoughts. "You're not talking about—The Monarch can't be ... Oswin Brahm?"

Francesca gave her eyebrows a lift.

"But that doesn't make any sense. Why would he work so hard to rebuild what he destroyed?"

"It's all part of his master plan. Tear down to build up."

Eden remembered the pamphlet. *Ad Astra per Aspera*. Through hardship to the stars. *Salvo Impetum*. Saving blow. *Sanctus Diem*. A holy day. The fourth of October. The day of The Attack—a catastrophic event that stripped the nation down to its barest, most vulnerable foundation. Then he swooped in like all the king's horses and all the king's men, determined to put Humpty Dumpty back together again. "What's he trying to build?"

"A utopian empire. One that will never fall. One that is completely loyal to him."

Caelum In Terra.

Another phrase from the pamphlet.

Heaven on Earth.

"Don't his followers care that he's building it on the graveyard of millions?"

"As long as they're not one of them."

Eden's stomach dropped. She pictured the charismatic billionaire. Hobnobbing with celebrities and politicians. Mingling with America's most influential at the Prosperity Ball, sitting like a king on his throne—knowing exactly what was coming. Because he'd planned it. A murderer. A villain. A demon disguised as a savior.

Francesca swiveled her chair to face Eden. "Did you really kill the Bryson's?"

"No." They'd been set-up. Just like Prudence Dvorak had been set up. She was no more a terrorist than Eden and Cassian. "Several years ago, you told Cleo the Monarch gave you that eye. Mona told us the Brysons gave you the eye. So we thought one of the Brysons might be The Monarch."

Francesca grimaced.

Cleo moaned.

"We broke into the Bryson's safe, and we found a photograph of Prudence with Lillian Kashif. Clay has a picture of him and Amir on his Perk account. We thought you were all on the same side."

"You thought wrong," Francesca said.

Amir and Prudence weren't with The Monarch; they were against him. They were part of The Resistance. And thanks to Eden and Cleo and Cassian, The Resistance was on the brink of extinction. Eden peered at the monitors. At the war zone overhead. At the dead bodies on the ground. The ones she could never unsee.

They'd gone horribly off course. But then, wouldn't most people have reached the same conclusion in their shoes? Thanks to the dead security guards at SafePad, they knew The Monarch had infiltrated the police force. It wasn't a jump to assume The Monarch had infiltrated other areas of the government, too. Like the NSA. Not to mention, Amir attended a Thursday night meeting at the Aigner's, parents of the late Melody Aigner. One of ninety-three Magnes Matres. The whole thing had been eerily similar to the Thursday night meetings the Bryson's hosted in Glencoe. Which meant …

"Amir's a spy," Eden said.

Francesca's hands balled into fists on top of the table. She stared hard at the monitors, where small pockets of soldiers had gathered into groups, as though conferring. Were they going to comb through the city? Flush them out of their hiding holes? When this was all over, would Eden and Francesca and Cleo be captured like Cassian? Would the entire Resistance be dead or imprisoned?

"How does he get away with it?" Eden asked.

"What do you mean?" Francesca replied.

"If this group—Invictus or Swarm or whatever they're called is meticulous enough to hide Oswin Brahm's true identity and carry out those attacks, then how is Amir able to spy?"

"Because of his mother."

"Lillian," Eden said.

Francesca nodded. "Every Magnes Mater is held in highest esteem. So are their surviving family members."

"Why?"

"Because they bore the Electus."

The Electus.

There it was—that word again.

"What's the Electus?" Eden asked.

"Oswin Brahm's special soldiers."

Eden looked at Francesca blankly.

"Weaponized humans," she said in a toneless, dispassionate voice.

Eden's mind twisted. Her thoughts churned. And a slice of pain cut through her temple. With a sharp hiss, she clutched the spot and squeezed her eyes shut. When she opened them, Francesca was watching her curiously.

"But my father—" Eden began.

"Destroyed a test group."

The words came like a hard, unsuspecting slap across the face.

"He destroyed the original six," Francesca continued. "But there are ninety-four others."

Suddenly, the puzzle came together in astounding clarity. Oswin Brahm cracked the code with Subjects 001 through 006. Then he tried again three months later. With a much larger group. This attempt hadn't ended in failure, like the obituaries led them to believe. The babies didn't die. The babies were alive. And now, they were no longer babies, but fully grown weaponized humans. Three months younger than Eden.

Which meant soon—if not already—their networks would come online. They would be activated. Ninety-four indestructible soldiers at The Monarch's beck and call.

Dread pooled deep in Eden's abdomen.

Only one incongruity remained.

"Ninety-three," she muttered.

"What's that?" Francesca said.

"You said there are ninety-four others. But there are only ninety-three Magnes Matres." Eden could remember each of their names. She could pull up in her mind's eye all ninety-three of the obituaries. Perhaps one of them had twins.

Then she remembered Francesca's words.

Always searching for the one who got away.

Eden pictured Dvorak in the photograph with the five other women—each of their names listed on the back of the pamphlet. But not Prudence. Her name wasn't listed.

Ninety-three names.

Ninety-four weaponized humans.

The one who got away.

"She didn't die in labor."

"None of them died in labor," Francesca said. "They were murdered. Coerced into drinking poison, led to believe that this would heal them."

"Why?"

"Because Oswin Brahm is a narcissistic megalomaniac who doesn't want his special soldiers attached to anyone but himself. The women were brainwashed. Led to believe this act of service would put them in his innermost circle. Then he killed them in secret and called them martyrs. Honored their families so they wouldn't think to question what actually happened. Pru was the only one who didn't drink the poison. The only one who escaped. The only one who knew the truth. Until she found Amir and told him."

Francesca sat up straight, staring hard at the screens

as the last of the soldiers loaded onto trucks. "They're not taking the injured."

It wasn't a question, but a statement. Confusing all the same. Why would they leave survivors behind? Why wouldn't they search the grounds? Why wouldn't they search the tunnels?

The trucks cleared out.

The helicopters stopped circling.

There was a long moment of confused silence. And then the jets flew over and the bombs began to fall.

42

Twenty-seven.

There were twenty-seven blinking dots on the map now.

All they could do was watch them appear, unsure of what they meant. Unsettled by what they could mean. There'd always been an odd number of them. Five dots when Jane and Barrett and Eden and Ellery made four. What was the fifth? And now, what were these?

Unease permeated Dr. Norton's cabin.

It doubled with the arrival of Ellery. Tripled with the arrival of another mother named Annette.

The air oozed with tension.

Like it did whenever Father was on the cusp of a rage.

Jack had certainly done a lot of yelling.

Jane kept flinching, waiting for him to strike.

Waiting for him to inflict pain. But he never did. According to Barrett, he never would. At least, that was what he told Jane earlier this morning, when he found her cowering beneath her bed during a loud argument. According to Barrett, Jack would not hurt Ellery. The reason he was so distraught was because he didn't want anyone to hurt Ellery, especially not the bad people.

Ellery knew the truth now.

Jack didn't want her to, but she did. Which meant Ellery's life would never be the same. When all of this was over—if it ever could be over—his daughter could not continue her life as usual. According to Barrett, this was why Jack had been hiding the truth. He'd been operating under the belief that Ellery didn't have to know. But now she did, and to his immense dismay, she wanted to be activated.

She wanted to be like Barrett and Jane.

Which was the reason for Jack's current yelling.

"You have no idea what you're talking about!" he hollered, so loudly Jane covered her ears. "Do you want to know what would come with those powers? Enslavement. I watched it happen, Elle. I saw Eden Pruitt point a gun at her own mother and pull the trigger. Against her will. Because a psychopath had control of her."

"But it doesn't have to be that way," Ellery shot back. "You said so yourself. It's not that way with *Jane*. Or whatever her name is. She's free from that control, which means we can be, too."

"But I don't know how!" Jack roared.

With a jump, Jane burrowed beneath her covers.

"And the only person who could give us a clue refuses to talk."

"Enough!" The sharp command belonged to Dr. Norton, who had come in through the front door with Ruth and Annette, the two mothers. The three of them had been outside, stretching their legs before dinner. "You are guests in my home. If you insist on yelling, I'm going to insist that you leave."

The house fell quiet.

The only sound came from the voices inside the television and seven elevated heartbeats. Jane's not included. She peeked out from beneath the covers.

"Look!" Barrett exclaimed. "That makes twenty-eight."

Another blinking dot must have appeared.

A prolonged beep followed his words. It came from the television, the same sound they heard on the day Jane was brave. The same sound they heard when Eden and Cassian's face filled Concordia.

More late-breaking news.

Several hearts skipped a beat.

"Interitus headquarters have been ambushed," a reporter said.

Jane clambered off the bed and ran on tiptoe down the hall.

In the living room, everyone stood stock still, staring at the television, which was showing footage of bombs falling from the sky, exploding in a city that already looked decimated.

"That's where they've been hiding?" Ruth said. "Washington D.C.?"

The footage changed to hand-cuffed prisoners being escorted into a helicopter. According to the reporter, eight members of Interitus were in custody. One of them was Prudence Dvorak. Another, Cassian Ransom. He walked behind Prudence smeared with blood and grime.

A strangled, choking sound came from Ruth.

"Many more have been killed," the reporter continued as Eden's face filled the screen. "18-year-old Eden Pruitt is believed to be amongst the dead."

Ruth's knees gave way. She collapsed onto the sofa while Alexander shook his head. Annette sat beside her and took her hand while two photographs replaced Eden's. A husband and a wife named Elmer and Eloise Miller, who lived in Bethesda and had been aiding and abetting Eden Pruitt and Cassian Ransom. Their home was raided, and the elderly couple had been shot dead.

Ruth moaned—an agonizing keen that sounded like an injured animal.

Like Kitty.

"She can't be dead," Alexander said, his voice cracking. "She can't be. It's not possible."

Nobody objected.

Nobody agreed.

"It's not possible!" he repeated on a shout, louder than any of Jack's.

Ruth began to rock.

Annette tried to hold her still.

Alexander kept shaking his head.

Ellery and Jack and Dr. Norton stood immobilized.

Barrett held the device that projected the map with the twenty-eight dots. He looked small. He looked frightened.

It was a scene of despair.

A tableau of agony.

Jane backed away, then spun on her heel and ran to her room. She slammed the door. And with shaking hands, she removed the folded map from her pillowcase of treasures. She stared down at the city she'd crossed off with a violent, repetitive X. As if that might cross it out of existence. Along with Father and every nightmare that belonged to her old self—Violet.

But now?

Ruth was in pain.

And Barrett was afraid.

Being brave once had not solved the problem. She needed to be brave again.

For Barrett.

For Mother.

The shaking in her hands moved up into her arms as she shoved the bulging pillowcase into a backpack. She forced the zipper shut, tucked the map into her back pocket, then snuck down the hall and through the living room. Nobody noticed her. They were too busy staring in horror at the television, watching footage of America celebrating. Oswin Brahm, popping a bottle of Champagne alongside the country's board of directors. Rejoicing over death. Calling it a victory. America might be sick, he said, but the tumor had just been removed. Now, more than ever, they needed to rally together and take every step necessary to eradicate the cancer for good. To ensure that it would never return.

This was their mission.

Jane had her own.

As quiet as a mouse, she stepped out into the night and walked in the direction the sun had disappeared. She trudged through the woods, fallen leaves and twigs crunching and snapping beneath her feet. Leaves and twigs crunching and snapping behind her, too.

She whirled around.

Barrett stood ten paces back, frozen in mid-step, his hands held above his head. "I should have known better," he mumbled. "Your superhuman hearing has always been better than my superhuman stealth."

He brought his foot down and looped his thumbs beneath the straps of his own backpack. Like all this time, he'd been packed and ready to go, too. "So, where are we headed?"

Jane stared at him

He took a few steps closer—slow and steady, as though not to frighten her away. "I'm going to make a pitch. I hope it will be convincing. Either way, I will respect your decision, whatever that decision may be. I only ask that you hear me out first."

Jane kept staring.

He took a few more steps. "I think Jack is right. I think you know how your system got to be the way it is. But I also think the *how* terrifies you. And that terror must be a really awful way to feel, especially when you're alone. I don't want you to be alone. I think you've lived too much of your life that way, which is no way to live. I think maybe you would like some company. And I also think that if I stay here ..." He nodded over his shoulder, toward Dr. Norton's cabin, no longer visible for the trees. "I might go crazy."

Jane's breath had gone shallow in her lungs. Her heartbeat, erratic.

Barrett smiled at her—a kind, patient smile. Because that's who Barrett was. Never demanding his way. Always asking for permission. Filling up the lonely, frightened places with words and stories and games and ideas and memories so filled with joy, sometimes she pretended they were hers.

Something cracked deep down inside—a tiny splinter that widened into a fissure. And up from that fissure rose a delicate bubble. It gurgled in her stomach, swelled in her chest, then rolled up her throat. She opened her mouth, and the bubble popped on her tongue. "Okay."

Barrett gaped.

Somewhere overhead, an owl hooted.

"Did you just—did I just hear—?" He looked around, as though checking to see if anyone else had heard it. Anyone besides the owl.

"Yes."

Barrett's face went bright with wonder. Like the sound of those two whispered words was a miraculous thing. "Yes," he repeated, bobbing his head. "All right. Okay, then. Where are we going?"

Jane handed Barrett the map.

He unfolded it and stared at the angry X over the city called Minneapolis. She wanted to run away from it. Instead, she was running toward it.

Because Jack was right.

Jane knew.

Father was the key.

It was time to go get him.

And Barrett was going to help.

43

Eden had lived through her fair share of long days—whole lifetimes unfolding in a twenty-four-hour span. She could think of several in the last two months alone. Starting with the day she came home to a ransacked house, only to be detained at the Eagle Bend police station, misidentified as a disturbed runaway named Ellery Forrester. Then there was the day she sliced open her hand and watched it heal before her eyes and learned the truth about who and what she was. There was the day her father was shot and almost killed and three more after that, when he hovered precariously between the living and the dead.

This, though, was the worst. Trapped in the White House Bunker as bombs fell from the sky. Cassian, gone. Cleo, injured on the floor, feverish as she came in and out of sleep. Francesca, a hostile acquaintance who kept chewing her fingers.

Eden found bottled water. A wholly inadequate first aid kit. Some pillows and blankets. She brought one of each to Cleo, who was beginning to shiver. There was nothing to do about her leg wound. Eden couldn't remove the dirty cotton without disturbing the blood clot that was keeping her alive. There was no point in cleaning around it, so she used the antiseptic and bandages to tend to the cuts on her face, the gash on her eyebrow—reminded of the time she'd tended to Cassian in the basement of Cleo's dormitory.

Voila. Tout au mieux.

Her heart squeezed so tight she thought she might suffocate.

Every cell in her body ached for him.

Longed for him.

Worried about him.

She shoved the pain and the panic down and focused her attention on Cleo—at times, coherent enough to understand where she was. To listen as Eden told her what was happening. Then she would slip away again, and Eden was left alone with Francesca and her own thoughts. She kept picturing Cassian in the back of a military truck. Where would they take him? What would they do to him? The government believed he was a terrorist. They'd executed Volkova. Would they do the same with his alleged followers?

Her stomach twisted.

She began to pace, stopping occasionally to check Cleo's pulse. And just when she was beginning to think the bombs would never stop—they'd be down here forever and ever—they did.

The bunker filled with a bloated silence.

One that stretched on and on—holding her and Francesca captive—as the jets cleared and all that remained above ground was an inferno of smoke and flame. Eden didn't move. She didn't even breathe until the hiss of the opening doors broke the trance.

Francesca picked up her semi-automatic.

Eden clenched her fists, prepared to fight when a hulking, hooded figure came into view.

"Asher," Francesca said with a relieved exhale, sinking into her chair. "What are you doing here? What happened to—?"

"He's dead," Asher said, his expression hard as flint.

Eden's heart dropped.

Another member of the resistance, gone.

Asher dropped a black medical bag on the conference table. He cast a dismissive glance at Eden, then peered at the monitors, zeroing in on one in particular. The solitary young man slumped in the corner of a small room—no longer still but stirring like the increasingly restless Cleo.

Asher rubbed his Adam's apple. "Brahm has to know he's here."

"I know," Francesca said.

"Why did they leave without him?"

"Leave without who?" Eden asked.

Her question went ignored. Neither of them acknowledged it at all.

"We're fifty minutes late," Asher said, checking his watch. "We need to administer the dose now or who knows what will happen."

Francesca dug her fingers into her short hair. "Xavier had the dose and now he's—"

"Dead." Asher opened the black bag and removed a variety of items, including a portable IV.

"The rest of the doses are in storage. We can't get to them without going above ground." Francesca pointed the remote at the monitors and changed the channel. A sky view of the city, where drones circled with the smoke. "If we're seen, ten to one, they drop more bombs."

"There are nine of us in bunker three. It's right by Metro Center." Asher hung the bag of fluids on the back of a chair, knelt beside Cleo—looking extra-large next to her smallness—and administered the IV. His touch far from gentle as he began removing the dirty bandages. "One of them can get to Xavier."

Cleo groaned.

"They've never administered a dose before," Francesca said.

"We're out of options, Fran. We wait any longer and who knows what could happen." Asher removed a packet of sutures like he intended to stitch up Cleo's wound.

Eden stepped toward him. He was obviously no doctor. "Are you sure you should do that?"

"Would you like to leave it open? Let her bleed out?"

Eden's face flushed.

Asher turned to Francesca. "One of them will have to find Xavier. Retrieve the dose. And get to the asset. I'll guide them from there."

The asset.

Eden looked at the screen again. A young man slumped in the corner of a room. A young man her own age. A young man with ... Eden tilted her head and leaned closer. A young man with shackles on his wrists. "Is that one of his soldiers?"

This got their attention.

Asher pinned her beneath a look of utmost condescension, like she was a small, inferior child getting in the way. Eden squared her shoulders and tipped her chin. She much preferred Francesca's hostility over his arrogant disdain, even if he was tending to Cleo.

"That isn't just a soldier," Asher said. "That's Brahm's five-star general."

Eden thought of the device back at Dr. Norton's. The fifth blinking dot on the map. The one that behaved differently than the other four. The one that never made sense, because why was there a fifth? Now, Eden knew. Here was the fifth blinking dot. Somehow, the resistance got him. Somehow, they were holding him prisoner. "What are you going to do with him?"

"Eventually, the same thing we plan to do with all of them." With an impassioned gleam sparkling in her good eye, Francesca curled her hand into a fist and brought it down on the table. "If Brahm is the snake, Electus is his head. We are going to cut it off."

Eden's blood went cold.

"After we rescue Pru and the others."

The others.

Cassian.

Yes.

She had to rescue him.

It was the only certain thing in a world that had gone topsy-turvy.

But how?

Thanks to her, the resistance was mortally wounded. And unbeknownst to the resistance, she was part of the snake's head. How quickly would they try to destroy her once they found out?

They certainly wouldn't help her. Which meant she

had to keep all of it under wraps and she had to convince Francesca to include Cassian in their rescue plans.

Right now, this was all that mattered.

This was her northern star.

Whatever it would take, for however long it would take, she would break Cassian free.

ABOUT THE AUTHOR

K.E. Ganshert graduated from the University of Wisconsin in Madison with a degree in education. She worked as a fifth grade teacher for several years before staying home to write full time. Now she's an award-winning author published in two genres: contemporary fiction of the inspirational variety and young adult fiction of the fantastical variety. She is currently pursuing the latter.

Shop direct from K.E. Ganshert at
K.E. Ganshert Books

Stay in the know! Join K.E. Ganshert's email list and receive 20% off your first order!

Made in the USA
Monee, IL
16 September 2022